SHADOWS OF MEMORY

CHILDREN OF SACRIFICE PART I

JADE T. WOODRIDGE

publicfrog
PRESS

Cover Photo: alameen .ng from Pexels
Cover design: Jade T. Woodridge
Editing: Jazmine Jules (The Manuscript Mender)

For information, contact the author through her page: www.jadetwoodridge.com

ISBN: 979-8-234-00266-2 (Print)
ISBN: 979-8-234-00267-9 (eBook)

Printed in the United States of America

PART I

Shadows of Memory

Contents

PROLOGUE

"Wait!"

Inside the cave, badly battered and unable to drag himself forward, the man watched in terror as the boulder rolled into place.

"Come back! Please—"

Blindly, his hands met the barrier and beating against the stone, desperate to be heard. A mercy, they'd said when they threw him in, for they could have killed him. He wished they had. This "mercy" was nothing but a thin veil for their cruelty.

He pushed and rammed the barrier until his ribs broke and his shoulder popped from the socket. Like an animal, trapped and crazed, he clawed at the stone until his nails broke and his fingertips were nothing more than broken flesh tipped with bone. He threw his head back and wailed in rage and agony.

"Curse you all! The moon and stars and sun above—you deserve none of it!"

He cursed them to the same darkness they sealed him in. He screamed until he lost his breath and cried until there were no more tears left to cry. He weakened, fingers swelling with rot, and legs stiffening with cold. Hunger rattled his bones.

As time went on, the weight of the mountain pressed down on him, forcing him back into the dirt until he was no more. Finally, the man closed his eyes, but there was no difference between the darkness of his mind and the dark tomb he lay in.

"You're dying," a woman whispered, her cold breath numbing his ear. "Are you not afraid?"

Just as his sight vanished with the light, so did his sense of time. A blink of an eye ago, he'd been afraid. But once he knew the truth of what death was, he was afraid no more.

Death was cold and dark. It was abandonment, ugly and spiteful. Death was . . . lonesome. He'd felt all of those each time they imprisoned him here. He'd feel it for an eternity.

"Lonesome . . . " the woman repeated, though the man had not spoken his thoughts. "We leave this world just as we enter it: reaching for something to hold on to."

The man inhaled a slow and raspy breath, his ribs creaking like brittle branches in the wind.

"Open your eyes," the woman commanded, and kissed his sunken cheeks.

He did so obediently, and the darkness opened up. He gazed up into the wonders of the starry night he never thought he'd see again. The man exhaled; mouth parting in a permanent sigh, his body . . . deflating.

"Take my hand," she whispered. "Let it be the one you grasp in the Dark, and I will show you that death can be beautiful, too."

Chapter 1

CHINEDU BREATHED HIS LAST wheezing breath early in the morning. His sunken eyes gazed at the rising sun, his thin lips parted in a gasp, and his skeletal hand rested against his chest. No one noticed his missing rasp until nearly noon.

Another gone. Despite the scarf wrapped around her head and face concealing her sorrow, Olun took her bottom lip between her teeth to stop it from quivering. Death was nothing new to her. Chinedu had contracted the Dry Sickness almost a month ago and, as horrible as it was to watch him waste away, it was expected. *This* death was expected of them all.

Regardless, Olun wept as she wiped the fine purple granules of sand and dust from his dehydrated limbs. "We'll make you handsome for the Goddess, ya?" she smiled a watery smile. In life, Chinedu had been a thin man. All of the Rohta were for food and water were scarce in the desert. Even more so as they entered their seventh year of drought. She remembered the man he'd been, a father of nine—all gone before him. A woman he'd loved who still lay amongst the sick, adding her wheeze to the chorus of painful coughs, gasps, and rattles.

"I hope you'll see each other soon," she whispered to him, passing the cloth over his concave chest and the grooves of his ribs. She continued talking to him about this and that as if he were simply sleeping. She dashed away her tears when her vision blurred too much to focus on her task, and decided to hum to him instead.

What hurt the most about his death, Olun thought, was the absence. When she had held his cracked hands the previous night, she'd felt life. Though faint, it was there. It was hope—he was holding on and *could* hold on. Hope that Ma Bright had taken pity on him, who'd lost so much, that She'd intervene when the Dark Lady came for him.

But his skin was cold and as devoid of life as a sack of grain.

When she was done bathing him, she carefully turned him to his side and folded his body, tucking his knees to his chest and arms crossed. This was the position Ma Bright put them in before birth, and, though it was the Dark Lady's touch that separated them from their bodies, the Rohta believed that one day Ma Bright would again cradle them against her breast and birth them into the world anew.

It was nothing to drag the blanket that bore his body to the shallow grave her clan had dug at her askance. They watched at a distance as Olun arranged him in the hole and covered him with sand. Each day, more and more sand would cover him, sweeping across his grave until the desert consumed him completely.

The sun beat down on Olun's covered head, and the passing breeze billowed through her thin robes to wick away the sweat. She returned to what was left of her clan. Their gaunt frames, like hers, were so thin the desert breeze could lift them up and away. The wild oombrak herd they followed across the dunes had long since moved on without them while they cared for their sick. Hunters had to travel farther and farther away, hauling back meat and water, their bodies pushed to breaking. How long would it be until they were too weak to travel? How long would it be until they were no more?

"I don't know how you do it," Oja, her little brother, sighed as she wove her way through camp. He was all eyes beneath a mass of black curls almost identical to her own. The lackluster ringlets coiled around his ears and about his shoulders. Olun pulled the scarf down from her face and took a deep breath of fresh air.

"Someone has to, ya?" she mumbled. *No one else wants to.*

When the Sickness came, no one believed it could be so devastating. Even grown men were afraid to approach the sick, covering their ears against their pain-filled, rattled breathing. But the sick deserved better than to be left to suffer alone and ignored. The dead deserved to be put to rest, not left to shrivel up in the sun because they were too afraid of the Sickness to touch their corpses. These were friends. Family. Loved ones. They deserved respect, and she would give them that.

Olun didn't fear the Dry Sickness. Well, she *feared* it alright—feared what it had done to her clan, what it was trying to do to her family. She feared having to witness their long, painful deaths—the blood spraying from their cracked lips as they coughed and wheezed, their bodies rejecting all moisture, their limbs shrinking, their cheeks sinking, their skin shriveling. She feared looking into the eyes of their corpses, but she did not fear death.

Olun didn't know why she felt this way. Perhaps she had more hatred and anger for the Dark Lady than fear. Whatever the case may be, she'd taken up the task of checking the sick throughout the day and preparing those who passed for burial. It may have been a tiresome service, but she performed it to give her people dignity in death. A daze overtook her at the sight of her pa; she smeared her sand-covered hand on her tunic, and Oja followed her gaze.

"Pa didn't watch the burial," he said with a shrug. "He said it's th'same as all th'rest."

"But Chinedu was his friend."

"So?" Oja said. "Everyone is friend or family. It makes no difference."

There was no emotion accompanying his words. No anger, malice, or hurt. Oja was six years her junior. He'd been so young when the drought began, and by the time the Dry Sickness spread, he'd come to expect such hardships. Such . . . losses. They did not faze him the way they did her. Indeed, all of those his age—what was left of them, anyway—responded to each loss the same way.

"Well . . ." she sighed. "At least tell him it's done, ya?"

"What'll you tell Chief Yannok?" Oja asked.

"There's nothing to tell. Elder Kikyel hasn't woken up, and she hasn't died yet, either."

"So . . . the same?"

Olun nodded. He followed her through the tent flaps and sat down beside her when she stretched out on her bedroll.

"Eat this," he said abruptly, giving her a handful of shredded dried meat. Olun wanted to decline, but the rumble of her stomach had her accepting the food without a word.

The two of them listened to the violent coughing that began from somewhere in camp. Oja picked at the fibers of the woven mat he sat on, and Olun focused on the meat slivers, the two unable to look at each other until it quieted.

"Do you ever think about leaving?" Oja asked suddenly.

Olun sat up, aghast.

"It's just something me, Fumi, and Tende were talking about, s'all." Oja looked down at his fidgeting hands again.

"Go where?"

"Casimir," he said with a shrug of his shoulders. "Maybe we could live there in the city or something until the Gathering. Then we could join another clan—"

"No," Olun said vehemently.

Oja grew angry. "*You* would've left," he accused. "If we'd made it to the Gathering this year, you would've left us to be with Yuhi and the Retryu!"

"That's different!" she shouted back. She wouldn't have been abandoning them. She would've been leaving to start her life. That was what was expected of all girls and young women. Her friends had met their lovers at the Gathering of the nomadic clans years ago. Olun was no longer a girl, and she'd been in love with Yuhi for years. Though he'd not asked her to be his beloved at the last Gathering, Olun was so sure he would have asked her this year had her clan had the strength to attend. But *next* year?

"Oh, s'I have t'have a reason?" he glowered.

"Where is your loyalty? Don't you even care about Ma and Pa?"

"I *do* care!" he snapped. "I do—but I—" he broke off and turned away from her.

"No one is ever going to join the Rohta for me," he said quietly after a time. "No one is ever going to *see* me, and if I stay here, no one will even know I'm gone."

Olun wrapped her arms around her brother and felt for the first time how much it all affected him. But he was still too young to understand that, even if he left, he'd still not be accepted. For if those of their own clan looked upon the sick with fear, how must the other clans look at them? It was something Olun had tried to shove down, the nagging fear that, even if they did survive the plague of the Dry Sickness for another year and had the strength to return to the annual Gathering, Yuhi and his clan would not want her. All of her friends and distant cousins in the Maris and Raida would turn her away, too. Oja didn't understand that, outside of the Rohta, there was nothing and no one. They only had each other.

***

Oja slept in Olun's arms, her body curled protectively around his small frame. Despite the heat and the sweat that dampened their clothes, he did not pull away, and Olun didn't let him go, either. In fact, as evening fell and the temperature grew cooler, they snuggled closer together. Olun didn't sleep, though. Her ears rang with the coughs and wheezes of the day, and her mind was heavy with the lingering thoughts of abandonment and death. When her heart raced, and hopelessness cast its dark shadow over her, she buried her face against her brother's hair and focused on his breathing. His soft, even, uninterrupted breathing.

"Your ma's not joining us tonight," Monta said gruffly as she entered the dim tent. "You know how she gets after days like this. So sensitive!" She sucked her teeth.

Monta, her pa's sister, was a large and stern woman. The plain ankle length kaftan she often wore, in addition to her temperament, presented her as more matronly than she was. Monta had no children of her own and was not the first person one would think of when in need of warmth and comfort, but she was the only one who seemed able to ground Olun. It'd always been that way. When her thoughts became too much, and she was overwhelmed by everything around her, Monta's stern voice and stable arms were enough to pull her back to herself.

Instantly, Olun felt better. She eased her arm out from beneath her brother and sat up. "She knows it's unavoidable," Olun said.

"That's what I told her—she can't keep avoiding you because you touched the deceased. Or *diseased*. Whatever."

"Both," Olun agreed. Her ma didn't like Olun to be around the sick. She hadn't gotten sick yet, but her ma always reminded her that one day her luck would run out. And if that happened, everyone in their tent would succumb to it.

"Maybe I should just sleep outside," Olun suggested not for the first time, and Monta waved the idea away as she always did.

"It's her own problem. She should deal with it instead of being so childish. But she'll deal with this like how she dealt with the nightmares that have you screaming and thrashing in the night all these years."

Her nightmares were well-known in her clan. With each year that passed, the louder and more vivid they became. Her screams filled the night; her sobs and strange recollections building an ever-thickening wall between her clan and herself. Each time she woke, she could remember nothing.

Olun was intrigued. According to Oja, who always asked what she dreamed each morning, her nightmares hadn't gone away. "How?"

"By pawning you off on me, like always!" Monta chortled, pointing to Olun's bedroll in the corner of the tent beside her own. "*I* would've silenced you with a pillow—*oh*, Olun, I only jest!"

Olun rolled her eyes. "She's scared, Monta."

"She's being silly," Monta countered.

"*You're* being mean."

"And you're pulling my last nerve." She unwrapped her scarf and snapped the sand from its folds. Olun pulled a blanket over Oja and moved closer to her aunt. When she was close enough, Monta let her rest her chin on her shoulder.

"You're too old for that," her aunt muttered, but didn't shrug Olun off as she undid her thick braid to comb through its soft strands.

"Let me?"

Monta grunted and relinquished her comb. Olun started at the ends, gently detangling the long black hair, picking out the dirt, and discovering many strands of gray. Olun kept her own hair short, but even long, her tight curls never revealed their true length. Monta was different from any of the Rohta and, frankly, any desert nomad Olun had ever known. The Rohta were long and lean, while Monta was thickly made, with broad shoulders and large hands. Her dark skin wasn't the deep black of Olun's, but a warmer darkness that peeled when exposed to the sun for too long. Like all Children of Ma Bright, Goddess of the Sun, Olun could spend all afternoon without her scarf and not once be burned. Monta stayed covered in her kaftan with a scarf about her shoulders and head as if to hide these differences.

Olun had always wondered about her pa's sister. The woman had been a mystery for all of her life. Monta kept to herself, even at the Gatherings when it was a time for celebration, friendships, and fleeting—yet passionate—loves. Despite her introversion and serious demeanor, she preferred the friendship and company of Olun's Pa and soft-spoken Ma. And, though she'd never taken a lover or chosen a beloved, Monta seemed content in raising Olun as her own, disciplining and teaching her as she wished.

"Did you know a group of boys wants to leave?" she told Monta.

Her aunt grunted again. "Unsurprising."

"Oja wants to go with them."

"Good."

Olun froze. "No, it's not—he is *Rohta* for better or for worse."

"What, so he should just stay here and die because he is Rohta?" Monta scoffed.

"No, but it just feels like he's giving up."

"It sounds to me, he's not giving up. He's *fighting.*"

Olun resumed her detangling as Monta lit a candle. "If you were on the verge of death and the only way to save yourself was to leave your home, wouldn't you do just that?" She asked.

"No," Olun mumbled, though she didn't exactly know what she'd do. "If I were dying, I'd want to die around people I love because who knows if leaving would actually save my life? I'd be dying anyway, and I wouldn't want t'be alone when it happened."

"That sounds very childish," Monta chided. "I would have liked to hear you say something about living your life—not dying for the sake of being loved."

"What good is living your life if you live it alone and without love?" Olun countered.

"I raised you better than that, my Olun."

Monta was disappointed, Olun knew, but she also knew she wouldn't be able to survive in this world without them. Without *her*. If she were being honest, that was the real reason why she hadn't gone with Yuhi. Though she'd been in love with him, she never took the steps to be with him. Not like the other girls her age who went after whom and what they wanted. They wouldn't still be waiting to be chosen at nineteen years of age.

No, for better or for worse, she would not abandon the Rohta. They were all she had.

Her pa burst through the tent, eyes wild and breath frantic. Oja startled awake.

"It's the Elder," he panted. "Elder Kikyel—she's woken!"

***

Elder Kikyel was silhouetted by the setting sun. They'd moved her out of the sick tent and by the fire in the middle of camp, but the circle that surrounded her was wide. Swathed in embroidered robes that swallowed her thin body, Elder Kikyel sat straight up and surrounded by cushions and bedrolls. Her ashen, upturned face caught the last of the sun's rays, and she curled her thin fingers into the sand as if a final goodbye to the small comforts of the living world.

"Olun," Chief Yannok called softly.

Someone nudged her shoulder, but Olun found that she could go no further.

"Olun, daughter of Oyelua and Liba, come forth," Chief Yannok, a small man with dull, wooly hair and a face like old leather, said louder, his eyes scanning the many, malnourished dark faces that gathered around them.

Just then, someone gave her a shove, and they parted as she stumbled forward. Elder Kikyel never lowered her face from the sky, though the sun no longer shone on her. As the medium between this realm and the next, Elder Kikyel—all Elders, really—bore insights that the rest often did not. She'd let herself waste away as her despondency lapsed into stupor. They'd all hoped that Elder Kikyel was pleading with the Goddesses in their own realm on behalf of the Rohta. They'd hoped she would wake with a way to end their suffering, but her words were only for Olun.

"There you are, my dear."

Time moved agonizingly slow as Olun felt all of their eyes on her. She crossed the sand and dropped down unceremoniously beside the Elder, sending a burst of sand across her knees.

"Why so nervous?" Elder Kikyel chuckled. "You had a lot to say while I was away."

"You heard me?" she gasped, eyes welling.

"Because they can't say it, I'll say it for them: Thank you, my dear, for your compassion. Every word and every song you uttered while caring for us was heard."

Olun sniffed and looked back at her aunt, needing her arms to ground her and stabilize her rising emotions. Monta's eyes were hard, and her arms rigid by her side. She stood beside her ma and pa, yet slightly apart from them as they held each other faces turning upward with reverence. Olun could see it in their faces, *the Elder has summoned our daughter!* While Monta looked ready to snatch her back.

"How've your night terrors been while I was gone?" Elder Kikyel asked, drawing Olun's attention back to her. Olun frowned. They all hadn't gathered to listen to them catch up with each other.

"Much of the same, Elder," she said softly. A spark of hope rose in her breast. "Did you ask—" she lowered her voice. "Did you take my petition to the Dark Lady? Will my nightmares finally end?"

"That is up to what you do next," Elder Kikyel turned her old eyes, sunken in her face, toward her. They were clearer than she'd ever seen.

"Elder," Chief Yannok cleared his throat and attempted to steer her back to the problem at hand. "What of the Dry Sickness?"

"Simple," she said softly, patting Olun's knee with such comfort despite the words she spoke next. "Olun should go to Her."

There was stunned silence before a murmur of confusion.

"What does that mean, Elder?" Olun recognized her pa's voice. He was close, but Olun could not lift her eyes from the skeletal hand on her knee. The pit in her stomach grew.

"No one looks at a single fiber and knows the entire pattern of a tapestry," the Elder said.

"My child isn't so insignificant as a thread."

"No, she's not," the Elder agreed. "No fiber is insignificant, ya? It adds its strength to the numerous other threads. It can also change a pattern entirely. Olun must go and lend her strength to a very old tapestry."

Whispers rose, questioning and speculating what it was the Elder meant. Olun looked up at her, meeting her sunken, sentimental eyes and thin, smiling lips. "Sometimes it's not clear where each thread goes or what pattern they create," she whispered. "But it goes somewhere, Olun. *You must go for the good of us all.*"

Chief Yannok, weary from sleepless nights burdened by hunger and death, voiced all of their confusion. "What you are asking is vague, Elder. The daughter of Oyelua and Liba must meet the Dark Lady? Will this end this cursed plague upon us?"

They all seemed to hold their breath, hope hanging in the air. Olun held hers, hopeless.

"Tell me, what is the cost of life?" When the Elder spoke, she looked only at Olun.

Olun was taken aback. She was asking for her thoughts? Her choice? There was no choice! Not good ones. Go, and they live. Stay, and they die. Go and die. Stay and die. What was one death if her ma and pa and Oja could live? Was this a test—surely to refuse would be to denounce the Goddess? To forsake them all!

Her voice trembled. "Are you asking me to choose?"

"I'm asking for your answer," Elder Kikyel breathed, her body swaying as if caught by a breeze.

There was a murmur around them.

Clips of what they said rose—*"This is all it takes?"* — *"The girl has always been peculiar,"* — *"Such a noble calling, why does she not answer?"*

Olun looked at her ma and pa, willing them to speak up in her defense. Willing them to do something. *Say* something. Perhaps it would be easier to speak her own mind if they did. To tell them all that she loved them, and though it would hurt her to leave them, she would be going with them all in her heart.

But they did not. Could it be possible that they felt the same as the others? Their peculiar daughter with a noble calling to end all of this with one answer.

Only Monta looked her in the eye, her lips pursed, and her eyes narrowed in the way she did when she was preparing to scold her. "Speak, Olun!" she demanded.

"If my death can save you all," Olun looked first at Chief Yannok and then Elder Kikyel, "I would be a fool to live."

Olun flinched as her ma unleashed a sorrowful wail. But it was Monta's look of disappointment, that haunted her dreams that night.

Chapter 2

T HE RISE AND FALL of desert dunes gave way to windswept plains of sandstone, bedrock, and parched soil. Dry wisps of grass pushed through cracks in the earth, and tangled tendrils of petrified roots coiled around rocks to claim the sun-bleached bones of unlucky creatures. Plateaus rose like monuments to the Gods so high Olun could scarcely see their tops. The strange creatures bleated and bounced along the base. They were smaller than the desert oombraks, Olun noticed curiously. Their long horns were straight and sharp, and their trunk-like noses shorter. The beasts paid their passing no mind, heads bowed to sharpen their horns against the purple rock, and grazed on the tough shrubbery.

Olun stumbled not for the first time since reaching the parched plains, wincing as she caught her foot on a jutting stone. Her leather sandals were made for traveling across soft sand, not this rough terrain.

"No fight in you." Monta sucked her teeth and roughly pulled Olun to her feet. Ahead of them, her clansmen marched on.

"How do you expect t'live, ya?" Monta muttered. "You can't even stand up for yourself."

Olun avoided her aunt's disapproving dark eyes and said nothing. What was there to say? *You must go for the good of us all. You must meet the Dark Lady. Olun should go to her.* They'd made up their minds.

She was not so naive as to wonder what these things meant. Olun returned her gaze to the rocky slopes and pointed peaks of the Zenika Mountains, where the Dark Lady lived. The realm the Great God banished Her to. The Goddess spoke through Elder Kikyel, who had deprived herself within an inch of her life. What was said, *must be.* Everyone knew this. And, though there had not been a sacrifice in all of Olun's years of living, who was she to fight this divine duty? Even if she was terrified.

My death can end their suffering, Olun reminded herself. *I'd be a fool to fight to live.*

And yet, she couldn't help herself from thinking of the possibilities.

***

"You don't have t'do this," Olun told her ma, who emptied her water-skin into a bowl. "You should save your water. It doesn't matter how I look."

"Hush," came her ma's soft reprimand. Behind a screen she erected to give them privacy, she unwound the scarf from Olun's head and face. The accumulated sand from their travels fell from its creases. She wet a cloth in the bowl, wrung it out, and proceeded to wipe her cheeks and forehead. Her dusty clothes were the next thing to be stripped away. The light fabric expertly dyed and beautifully embroidered fell to the ground in a heap. Discarded. *Why didn't you fight for me?*

Olun lifted her arms and turned as her ma instructed, trying not to look at the tears in her eyes as she repeated the process of wetting the cloth and wiping it across her body, bathing her only daughter for the last time. They camped just before the jagged rise of rock that led into the mountains. A pillar of rock, like a monument to the Dark Lady herself, arched over them. A gateway to Her domain.

"You must look your best for Her, ya," her ma said, voice breaking. "I haven't done much for you, but this . . . I can prepare you for this."

You shouldn't have to, Olun turned her back to her ma, shivering as the cloth passed across her shoulder. *Don't make me do this.*

"This is for the best," her ma said more to herself than to Olun. "Yes, this is best."

What do you know about what's best? Her ma wasn't the most affectionate. Not in the way most mas were. She didn't touch or hold Olun like the other mas did their babes, either. She was too sensitive for that. Too afraid that she would upset Olun and unable to figure out how to calm her when she did. Too *feeling* in the sense that most things affected her ma more than they should, like it did Olun. It was Monta who had done the bulk of the rearing—Monta who had been a ma to her than ever her ma was.

Olun remained silent; her anger was but a blip. Olun never denied her ma's love for her, despite her distance. Her ma was, by all means, a good Rohta woman: Dutiful to the Goddess and the man she took as her beloved, Olun's pa. Her love was in the little things she did. The clothes she dyed and stitched for her, the treats she saved for her. The way she bathed her now. *You're my daughter,* her actions seemed to say. *And, though my heart breaks, I believe this is best.*

She came to the little scar on Olun's hip and snatched her hand away. Her full lips pursed and Olun felt her ma's love and heartache shift to fear as it tended to do when she saw it. Scars were visual proof of moral and physical failings. One had to have made a mistake in order to cause damage to oneself. One had to have been reckless or lacked common sense.

Olun resisted the urge to touch the scar at the back of her head, hidden from view beneath her dense curls. While she'd earned the scar on her hip by foolishly trying to impress a boy, she'd had no memory of this scar. It was deep and jagged. However she'd gotten it, it was clear the Dark Lady had been close.

She knew the nature of her ma's thoughts. Had the Goddess marked for death years ago? Were all of her flaws and imperfections—the night terrors—meant to separate her from the living? *It certainly makes their decision easier . . .*

When her ma did not resume her bathing, Olun wrapped her arms around her naked body as if to shrink herself.

"Ma?" She whispered. *Do you still love me?* She didn't turn to look at her ma, afraid of what she might see.

Her ma hesitated. Her hand stilled for long enough that Olun thought she would spin her around and pull her into the hug Olun longed for. But she resumed her washing, passing the cloth over the rest of Olun's body, avoiding the scar as if it were a disease. She finished without another word to Olun or to herself.

The beautiful length of woven cotton her ma took care to drape over her small frame was dyed in various hues of purple with patterns of the desert bleach into it. Stars, moons, oombrak, the dunes. The garment had been intended for her first night with her beloved. How special it would have been to be wrapped in something so precious by someone she loved, and to be unwrapped so preciously by a lover. Olun swallowed hard. This would never be.

And dressing up a scar did not hide the fact that it was there.

Perhaps Olun *was* the weak thread threatening the integrity of her clan. Olun wasn't strong. Had never been strong. If she were a thread, she was a weak one, damaged and frayed. One weak thread can cause a rip. And everyone knew that even the smallest rip weakens the whole. Maybe all that stuff about strength was to give her courage to accept what must be done.

No one knew what to do with her when they came to the arch. The final instructions Elder Kikyel had given them had been vague. *The girl must be taken to Zenika's Mountains. There, she will give her life and set her people free of the curse.* In the end, they'd decided to bind her limbs so she could not run from whatever was to be her death. Exposure, thirst, hunger. Devoured by a creature hidden beneath the sand or in the rock. Whatever form death took, and however long it would take, Olun told herself she was ready for it.

She didn't struggle as the leather bit into her wrists and ankles and thanked them. Though she knew what her fate entailed and was prepared to accept it, she didn't trust herself not to run after them once they'd gone, chasing the wind of her pa's prayers and her brother's tears.

"Come with me," Oja begged. "We'll go to Casimir—"

"Shhh," she kissed his cheek. "I'm doing this for you, too, ya?"

He jerked away from her in anger. "You're *not* doing this for me! If you leave me here, Olun, I'll never forgive you."

Olun nodded solemnly. It didn't matter if he couldn't forgive her. It only mattered that he lived.

Her aunt was the last to approach her.

"When we go, cut yourself free and go int' the mountains," she said quickly under her breath. Something cool and heavy was pressed between her bound hands. Before she could look at it, Monta dropped a cloak over her shoulders, enveloping Olun in her scent.

Confused, Olun glanced up at her, then to where the rest of her family prepared for the long and arduous journey back across the desert. Back to where the rest of their clan lay dying.

"No," Olun whispered.

Monta ignored her. "Once you're free, you'll want t'build a fire. Stay by its light, Olun. In the daytime, you'll follow the path through the mountains. It's not seen at first, but you're a keen girl. You'll find the path. Find shelter, too, just before it gets dark, ya? Do you hear me? *Do not travel in the dark.*"

Even if she wanted to do as her aunt said, Olun knew there was nothing past the mountains. Nothing but stories, and high in the peaks beyond the clouds, the Dark Lady.

"*No,*" Olun said again, letting the knife slip from her hands.

"Remember that question I asked you?" her aunt hissed. She picked up the knife and again pressed it upon Olun. "Go t'the Ithoumi Village hidden in the mountains. My brother'll shelter you."

At this, Olun looked at her in bewilderment. "Village? Your brother?"

Her pa was Monta's only brother, and Olun was absolutely certain he was desert-born and raised.

"It's *my* village, Olun. I was sent away for my health when I was a girl. I thrived in the desert with your Pa's family as my own."

"No—but there's *nothing* in the mountains." She expected Olun to believe that a whole village lived up there? No people would dare live in the mountains—all the stories said so! And besides, what kind of people would give up their sick child?

"They are monsters!" Olun sobbed.

Monta drew Olun into her arms to rock her steadily. She smoothed Olun's tousled hair lovingly, lulling her into calm. Monta was always good at that, soothing her upsets and quelling her panic before it had a chance to grow. Her fingers made their way past thick curls to the small, puckered scar on the back of her head.

"I know you've no memories, my Olun," she said softly. "But, when you were so very small, I told your Pa that I wanted to return t'the mountains and that I wanted t'take you with me."

The air seemed to have been pressed from her lungs.

Monta continued quickly. "Even back then, the clans were on hard times, and your Ma and Pa agreed you'd be better off. A better chance at life, they'd said. So, we went up into the mountains of my birth and stayed with my brother and his family for a season."

"You—you are lying to me," Olun whispered.

"It's the truth, my Olun."

"Then why'd we leave, ya? Why don't I remember?" she demanded frantically. *Why now and not back then?* Why hadn't her parents said *anything*? This is the second time they were giving her up—?

"You were a child. You didn't remember, so I thought it best not to remind you of such things."

"Such *things*?" Monta wasn't making sense—wasn't *answering* her! What happened—"

Monta's face sagged. "I wish I could tell you everything, but there just isn't enough time."

"You had my whole life to tell me," Olun said coldly. But, in the end, what did it matter? She was going to die anyway. Why tell her about them now at the end of her life?

"The important thing is they'll help you, my Olun." Monta said firmly. "They'll remember you—*go to them!*"

"Why can't you come with me?" she said abruptly, the question a surprise even to herself.

"Olun—"

"Answer me, Monta!"

"Because I don't belong there anymore, my Olun," she relented. "Perhaps I never really did—but *you?* It may not seem like it now, but this is a blessing in disguise! Perhaps *now* is your time to go back there."

"And do what?"

Monta smiled and thumbed away Olun's tears. "Live."

Olun turned away, willing to drown in her own tears than let her aunt comfort her. She wanted to believe her—wanted to believe she could *live*. There were so many things she had not experienced, so many things she had yet to do. A night spent with a lover, perhaps? Waking without the terror of her nightmares looming over her—a truly sound sleep?

But Monta was *wrong,* and those people in the mountains? No such people lived there—and if they did, there had to be a reason they'd been exiled there. Monta had lied about everything—how could Olun trust her now? How could Olun believe that what Monta said was to benefit her when the very action of running away meant certain doom for the people her aunt supposedly loved?

"I don't believe you," Olun sobbed. "I don't believe a word you're saying t'me!"

"And you would rather believe stories of monsters and mythical beasts?" she said tersely.

"I can't," Olun inched further away. "Oja'll *die* if I don't do this. You *all* will—"

"You don't know that," Monta said tightly. "I will allow you this grief—but you *will* get up, and you *will* start again. Do you hear me?"

Olun shook her head frantically, clenching her eyes shut to stem the unrelenting flow of tears. *We live, we suffer, we die. Life, Suffering, Death. When our bones return to dust, and Her breath carries us across the land, we begin a new journey of Life, Suffering, and Death.*

This was what Elder Kikyel preached.

This was the way of the living.

This was the way of her short life.

Olun smoothed her fine clothes as best she could with her bound hands and lay down. True to her ma's word, she would look her best when she walked into the Afterlife to meet the Dark Lady. There was no turning back.

"Sacrifice," Monta said just before her parting. "Doesn't have t'mean death. Remember that, my Olun."

CHAPTER 3

C OOL METAL SLID BETWEEN her wrists, and the leather of her bindings fell away.

Parched and weak with hunger, Olun blinked up at the strange men surrounding her. They were enormous—Olun wondered vaguely if they were the creatures the Goddess sent to kill her. One crouched before her, lifting her thin, limp wrist in his large, calloused hands. He wore his dark hair pulled tightly back from his face and gathered in a braid. His face was stoic, and his dark eyes appraised her somewhat lackadaisically. His clothes were strange; a shirt reaching his knees with a wide belt cinching his waist. Around his shoulders, he wore a furred cloak. The thick fabrics and leathers were dull and unfamiliar.

"She is quite thin, but not dead," he told the others.

The formal pronunciation of his words confused her as much as the words themself. *Not dead?*

"Who . . . ?" Olun croaked and tried to lift her head. She'd curled beneath her aunt's cloak after her family had gone, tossing away both the knife and food her aunt had left her in secret. She was weak and not at all sure she wasn't hallucinating.

"Can you stand?" the man asked.

Olun carefully uncurled her limbs. Whether or not her stiff legs would hold her weight was another story entirely. She nodded nonetheless.

"Who . . . are you?"

"I am Genta," said the man. "I have come to bring you to the Ithoumi Village."

***

They traveled by day, stopping when the shadows crept up the rock to start a fire. Olun followed as if in a daze, reluctant to go anywhere with such strange men but unable to fight them off. The flames danced off their spear tips and the wicked recurve of blades she'd never seen before. A monstrous weapon for monstrous men. If they thought to scare her into compliance, using their blades against her should she rebel, it worked.

The men were curious about her as well, especially when she refused their food and water. Even more so when her night terrors had her thrashing about with more might than they believed her small, malnourished body capable of. But, as if under command, they did not touch her. It fell to the man called Genta to wake her from her thrashing. And when she woke, weak and weary, it was he who pinched her jaws open to force her to eat and drink.

"We still have two more days of hard travel ahead of us," he said gruffly in his strange cadence, unaffected by her weak struggles against his grip. "I will *not* bring back a corpse."

She didn't like his roughness and wished he'd just leave her alone like the others, but she stopped her protests when the next thing out of his mouth was a threat to throw her over his shoulder like a hunted beast if she continued to be difficult. Perhaps he should have. Her night terrors had weakened her so much so, it had taken an extra day for the Ithoumi Village to come into view.

Dirt footpaths shifted to cobblestone beneath her feet. Olun gaped up at the rock-cut homes ascending the mountainous terrain, some having been chiseled into the sides of cliffs. Pillars of stone and round mud brick houses and wide thatched roofs created streets and alleyways. Fires sprang from pits, and torches lit windows, setting the village aglow. What seemed like the entire village welcomed them with booming drums and the thrum of strings of celebration. Olun never imagined such a place could exist outside of the metropolis of Casimir.

"Is *this* the Afterlife?" she whispered in awe, and Genta looked down at her curiously.

"You tell me," he said and urged her forward with a hand on her shoulder.

The musky scents of incense, cooking meats, and bread mingled together as Genta ushered her forward through the streets, the curved walls of homes blocking her view of the cliffs. She didn't see much else as he ferried her through the street, past curious eyes, and excited shouts and whispers.

"Is that her? Sickly little thing." — *"The little desert girl!"* — *"Such a strange choice, if you ask me."* — *"This proves Vasc has not been right in the mind."*

She kept her eyes to her feet, afraid to look up into the eyes of the curious crowd that had formed for their arrival. If these people were the spirits of the forsaken—apparitions of a time long ago—they were not at all what she expected.

"You have arrived!" Olun jumped at the gleeful boom that met them at the top of a series of steps just before the plateau. The man who approached her was tall, like the other Ithoumi men. Chest hair curled up from the collar of a simple, yet beautifully made, tunic stretched over a jovial, bouncing belly. But it was his face that struck Olun. With a pang of shock, she saw just how much the man resembled Monta.

"Our arrival was delayed," grunted Genta, glancing around at the festivities with apprehension. "And yet it seems we have arrived on time."

The big man laughed and clapped him on the back. "Of course, the Elder told us delays were to be expected—but no more than a day, he said."

Genta grunted again. "How convenient," he muttered.

To Olun, the big man cooed. "You have grown into a striking young woman! I almost did not recognize you, my dear Olun."

Monta *had* said that he would know her, though as similar as his features were to Monta's, Olun had no other recognition of him. The big man looked over her head, expectant eyes filled with hope as he scanned the crowd behind her.

"She was not with the girl," Genta answered his unspoken question solemnly.

The big man's face fell momentarily, and he turned his attention back to Olun. "Come, we must get you situated. There are many people waiting to meet you."

He swept his arm toward the center of the plateau, where four striking men and women stood before a large fire. Olun gazed at them warily, taking in the placidity of the plump woman dressed in a deep, dull green, and the haughty height of the man's head to her left. He wore fine leathers and fabrics that showed his strong physique despite his age-bowed back. The other two men and women with them, similar in face and size, looked on in matching curiosity laced with apprehension.

How had they known she was coming? Did Monta know they would come for her? This man had mentioned an Elder—why would *their* Elder speak of her? These questions and more swirled through Olun's mind at dizzying speed.

"Why—" She began before the swell of whispers caught her attention again.

"He has returned!"

"How unfortunate."

"Madness, simple as that!"

"Watch what you say!"

The voices contended with one another, morphing into a garble of indistinguishable words pulling her in every direction until her eyes settled on the rugged man they parted for. He lumbered through the crowd with a noticeable limp. His messy black hair fell unbound down to his elbows, with a mix of matted and twisted strands to form cords and braids. Various items swung from them in his uneven gait. His broad shoulders sat at a slight angle, and his face was an ugly twist of scars stretched as though the flesh had been bound together again. Olun took an involuntary step back, bumping into the big man.

". . . very weak," she caught the end of Genta's observation, oblivious of her terror. "Closer to death than I would have liked to see."

"We cannot postpone what must be done tonight . . ." the big man replied.

Their conversation, too, faded away. Olun couldn't breathe—her head spinning. The scarred man drew closer and closer, trapping her in his feral gaze. *Had the Dark Lady sent him to collect her? A monster crafted of shadows and sorrows to do Her bidding?*

The man's eyes widened as she fell to her knees. His slow gait quickened to a lop-sided gallop and his twisted face neared hers. The last thing she saw was the glint of his deep-set, milky white eye reminiscent of the moon.

Chapter 4

"**S**he has no business being here." A young woman's shrill, contemptuous retort stirred Olun to consciousness.

"According to the Elder, she does," said a second woman, older, by the sound of her sagely voice.

Olun cracked open her eyes, groggily finding her bearings. She lay beneath a pile of blankets on a wide, soft bed. Walls of stone kept in the heat from a bulbous, freestanding fireplace in the center of an open room, its thick neck carrying smoke up to vent out of the ceiling. Candles perched on built-in stone shelves, illuminating walls decorated with various childish illustrations and tapestries. Curiously, Olun craned her neck to see the rest of the space.

"Because she went missing?" hissed the younger woman, drawing Olun's attention to the far side of the room. She paced like a cornered beast, her long, black braid whipping like a tail.

"I went missing, too, Naleda, and *I* am not Elder." She laughed humorlessly.

"He is not made for this," reasoned the older woman, Naleda, while watching the young woman from where she sat cross-legged at a low table. "What a toll this life has taken on him. At least this way, he can be free of his responsibilities to the Goddess and Elder Vasc."

"Free?" The younger woman scoffed. "He will never be able to live a normal life. Didan is damaged, you know as well as I how bad his wounds were. He will not be able to wield a hammer or a weapon. He will not be able to father children or feed a family. He has half of his sight! There is *nothing* left for him except for life as Elder. Do you not care about any of that?"

"I will not have you speak to my mother this way." Olun recognized Genta's hard voice.

"Maybe I should be speaking to *you* this way," the young woman fired back. "You are the one who brought her here! You never wanted Didan to succeed in anything. Of course, you would be the one to bring the girl here."

"So, it was I who conjured her from thin air just to push my brother into exile?" Genta sneered. "You have *quite* the imagination, Syndra. I applaud you for it."

"Enough," snapped Naleda, her voice dropping to a fierce whisper. "Syndra, I understand you—I really do—but this *has* to happen. There is no other way—*let me finish!*"

Olun flinched at the woman's reprimand, getting a glimpse of the younger woman—Syndra's—combative yet surprisingly beautiful face as she bit back her interjections.

"His injuries will make it hard, but not impossible for him to live the life he wants. This girl will take his place and set him free, I'm sure of it. He is here because he knows it, too."

"No, he has come here because you are taking away his purpose in this village," Syndra laughed bitterly.

"A village he has spent the past ten years running away from," Genta said. "He gave up his place here long before this girl arrived. One would think you, of all people, would be a little happier since you can finally act on those feelings you have never let go of."

"Should we really be happy that you have brought back *another* thieving desert dweller for your collection—"

"Hush, both of you!" Naleda groaned. She crossed the room to sit by the oven and stared into the coals. Despite the warm glow of the fire, her black skin seemed ashen, and her eyes hooded with exhaustion. Olun could not begin to understand the emotions running through this woman if what Syndra had said was indeed true.

Syndra took a knee beside Naleda. The hand she placed on her shoulder seemed to Olun more commanding than comforting.

"We are healers," Syndra said. "We defy the Goddesses each time we use our craft. Each time we stitch a wound or deliver a baby—*we* are controlling the ebb and flow of life. Naleda, you brought Didan life not once but twice. If you are so worried about who will free him from his burden, then *you* should do it. We all should praise *you*."

"First she takes pieces from him, now she saves him," Genta muttered, rolling his eyes. "You are just as fickle as he is."

Naleda patted Syndra's hand. "If you truly believe that, then I have failed as your teacher. Now get out—*both* of you."

Syndra seemed to linger in challenge before she followed Genta out, the leather flap snapping behind her like a whip. Naleda sat pondering for a time and sighed. She stood up and crossed the room to Olun, who clamped her eyes shut.

"Olun," Naleda called sternly, stroking her brow. "It is time to wake up now."

Nostalgia rose in Olun's breast, the command one Monta would have given. She opened her eyes to stare up at Naleda. She was, Olun recognized, the woman in green from the plateau. She was full-bosomed, up close, her dark hair piled high on her head gave her a larger-than-life look. Her smile was warm and grounding; round cheeks rose like clouds to allow the sunshine of her smile through.

And yet, Olun found nothing about her familiar.

"I . . . I should remember you, ya?" Olun croaked with dismay.

"It has been thirteen years," she said warmly. "You were only a child when we last met."

"I remember nothing."

"I was confident you would in time." Naleda's brows knitted together with concern. "Perhaps the injury was too severe."

Naleda reached to touch the place where Olun's scar was hidden beneath her thick hair, but Olun jerked away. "Severe?"

Naleda nodded. "You vanished. Days and days passed by, and we had given up hope of finding you. Then my son came out of the caves with you in his arms. I was the one who stitched your head, but it took many more days for you to wake."

Olun drew up her knees, hugging them as tightly as she could to stop her shaking. *Why hadn't Monta said anything sooner?* Perhaps it was the shame of the scar she bore that had kept her aunt silent. It was ironic, really; scars were meant to remind them of their punishments, but Olun could not remember what she'd done to cause such an injury. What had she done to be punished like this, and why had the Dark Lady taken that memory?

Naleda patted Olun's knee sympathetically. "Head wounds are tricky. Sometimes memories return, sometimes they do not. You are lucky to have woken up at all."

"The woman who left—" Olun wiped her eyes, remembering what Syndra had said. "Was she hurt back then, too?"

"Naleda," came a quiet call from behind the leather door. "We are ready."

Naleda grunted her response. To Olun, she thumbed away her frustrated tears. "Let us get you presentable, dear. Tonight is a night of celebration, not sorrow."

"I don't understand what's going on," Olun tried to stem her rising panic.

"The Dark Goddess has spoken to Elder Vasc at last," Naleda replied somberly. "*You* are to be our next Elder."

***

This is a dream.

Night was fully upon them when Olun emerged from the dwelling, numbed by her confusion. She'd had no words for Naleda's revelation. She wasn't all that sure she was awake, either—this was all too far-fetched to be real. In fact, the only thing that made sense was that this was all a dream, and it began the moment she'd set foot in this place. Olun shivered beneath the drape of the kaftan Naleda dressed her in, her thin body and short curly hair washed clean of her travels and neglect, and went along with it. Perhaps this dream would reveal its secrets before it descended into nightmare.

The villagers watched her as she climbed the stairs to the plateau for the second time, their smiles subdued and their curious excitement contained behind their hands. Olun tried not to look too hard at them, embarrassed by her previous entrance, and afraid of who she might see amongst them. The big man stood in the glow of the bonfire, as large and as bright as the flames themselves. *This is what Monta would look like if she smiled,* Olun thought. *Or laughed, or played.* It was then that Olun realized how serious of a woman her aunt was.

"This is Zafre," Naleda reminded her when they approached. "You may not remember, but he is the Chief of this village, and my Bonded."

Bonded? Olun frowned at the unfamiliar term. But what was even more shocking was that *Monta's brother was a chief!*

Naleda continued her introductions, gesturing to the three other people who had first stood with her. "And these are his Doyens: Hujak, Master of the Hunt; Zayeer, Master of the Herd; and Helima, Master of Crops—"

"Crops?" Olun perked up. Her clan got their rice and grain in Casimir when they could afford to trade for it. Was it really possible to have such things so far away from Casimir? *I guess in a dream, anything's possible,* she smiled wryly.

"We will show you," Helima said kindly, though her gray eyes poured over her in scrutiny. "And you must know that Naleda here is our final Doyen: Master of Healing," she finished.

"She is nothing but skin and bones," acknowledged Hujak, frowning at Olun. The tall man with the bowed back regarded her as if she were a nuisance. Beside him, the man who resembled Helima—Zayeer—stroked his peppered beard with concern.

"You are right," said Naleda pointedly. "Let the girl have a meal first and be settled. Has anyone seen where Vasc has gotten to?"

"The man is probably halfway up the mountain by now," Zayeer chuckled, the three Doyens migrating away from her.

Again, Olun noticed the formality of these people's conversation. Desert folk were looser with their words, and their tones quick and snappy. These people chose their words carefully, spoke slowly, and tediously dragged out their sentences. It was a lot to wrap her head around.

Naleda sat her down on a cushion before a grand feast. Roasted and boiled meats, some of which Olun had never seen before—*fins* and *scales?* Sweet-smelling breads drizzled with sap, fragrant sticky rice, clotted creams, and *fruit!* Water and tea and a spiced fragrant one she couldn't name! Unbridled emotion washed over Olun. *This is no dream but the Afterlife.* Her breath hitched, and her eyes watered with a sob threatening to pull her under. Such indulgences could not exist beyond the stone pillars of the Gate.

She devoured all that was put in front of her, her face full and alight with as much glee as greed. She licked sweet cream from her thumb and sampled various fragrant breads despite the painful protests of her stomach, shrunken and weak from weeks of malnutrition. Naleda and others chuckled at her sudden enthusiasm. "Take it slow," Naleda chided. "There is more where this came from."

More? Olun slowed and nodded, mouth too full to reply. But Naleda was already ushering her observers away to give her a little privacy. Olun watched her return to Zafre's side, joining conversation with him and the others introduced as Doyens. Guests danced to the rhythms of the drums and strings, drinking and eating and laughing together. She drank the dark, fragrant beverage poured into her cup, so sweet it made her feel as if she were floating. It was cold, but warmed her insides. This, she found, wasn't half bad! Olun smiled to herself, downed the cup, and poured herself more, watching the festivities of the night. It reminded her of the Gathering. But something still seemed off to Olun. *Wrong,* even.

In the sea of glances, she saw Genta. He'd cleaned up since she'd last seen him, having traded his traveling clothes for an embroidered robe and his tight braid for loose curls swept back from his face. Olun reached out involuntarily to grasp his robe as he passed, the only face of whom was truly familiar.

Genta regarded her with disinterest, and—if she were being honest—disapproval. He pulled his clothes from her fingers and continued on. Dream or not, she concluded, there would be no ally in this man.

She put her cup to her lips and watched him from its brim.

"If you keep drinking like that, you will faint again," Olun jumped as a boy plopped down at her left. "Genta brews it quite strong, you see, but it is *very* popular!"

Olun eyed the beverage suspiciously, her head and body so light, she swayed.

"Have you never had wine before?" he laughed. Behind him, a group of boys and girls giggled and whispered behind their hands.

"Wine?" Olun chirped. She'd had wine before, and it did *not* taste as good as this. In fact, the wine she knew was bitter and so dry, she'd rather eat sand. The boy and the others laughed harder. *He couldn't have been no older than Oja,* Olun thought with a pang. All at once, her family came flooding back to her, and the awe of this strange dream began to dissipate. She put down her cup and pushed away her plate. *You shouldn't be here,* she scolded herself and patted her cheeks. *Okay, Olun, time to wake up now!*

"Leave us, Bana."

Olun froze, a shiver of fear traveled up her spine as the mangled, scar-faced man from before lowered himself down on her other side. The children scattered, and the boy scrambled to his feet obediently, pouting as he left them together in silence. Olun wanted him to come back—or Naleda, for that matter. *Someone* to rescue her from this man. If this were a dream, then she should have control over it, right?

But Olun noticed the villagers giving them a wide berth. No, they avoided *him.* He must be a terrible, terrible man for the Dark Lady to do this to him. He had to be, for his own people to regard him with such tense apprehension.

This must be the nightmare. Olun shivered, and the man mistook her dread for cold. Without a word, he removed his shawl and draped it across her shoulders. Hesitantly, Olun glanced at him from the corner of her eye. Instead of the feral man she expected to see, he was finely dressed just as she was, a strange contrast to the messiness of his hair and patchy beard. Beneath his mane of hair, his profiled face showed his unmarred side. He was young, with full lips and high cheekbones. His dark skin was smooth and, dare she think it, handsome? Or perhaps it was just wine.

He watched her, too, roaming over the details of her face with just as much interest. Olun dropped her eyes to her lap immediately, the fine hairs on the back of her neck prickling as her intimate observations were noticed. She hiccuped.

"I am Didan," he said quietly.

His voice was dragged as if a heaviness weighed down his tongue along with the corner of his lip. A result of his many injuries, Olun assumed. One of his many punishments. This was the man they argued about in Naleda's home. This was the man she would be replacing as their Elder's successor. His name meant nothing to her, but the gentleness in his voice pulled some semblance of familiarity she could not place.

The drums quieted, and all chatter ceased. When all eyes turned toward the fire, Didan grabbed her arm so suddenly, she couldn't even cry out.

"Do *not* drink," he hissed, the gentleness gone from his voice.

Though there was hardly enough force behind his grip to bruise, his touch awakened something buried deep inside of her. A recognition—or perhaps a memory—of pain so intense, she reeled back in shock.

Didan jerked her closer until she looked directly into his disfigured face, his blind eye as pale and glaring as the full moon. "Do you understand?"

Olun nodded fiercely even though she didn't, in fact, understand. Didan released her arm just as suddenly as he'd grasped it, and the pain she'd felt dissipated. He climbed to his feet as Naleda approached and limped away.

"Come along, Olun," Naleda beckoned, oblivious to what had occurred, and Olun couldn't think to tell her of it. When she could, she was already before a wizened old man.

This man was unlike the haughty Hujak or the contemplative Zayeer. He was thin, with a face pulled by wrinkles that sagged his eyes and lips to jowls. His hair was stringy, stark white at the roots, adorned with river stones and bone. He leaned on a staff and assessed her with muted eyes as if he were not completely present. As if he tried to shrink into the recesses of his mind. When he held out his bony hand for hers, Olun paused. She hadn't feared Elder Kikyel, but she feared this Elder and his dead eyes. There was a void in him—a blackness in place of the very thing that gave life meaning. He curled his fingers into her palm, insouciant of her repulsion.

"As it has been since the Firsts, there has been an Elder to bridge the gap between the living and those departed," he began in a strong, commanding voice despite his appearance. "We are corporeal mouthpieces for the Goddess and spirits alike."

Olun knew this to be true; every clan had an Elder for spiritual guidance and enlightenment. Her eyes watered at the thought of Elder Kikyel. Though she'd condemned Olun to death, she'd still been an ever-present fixture in her life. Perhaps this was why Olun obeyed her so easily. This Elder heaved a put-upon sigh, his sagging face benumbed.

"My duty to the Dark Goddess has blessedly ended, for She has set her sights on another," he continued. "Child of the Goddess, gifted with abilities none but She can understand. So great and so terrifying these gifts are, we often lose our way."

All at once, a wave of murmurs passed over the villagers. Olun followed their pointed glances toward Didan, standing stiffly beside Syndra, his disappointed eyes never leaving Olun.

"Goddess of the Night, Farrier to the Great After, bear witness as Olun of the Rohta begins her life anew as Your disciple. May she never stray from Your side."

"May she never stray from Your side!" the villagers repeated.

"May she never lose herself to the dark."

"May she never lose herself to the dark!"

Elder Vasc lifted a beautifully carved stone bowl above his head. When he brought it down again, he beckoned Olun to take it. "This is the Stream that flows through these lands beneath the surface, like the veins of life that flow through us all. *Connecting* us all."

She let him gently place the bowl in her hands, and everyone seemed to hold their breath, waiting for her to take the final step. Didan had warned her not to drink, but everyone waited for her to do it. Just like that evening when Elder Kikyel told her of what she must do, and all eyes landed on her. All hopes, all emotions—*everything!* What would happen if she didn't? What would happen if she *did?*

Her breath shortened, her mind grew frantic. They weren't asking her to give her life, but they were asking her to give *something*. They waited for her to *do* something. Olun closed her eyes. *I want to wake up! Please—I don't know what to do!*

But she heard Elder Kikyel's question, *"What is the cost of life?"* Was this it? If she drank, would she finally wake up?

The water was ice cold and pure—the best she had ever tasted. It met her lips like a kiss, sealing the covenant of soul and spirit, the Stream flowing to every inch of her.

CHAPTER 5

T HE NIGHT PASSED IN a blur. Olun vaguely remembered following Genta through the moonlit village, the houses growing fewer and farther between. Her legs ached as they climbed a steep path to a round, windowless hut at the top of a hill. Inside, he lit the coals in a free-standing oven, providing light and warmth.

Olun looked around at the curved stone walls and up at the webs strung along the thatched ceiling. The hut was a little more than a room, with a bed, an oven, and a crooked table propped up against the wall. In her slow pivot, she saw the dress her ma had made, now stained and soiled, and Monta's cloak neatly folded by the door beside Genta.

"My father says that you will not begin your duties tonight," he grunted. "You are much too fragile for that right now. You will live here for the time being, so welcome home."

Home. Olun stared at him vacantly. This was not home.

When he left, she crossed the room to snatch her ma's dress and her aunt's cloak into her arms. She breathed in their scents deeply. *This* was home. She nuzzled their clothes, sinking to the floor. It carried the warmth of the desert, the memories of love, and the sweat of resilience.

Their essence clung to the fibers like the desert dust that coated their skin.

***

Morning did not erase the gloom of the stone walls around her. In fact, had it not been for the distant sounds of the village waking, Olun would not have known the sun had risen. This place was like a tomb, and just as cold were its lingering ghosts of sorrow and angst. The only times Olun had felt so full of hopelessness and sorrow were after waking before the wisps of nightmares faded into nothingness. But the events of the previous evening had not disappeared from her memory. Her head throbbed, and her bloated belly ached, further proof of the night before. It was as if Ma Bright herself had placed such a feast into her hands. And yet, this place—these people—that *man*—

"It wasn't a dream," Olun gasped.

Heart pounding and still clutching the dress and the cloak, Olun stumbled into the world outside. Instead of desert, she was met with the emptiness of a dirt yard and a dilapidated stone wall. Beyond it, a winding dirt path led down to another stone hut. Stone steps and homes that clustered together into a living mass further down. Olun shaded her eyes to get a better look, leaning on the wall that poorly separated her bare yard from the path.

She'd never been in a village—at least, did not *remember* being in a village. She'd never even been into the City of Casimir, despite the annual Gathering of the clans that took place outside of it. But she'd seen the towering buildings in the distance. These buildings were small, rounded like baskets with coned tops.

The villagers were already well into their morning. The bleating of beasts somewhere in the village met her ear as well as the faraway clinking of tools. Olun closed her eyes as a soft breeze swept the various scents of roasting meat, bread, and smoke to her nose. Her stomach groaned uncomfortably, remembering the feast from last night. Olun covered her mouth against the onset of sickness, but it was too late. Her stomach violently purged the decadent foods and drinks she'd had no business consuming.

And yet, how easy would it be to stay in this place, gorging on food every night? Without famine, without sickness, without death? Olun knew how inappropriate those thoughts were. She'd been obedient to her Elder and her Goddess all her life. She should not be here—in the village, as its Elder, and certainly not *alive*. For what did it mean that she lived? What would happen to her people if *her* Elder's instructions were not met?

When Olun finished, fatigue had her drooping against the wall, but the sight of Didan loping up the hill toward her, his crooked frame and dragging gate unmistakable, bolted her upright. His scars, twisted to an ugly sheen, were just as horrifying in the daylight. Olun backed away from the wall, her only options for escape being further up the path, where nothing seemed to exist other than rocks, or back inside. Olun chose the latter. She hugged her knees to her chest, her ma's dress and aunt's cloak not once leaving her arms. What did *he* want? Not just that—what had this man done to offend the goddesses? These people lived in the Ithoumi Mountains—home of the exiled Goddess. They *worshiped* Her! Olun realized it didn't matter what he'd done—all of the Ithoumi were terrible.

Yet, Zafre's smiling face flashed before her eyes, a face so similar to her aunt's she could cry. *Did that mean Monta was terrible, too?*

"May I come in?"

Olun jumped, startled by the sudden sound of Didan's slurred and slowed speech. Retreating to the back of the dwelling, she caught sight of an iron rod by the fire and wielded it in her shaking hands. "No!" she cried.

There was silence as she waited for him to leave, or to force his way in, but he spoke again. "Walk with me? I wish to speak with you—"

"I don't want t'go *anywhere* with you!" she screamed, shocked by such a question. He was the last person she expected to have at her door—the last person she would ever go anywhere with! Even without his scars, he'd made it perfectly clear the night before when he'd grabbed her that he was not a man to be trusted. Had he forgotten what he'd done, or was he here because he hadn't forgotten what *she* hadn't done?

"I—I want t'speak to the Elder," Olun said to him, voice quivering. "Where's he?"

"You can speak with me if you like—"

"I *don't* like!" she cried incredulously. Why wasn't he understanding? "The *other* one— I want to speak to him!"

There was another pause. "Elder Vasc has left the village. He is no longer needed."

No longer needed!? "He's coming back, ya?"

She heard him take a deep breath and exhale slowly, but he didn't answer her.

"I want to see Zafre then. Bring him!"

"The village *Chief* is a very busy man," slurred Didan and Olun noticed the way he dragged out the word 'village,' running it into the next word as if his tongue momentarily ceased function.

"Then Genta—he's the one who brought me here!" Olun couldn't help her hysteria from pinching her voice. "I need t'see him now!"

"Are you ill?" Didan asked abruptly. "I could—"

"Go away!" she cried. If *he* would not do as *she* said, then why entertain this further?

"Leave me alone—go away!" There wasn't much in the little hut to throw, but Olun suddenly found herself throwing anything she could get her hands on. A bowl shattered against the wall with the surge of anger. A sandal hit the door flap and tumbled to the floor; the objects were a useless defense, but she would fight him with whatever she had to keep him from touching her. From *hurting* her again.

"Go away! Go away! Leave me alone!"

"I am coming in—" Didan said quickly, but Olun shrieked, never ceasing her onslaught of projectiles. She didn't want to be there, didn't want *him* to be there. It was all too much and happening far quicker than she could keep up with.

The door flap fluttered.

"Are you as foolish as you sound? Don't you understand—I said *go away!*"

When the clothes in her arms were the only thing left to throw, she stopped and curled around them like a child in the womb. Olun rocked back and forth, hugging the clothes and imagining her aunt rocking her. Hoping with all her might that he would leave her alone.

"Very well," Didan said softly.

Olun didn't know how long she lay curled around the ball of clothes when she finally managed to crawl to the door and lift the flap. Left outside of her door was a basket of food and drink. Her stomach flipped and seized with renewed hunger, but she didn't touch it. Instead, she glanced left and right, fearful that Didan still lingered in wait. But he'd done as she'd demanded.

She left the basket outside. Food and drink would only prolong the inevitable. She thought of her brother. He still had a long life to live, and he was so sure that he would not be able to live it among the Rohta.

But he was wrong. Oja just needed to wait a bit longer—wait for her to set things right.

Olun took off the kaftan Naleda had dressed her in, noticing for the first time how beautiful it was. Its dull color was offset by expert stitching around the neck, sleeves, and hem. It was yet another thing Olun would not be needing. She carefully folded it and set it on the bed, then quickly dressed herself in her ma's flamboyant wrap. Soiled with travel and her own filth as it was, Olun would wear into the Afterlife as intended. She would die a Rohta. Lastly, she draped Monta's cloak about her shoulders and stepped out into the evening.

Elder Vasc had gone, and it was clear Didan would not fetch Zafre or Genta. It didn't matter to Olun either way. She would only tell them all that they'd made a mistake. That her fate was to be her clan's divine sacrifice. That her life should end at the pillars beneath the mountain.

With one last deep breath, Olun raced down the hill, skidding around the curves and taking the steps two at a time. She pushed past startled villagers, deaf to their calls and blind to their gestures. She ran faster and faster, not slowing until she left the village with its odd homes, monstrous men, and disillusioned people behind her.

CHAPTER 6

Hɪɢʜ ᴄʟɪꜰꜰꜱ ʙʟᴏᴄᴋᴇᴅ ᴛʜᴇ setting sun, and rocks stretched the shadows from cracks and crevices. The sky was a tapestry of soft lavender streaked with pink, and shadows clung as heavy as the cloak on her shoulders. But Olun wasn't afraid of the dark. Not really. *"If there's one thing you can count on . . ."* Monta had told her once when she was small and her nightmares had made her fear sleep, *"It's that Night always becomes Day."* This kind of darkness was only passing.

If she traveled night and day, resting only when she had to, her travel time would be cut in half. It wasn't ideal, but then again, nothing about dying was ideal. There was something else Monta had told her about these mountains, Olun was certain, but she could not focus her thoughts well enough to remember. Monta had said so many things—too many for her to discern the lies from the truths.

"Go to the mountains," she muttered, deepening her voice to mimic her aunt's. "It's your time to live." Olun had already been alive almost twenty years, and *now* was her time to live? Ha! By her age, her ma had been a mother of two. And live *here?*

"May she never stray from Your side," Olun continued her muttering. "May she never lose herself to the dark."

These people were backward. They leave their mountain in search of lone, young women that they could claim as their Elder. Elders were not chosen that way—at least, not in the desert. In all actuality, Olun didn't really know how Elders were chosen among the Rohta, but she was certain it was not by *kidnapping*! But, then again, the Ithoumi worshiped the Dark Lady. There was no telling what kind of rules She played by. If Didan was any indication, She treated her people horribly. A quick death as Her sacrifice would be better than living a lifetime bearing the scars of Her abuse.

"Will you have the strength to face Her in the Great After, then?"

The question took Olun by such surprise that she slowed and thought. Her life had not amounted to much. She'd had no skills, other than her patience with the sick and dying. She'd had no purpose other than as a burden to her clan, keeping them awake with her night terrors and sporadic emotions. By the light of Ma Bright, she'd received two shameful scars, one of which she should've already repented for becoming the dutiful daughter that she was. She'd *die* for them, just as they wanted.

"I'm doing what She asked," Olun said. "That should be enough, ya?"

"Is it really, little one?"

"Enough already—" Olun released a long, helpless groan and stopped. *Who am I talking to?* She glanced about herself, bewildered, as if waking from a trance. There was no reply from her thoughts or otherwise. Olun pinched the bridge of her nose; that wine was strong indeed. It wouldn't surprise her if she were still feeling its effects. As if to prove her correct, a stone skidded behind her, hitting the dirt below with a crack that echoed down the canyon. Olun spun around to face the direction of the sound and was met by nothing but the empty path and cliffs shadowed by the receding light of day.

Delirium, she told herself, despite the nagging whisper of a memory. The sooner she was out of the mountains, the sooner all of this would be over.

"*Long ago, your life was spared at the expense of another's,*" her thoughts chuckled humorlessly. "*How eager you now wish to throw it away.*"

But then . . . those weren't her thoughts at all.

"Hello?" she called, spinning around desperately to find the person such voiceless mockery came from. This hallucination—no, *delirium*—was neither from wine nor exhaustion. Something was very, *very* wrong!

When Olun looked behind her again, she saw it. A flicker of yellow eyes from the shadows of the rocks, the creature's body blending so seamlessly she would have lost sight of it if it hadn't been creeping steadily closer.

"What're you?" She murmured.

Its lips peeled back, revealing white, dagger-like teeth. It released a possessive cry—the distant sounds she'd heard in the night during her journey into the mountains. Then she remembered the important thing she'd struggled to recall: *Do not travel in the dark.*

With a cry of her own, Olun turned and ran toward the shelter of the rocks. Behind her, a roar more terrible than the last echoed through the cavernous path. Claws scraped against rock and shifting dirt. The creature let off another cry of chase, and Olun risked a glance over her shoulder. Propelled by four powerful legs and massive claws, it gained on her at frightening speed, its yellow eyes focused.

The creature pounced, swiping one great paw, catching the billowing fabric of her clothes, and knocking her sideways against a boulder. Olun struggled to free herself from the creature's tangled claws. It opened its mouth, and without thinking, Olun shoved a rock into it.

Teeth the size of her forearm clamped around the obstruction with a crunch.

A horn sounded close by, startling the beast. It looked up, ears flattening, and a great hiss escaped its mouth. The blare barely registered to Olun as she threw her cloak at the beast and scrambled away. She sobbed hopelessly as she wedged herself between a gap of rock just barely wide and deep enough to shelter her.

The creature roared again, free from the tangles of her cloak and clawing at the opening desperately to reach her. Each strike brought it closer and closer. Spit from its roars and hisses spattered her face. Olun could hardly breathe, her body wedged so tightly between the rock walls. There wasn't even enough space to manage a gasp when a single claw grazed her shoulder. Its claws grew nearer and nearer, its gums pink, its fangs webbed with drool, its yellow eyes fixed on her own. Olun couldn't look away even as her body tensed for pain, locking her limbs into place. As she watched the creature struggle to widen the gap, she knew there would be no fighting it. There would be no stopping this death. In this moment, Olun realized how terrified of death she was—she *didn't* want to die! Not like this, not starving at the base of the mountain, either. Not *alone*.

"*Dark Lady*—" she sobbed. "*Please!* Have mercy!"

The deep blare of a horn sounded again, so close this time. The creature screamed as if struck and fell away from the entrance. Shouts came from outside, hollers accompanied by clacks of stones striking against each other. The glow of the torch illuminated the creature as it paced back and forth in front of the crevice, its tooth-filled maw agape and its black, leathery tail flicking back and forth. It took a swipe at the men, not yet ready to concede defeat despite the intrusion, before it hissed and disappeared from the entrance altogether. Three men bearing torches and brandishing an assortment of weapons blocked her view of the creature. Suddenly, Bana, the boy from the other night, appeared before her.

"She is alive!" he shouted, reaching in.

Though there was certainly enough room to extend a hand toward him, try as she might, her body *would not do so*. Bana grunted as he wedged himself in enough to take hold of her arm and, with unexpected strength, wrench her from her hiding spot.

"I have her!" he called as Olun toppled against him, her legs refusing to let her stand.

"Get her out of here, Bana! *Now!*" Olun recognized Genta.

He swung a rope above his head; the stone tied to the end whistled with each rotation. His focus was for the creature which, though it had retreated to higher ground, had not given up the fight. It flattened its ears and struck at the group, baring its claws. Didan, of all people, thrust his spear at it, backing it up. A third man helped the pair drive it back further.

"Come on," Bana said as he hoisted her up onto his back effortlessly and took off in a trot.

"What if there're more?" Olun said hysterically, her arms wrapped tightly around his neck.

"The sun has just set," Bana said matter-of-factly, his voice breaking in the awkward squeak of a boy on the cusp of manhood. "It is not dark enough, and they do not hunt so close to the village. You must have found a straggler, Tiny Desert Girl!"

A horrible shriek echoed through the canyon, and Olun cowered against his back. "Is—is that thing real?"

"Echrol," Bana grunted, slowing. "Can you walk, now?" He lowered her to the ground, holding her arm until he was sure she could stand on her own. The shriek was just enough to unfreeze her limbs to follow Bana's brisk pace.

"They are powerful predators, but Manuk and my brothers will not let that one get to us," he assured her. "And we are too close to the village now anyway, so we will be okay. They do not like us very much."

"Your brothers?" Olun asked dumbly.

"Genta and Didan."

"That creature could kill'em," Olun mumbled, thinking of Didan. He was not only lame but half-blind. Did these people not care about their cripples?

"Who?" Bana asked, then, at the wide-eyed, *who else?* expression she gave him, laughed. "Didan? He will be fine. Even if he were alone, an echrol would think twice about making a meal of him. But you, Tiny Desert Girl, you are an easy snack."

Tiny Desert Girl. He'd said it before. Bana stood half a head taller than her. His lanky awkwardness told her that he'd only grow even taller and fill out into a robust man like his pa and older brothers. Olun couldn't help but think about her own brother; next to this boy, Oja would look like a child fresh from his ma's bosom. Bana had not suffered death or endured malnutrition. He had no idea what was beyond the mountains and their abundant food and unending flow of water.

Oja won't survive on his own. Olun stifled another sob. He's small and weak, and if things didn't get better for the Rohta . . .

"What I struggle to understand is," Bana mused ahead of her, "*Why* you ran away. I mean, Genta told me he *cut* you free. He said if he had not listened to Elder Vasc and come when he had, you would be nothing but a corpse by now."

"It's what I'm supposed t'be," she said quietly.

Bana snorted, glancing at her as if to figure out whether or not she was joking. When Olun said nothing else, he shrugged.

"We should get you back. My mother is a great healer—she will fix you up! She is an amazing cook, too! You need it—"

"This makes no sense," Olun wiped her eyes.

"What?"

She wasn't supposed to be here. She wasn't supposed to be *alive*. She was supposed to be left at the base of the mountain, like Elder Kikyel said, yet she was *here* and couldn't leave. She was so afraid—so confused! And the voice from earlier, chiding her as if it knew her—

"You look sick," Bana said, falling back to her side.

"You have t'let me go," Olun said, breath coming out in hysteric gasps. "I—this isn't right!"

Bana lifted his hands to calm her. "You are just in shock. Take a breath—"

"No!" she moved out of his reach. "I'm not one of you!"

"Sure, you may say words kind of funny, but you *are* one of us now, since the Stream connects us—"

"You don't understand!" she cried. "I'm supposed t'be *dead!* My clan—I'm their sacrifice! I have t'die so they can live! So my brother doesn't have t'risk his life and my aunt and ma and pa—" she broke off, gasping. *Why can't I breathe!*

Bana thumped her on the back like a drum.

"If you were *supposed* to die," he said through her hysterics, "The echrol would have eaten you before we came."

"I ran," she squeaked.

"So . . . you do *not* want to die?"

Olun didn't *want* to have this conversation with him. Not only that, but she didn't want to admit it aloud. She'd had a moment of weakness—a moment of fear. What did that make her if she let dozens of people suffer and die because she ran from her duty?

"*And,*" he snorted. "Your Elder said to leave you at the base of the mountain. *Our* mountain. Could that not mean you were meant to be found by us? Father says that sacrifice does not always mean death."

Olun froze. *Monta said that, too.* Even if what he said was true and she was indeed supposed to have been found by Genta, Olun still longed for Elder Kikyel's guidance, her ma's rare hugs, her brother's laughter, and her pa's encouraging smile. For all of the hurt she'd felt at Monta's confessional, Olun needed her stern words reminding her to fight when it was so easy to give up.

"Oh!" he gasped. "Do not cry! I am sorry—whatever I said, *I am sorry!*"

Bana thumped her back again, at a loss for what to do. "Hey, look! Genta is here. We can all go home now, what do you say?"

Olun didn't look up from her hands until they were roughly jerked from her face.

"You want to feed yourself to an echrol, be my guest, but do *not* bring my brothers into it!" Genta shouted.

Olun gaped up at him in shock. He towered over her like a pillar of stone, solid and immovable.

"I—I—I didn't ask you t'come for me," she sputtered, shrinking away from them both.

"No?" Genta spat. "You made quite a scene this evening. You had to have known that my brother would come after you, and us after him."

"Is Didan alright?" Bana squeaked with worry, but Genta shrugged him off.

"I *didn't* know," Olun sobbed. He'd been the furthest thing from her mind. Why would he come after her? She would have thought that, after he'd grabbed her the other night and how she'd spoken to him that morning, he'd be glad to see her gone.

"Have you really no memories of him? Of *us*?" Genta demanded, amazed by the depths of her ignorance. Pity flickered once and only barely.

. . . Your life was spared at the expense of another's . . .

"This is not your desert," he continued his tirade. "What makes you think you can make it on your own, weak as you are? Though the burden is mine to care for you, trust and believe, if you try this again, I will not even collect your bones."

"Hey! You go too far, Genta," Bana argued, but Genta held up his hand to silence him.

"You should've left me there in th'first place!" Olun cried helplessly.

Genta glared at her for a moment longer. "Yes, maybe I should have." He stalked toward the village and the throng of onlookers.

"Manuk is making sure the creature has gone," Didan said quietly to Bana behind her. She was too stunned and embarrassed to face them. One of them touched her, perhaps to coax her along, but it made little difference. The adrenaline that kept her going was no more. She felt everything—the blood that oozed from the scratches on her body, the bruises, Genta's ire, Bana's discontent.

An arm circled her waist, and Olun slumped blindly against the body it belonged to, no longer able to keep herself upright. Her muscles loosened; safety, a feeling she dared not process in light of her escaped Rohta duty, washed over her. The heat of his body dulled the chill of her helplessness. *I will protect you . . .* the words rose from her memory.

"You are safe now," Didan murmured and lifted her into his arms.

Chapter 7

He watched centuries of unshed tears sparkle in her eyes like starlight in an endless night. When she took his hand, he felt the cold of abandonment and the painful prick of possessiveness.

"Come with me," she whispered. "Forget all your woes."

"There is nowhere to go," he said, pulling away from her in sudden anger. There was nothing but darkness. When he traveled close to the surface and saw the light streaming in through the rocks, he was unable to touch it. It was as if there were a barrier surrounding the ray. Teasing him. He stood by that stream of light until it faded into night.

"Let me be your guide," she said.

"You were my guide!" he shouted angrily. "You guided me to these mountains, and then you guided me to my death. Where now do you wish to take me?"

One by one, green lights twinkled into existence above him. Hundreds—thousands of them, like stars in the sky. He could only stare in awe as silent tears trickled down his cold cheeks.

"To peace," she whispered.

***

Tula hummed a pleasant tune outside, enticing Olun from sleep. She palmed her eyes and sat up, surprised by the wetness of her cheeks. *You were weeping in your sleep,* she reminded herself. Olun stared up at the ceiling, searching the darkness for the dream that evaded her by day. At least it hadn't been the screaming one, again. She'd given Tula, the woman who'd taken it upon herself to nurse Olun back to health, such a fright two mornings ago.

"The girl is plagued by fits," Genta had hissed angrily to Tula, the latter visibly shaken by the ordeal. "This is ridiculous, come home! If she hurts you—"

"I'm fine, love," she'd hissed back. "But I must stay, at least until she's able t'care for herself."

Olun had cocked her head at the familiar cadence of her voice, as if each word were made for song instead of conversation. This woman was not Ithoumi born and bred. By firelight, Olun had seen that she was young, perhaps a couple years her senior. Her dark skin glowed flawlessly in the warm light, illuminating full lips and round cheeks that fit perfectly on her equally round face. But Olun had said nothing to her then and kept her thoughts to herself now.

Tula's song ended, and after a short pause, began again. The hardy smell of porridge soon accompanied it. For four days, after exhaustion and poor nutrition finally caught up to her, Tula made sure Olun ate and fed her when she was too weak to feed herself. She cleaned her scratches and reapplied the medicine Naleda supplied. Tula even began the process of refitting old clothes to Olun's small frame. Most importantly, she kept people away.

Naleda looked in on her, Bana curiously asked for details to report back to his friends, Zafre and his Doyens wanted to speak to her, and a host of other villagers whose voices she did not recognize came by hesitantly.

"Let her catch her breath!" Tula told them all. "Stop hovering—no wonder she doesn't come out!"

Though Olun longed to see the sunlight, she couldn't bring herself to step out into her new reality. She was alive. And she'd forsaken her people. Depression became her cage.

Tula poked her head in just as Olun lay back down. "Would you like to join me?" she asked, always with a smile. And, like always, Olun didn't answer. She didn't want to like this woman—she didn't want to like any of them. There were so many reasons why she shouldn't, but the most important one was that they were beholden to the Dark Lady. But something about Tula was different.

She reminded Olun of the desert warmth, and her voice brought her back to the annual Gathering of the clans. Whether this was a trick of the Dark Lady and the Ithoumi people, Olun couldn't say, but she found herself relaxing in Tula's presence. Like always.

Tula flitted around the little room, lighting candle nubs and stoking the stove into a gentle glow. The room was only slightly brighter than before, but no less warm. Again, Olun felt suffocated, as if locked in a tomb. But Tula was unaffected.

She twisted her lips at the sparse space. "We'll have to work on this. If I'd known they were putting you here . . . *San'da daan!*" She sighed, and Olun sat up at the familiar phrase: *It is what it is.*

"Oh good, you're up!" she trilled and ducked back outside to retrieve their breakfast. They ate by the light of the oven and in comfortable silence. Each breakfast Tula prepared was rich and sweet, and after their evening meals, she'd slather slices of bread in a thick, sticky syrup for them to eat with tea. Sweetness was a delicacy among the desert folk. It was expensive to trade for at the Gatherings and even more expensive to get from the city. It was as if she did this to entice

Olun into eating more. It worked just as it had the night of the feast, and she begrudgingly indulged in a morsel.

"You're looking well," Tula acknowledged. "Better and better each day—Good food and sleep will do that."

Olun stared at her food. *Better and better, while I know my people are getting worse and worse.* The pain in her heart was almost too overwhelming to breathe.

"I know this all may seem like a lot," Tula said softly, leaning forward to rest her hand against Olun's knee. "But we'll get through this. Us desert folk must stick together, ya?"

Olun gaped at Tula, the pieces finally clicking together.

Tula's smile broadened. "I'm from the Maris to the East."

"I knew it," Olun gasped. Tula's familiar words and the way she all but *sang* them were wholly different from the tedious way the Ithoumi spoke. Not only that, but Tula's features— soft curves, rounded face, broad forehead—were indeed *Maris!* Had she been brought there like Olun had? Why hadn't she run away? What of her family? She had so many questions for Tula, so many that she could hardly get out one!

Tula poured them water and urged Olun to drink.

"I was visiting my Nana in the Retryu when I was younger than you," she said. "My fourteenth year, maybe? It was during the time the Ithoumi came down to trade with the Retryu in their summer settlement near the mountains."

So the stories of mountain monsters stealing away girls are true, then, Olun thought bitterly.

"I met a handsome Ithoumi boy, and when they packed to leave, I went with him."

Olun blinked dumbly. "Genta is your beloved?" She'd called him *love*, but the idea was just too farfetched to believe.

"We are called *Bondeds* in the village," Tula explained. "Life partners. For me, there is no one but Genta, and I'm the same for him."

Olun grimaced at the thought of Genta. His cold, penetrating stare and his biting words left nothing to be desired. He was so quick to anger, easily a bully, too. The man, like all the other men she'd seen in the village, was tall with a body that appeared to have been chiseled from stone—one of his arms could easily lift half a dozen of her small and lean brethren. Even Didan, a cripple, was still just as imposing in his size. It was more believable to think Genta had thrown Tula over his shoulder and stolen her away like the stories.

"This is a lot to take in, I know," Tula continued. "Change affects us differently. It is no right of mine or anyone to judge you for how you deal with it, but I hope you'll let me in?"

Olun didn't know what to say. On the one hand, she was pleased beyond belief to have a desert sister here in the mountains. On the other, would Tula retract all niceties once she discovered what Olun really was? She was Desert Kin, after all. She would know more than anyone in this village of the traditions and duties of the desert.

Tula waited a moment longer before clearing away their breakfast.

"I could use a nice, relaxing bath," she announced abruptly. It wasn't until they were on their way through the village that Olun realized she'd agreed to go, too.

Chapter 8

They stopped by Tula's home first, toward the middle of the village. Olun kept her eyes low, cognizant of the curious stares her sudden appearance garnered. "I'll just grab us some soaps and clothes, then we'll be on our way," Tula said cheerily. Olun nodded, eyes still downcast, but an unusual sound lifted them.

Inside a fenced yard, little creatures scratched at the ground with taloned feet, clucking and bantering in an assortment of sounds. Olun approached the fence with hesitant curiosity. The creatures were barely tall enough to reach her knees. The bubble eyes on either side of their head were almost comical as they blinked independently. The creature had to turn its head from side to side so that both eyes could see her. Its nose was hard and smooth, like a shell, sharp and slightly hooked as it pecked pebbles out of the way of its scratching talons.

"Bimi," Tula explained. Indeed, that was the sound the little feathered creatures made. A middle-aged woman came from around the side of her house, a covered basket in her arms.

"I was just about to leave this at your door!" she laughed. Her curly black hair was braided upwards in a youthful style, but the lines about her eyes gave away her years. Her white smile was just as inviting as Tula's, but now that Olun knew where Tula was really from, all she saw were the differences. The woman's broad shoulders, angular face, narrower eyes and nose, skin a degree or so lighter than the black skin of those who endured the desert sun day in and day out.

"This is Willa, my neighbor," Tula said, slipping back into the formal tongue of the villagers as she made her introductions. "Willa, meet Olun. She is still finding her way, and I thought to take her to the bath caves."

"Ah," Willa smiled at Olun. "I was at your ceremony, little Elder. It is nice to make your acquaintance. Tula is a good girl. You could not have found a better guide."

Tula smiled modestly and leaned against the fence. "What have you got for me?" she asked, peering into Willa's basket.

Olun found herself looking, too.

Willa carried brown eggs, far larger and more solid than the soft-shelled ones the desert serpents buried. Olun counted a dozen of them, perhaps more. "You can have some, too," Willa nodded to Olun.

Tula clapped her hands excitedly and accepted the basket. "Thank you, my friend!"

Olun waited by Willa's fence, watching the little bimi while Tula brought the basket of eggs inside in exchange for bathing supplies. The woman had returned to her chores, put off by Olun's lack of engagement.

"I'll teach you how to cook them," Tula announced when she came back, easily taking up the quick, sing-song intonation of the Maris. "Bimi eggs can be cooked many ways. Oh! And Bimi themselves are good meat, too."

"Why don't you have them?" Did these people treat her differently because she was from the desert? Would they treat Olun as less than?

"Genta doesn't like bimi," Tula sighed. "He says they eat everything and are messy little things. But they're cute, ya?"

They eat everything? Olun thought about the little bimi wandering into her tent and using its sharp beak to scoop out her eyes. She shuddered at the thought.

"But Willa's bimi lays enough eggs for us, so it's alright. It would've been a lot of work taking care of so many bimi and a baby."

"You have a child?"

Tula shook her head and said nothing else.

***

The stream glistened as it cut through a narrow valley, flowing gently over pale rocks below. Like a ribbon of fine silk caught in the wind, it danced in and out, curving with the valley's cliffs on its way down the mountain. Women waded to their knees, pulling greens from the water. Children splashed on its banks. Plants grew between dark, damp rocks. Downstream, the water moved quickly, churning into rapids. Little girls sat on slick rocks, moistened with spray, dipping nets into its currents.

Olun didn't know where Tula was taking her, but she got the feeling that the woman was intentionally leading her through the more scenic parts of the village. Regardless, Olun was enamored. This village—the *mountains*—was a completely different world. She stopped in her tracks completely to gaze down into the valley. Across the stream, a scattered herd of what appeared to be some form of oombrak bleated. Their bodies certainly were the same as the herds in the desert, but they were smaller—perhaps five or six feet tall from hoof to curved horn. Their fur was shaggier, and their tusks barely protruded from the corners of their lips.

Tula followed her gaze with a smile. She pointed to the herd that bounced from rock to rock, grazing on the tough shrubs that grew between.

"Those are ootingla," she said. "We get our furs from them. Milk, fat, oils, meat. Zayeer—you met him—is the keeper of the herd. A Doyen."

She pointed to a cluster of children, each holding crooks as they watched over the herd. "Bana is down there," she explained. "You'll find that Zafre and Naleda's sons are very different from each other; Genta followed his father's footsteps as a stonemason, and Bana *loves* those creatures. He is apprenticing under Zayeer to be a herder."

Tula chuckled. "It's been the talk of the village that Genta will take over as Chief from his father, and Zayeer has already named Bana Doyen of the Herd—something that's unheard of since Bana is so young and Zayeer is nowhere near old enough to retire from his position."

She said nothing of the middle son, Didan. But Olun knew all that she needed to know about him: once looked upon as the next Elder, now deformed and whispered about like a pariah. He had no place in the village. Olun was thankful she hadn't come across him again after the echrol incident, especially since the contradicting feelings his touch stirred within her were unnerving. Twinges of comforting familiarity laced with vague memories of fear and pain. Who *was* he?

"We'll develop a routine," Tula spoke, whether to Olun or simply to voice her thoughts. "Yes, and projects, too. Didan's home is a little dank and unlived in, but we can make it more comfortable for you."

Didan's home? It took Olun longer than it should have to understand that Tula was talking about the hut she stayed in. *Didan* lived there? *No wonder it feels so suffocating and uninviting.*

Tula continued, neither giving Olun the time to process a response nor unperturbed by her silence. "We'll decorate. More fabrics of your own making, and your own dishes! Soaps and oils, too. Naleda has a wonderful store of dried herbs we could use, or we could collect them ourselves. Yes, that's what we'll do!"

Olun still stewed on the realization that it was Didan's home she stayed in when Tula led her through a narrow cave opening. Torch sconces illuminated their way through a winding tunnel.

"Don't be afraid," Tula said when Olun drew closer to her side. The tunnel opened up into a high-ceilinged cavern. Torches and lamps burned high, revealing long, sharp rocks pointed like teeth from the darkness above, and reflected their light from the clear pools below. Men and women undressed on rocks and soaked in the steaming pools. Others waded to their waists, washing soap from their hair and bodies. Trickling water mingled with the murmur of quiet conversation.

"The bath caves," Tula trilled. "Much better than washing in a basin."

Tula found them a spot amongst the other women in the surprisingly well-lit cave and set down her basket of bathing supplies. She stripped out of her clothes while Olun looked around, still in a state of disbelief. Steam rose from the water like old friends ready to take her hand. How did all of this exist here in the realm of an exiled Goddess when her clan suffered beneath the gaze of Ma Bright, the Goddess supposedly so full of life and compassion?

Tula dropped beneath the surface briefly, coming up to smooth her long black hair from her face, the strands immediately curling to ringlets. She watched Tula, so at home in this world. If it weren't for her appearance or the way she spoke, Tula would be no different from the Ithoumi villagers who bathed around them. Tula beckoned to her and Olun felt a surge of panic; she'd never been *submerged* in water before. She eyed the water apprehensively, stepping back from its edge.

Tula pulled herself up to sit on the edge and patted the spot beside her.

"Here, let us just sit at the edge, that's right. Now hang your feet down in there just like that. Doesn't this feel nice?"

There was laughter in her pleasant voice. Tula reached behind them both to grab a cloth and a soft-smelling soap. After lathering up her own hair, she passed the soap to Olun.

"Let me know when you want me to get your back," she said and continued bathing.

Gradually, Olun disrobed and splashed the warm water across her body. *I deserve this scar,* she thought as she gingerly dabbed the healing wound of her failed escape. *I deserve this punishment. I deserve this pain.*

"It will heal," Tula said, sensing the nature of Olun's thoughts. She, too, was desert-born after all. "I've heard Naleda say that scars don't remind us of our mistakes, but of our own mortality."

What did Naleda know? Though the woman had been kind to Olun and doctored her scratches when Bana and Didan had called for her, Naleda was still just an Ithoumi woman. In the desert, scars were moral blights. Scars were both proof of weaknesses and punishments for them. Olun glanced at Tula. Had she been so long removed from the desert that she'd forgotten this?

"Are you . . . *happy* here?" Olun asked, voice low. She glanced around herself nervously, but the bathers paid them no mind.

"I have challenges, like every person," Tula thought for a bit, toying with the little white beads on her necklace. "But yes, I'm happy, Olun."

"I don't know if I'll ever be," Olun said, fighting the urge to cry. Again, she wanted to confide in Tula about what was expected of her and the burden of knowing what her inaction was doing. But, like that evening running from the echrol, Olun was afraid.

Tula let a thoughtful silence pass between them before she spoke. "I used t'feel the same as you, believing happiness would never smile down on me."

I knew it, Olun thought. No desert folk would ever be happy in the mountains, living in a village instead of roaming.

"When me and Genta lost our first baby, I was so sure my life would never be complete ever again. Then it happened again and again, and I knew I wasn't meant for joy."

Whatever it was Olun expected to hear, it was not this. "I'm so sorry, Tula!"

Tula held up a hand against Olun's sympathies. "Let me get your back," she said suddenly, climbing out of the pool to sit behind her.

Tula passed a cloth across Olun's skin, soaping her in silence. She dipped a bowl into the pool and poured it over Olun's back to rinse the lather and sighed.

"I wouldn't have gotten through it all without Genta," she said. "When I felt my lowest, Genta never left my side. He lifted me up and showed me I could be happy again. That *we* could be happy again. I couldn't ask for a better person as my Bonded."

"But isn't he t'blame?" Olun blurted, turning toward Tula. "He took you from your home—he's probably the reason you can't leave, ya? A man like that you should be hating, not praising."

Tula was visibly taken aback by her outburst.

"I made my choice long ago t'be with Genta, and it's always been *my* choice. Don't confuse what I've told you with what you *think*. My home is where I make it. Isn't that the way of the desert?"

The slower she spoke, the more she sounded like one of the Ithoumi, Olun noticed with distaste. But Tula was right. They made their home wherever and with whatever they carried.

"We all make choices every day. You made a choice to come here with me, ya?"

"Not everyone has a choice," Olun mumbled, looking away.

"*Everyone* has a choice," Tula said somberly. "And I for one choose t'be *happy.*"

There was nothing more to say. Whatever else was expected of Olun, happiness was not part of it. She washed her short hair and splashed herself clean while Tula took another dip and waded briefly to the other side of the pool, where an elderly woman beckoned her.

When they finished, they dried, dressed, and navigated the tunnels back into the light of day. Olun kept her eyes low, watching the swish of her borrowed dress sweep the dirt path. It would have to be hemmed, Tula had said. Olun didn't care. She listened to Tula greet passersby and felt their curious eyes upon her, but again, Olun didn't care.

That's the difference between Tula and me, she thought. *She wants to be here, and I can't even leave . . .*

Chapter 9

G ENTA ATE ACROSS FROM Olun, his short, manicured beard catching the crumbs of his buttered bread. He brought his bowl of porridge to his lips, slurped quietly, and poured himself a cup of wine. "This isn't as strong as the one you had before—so do be hesitant!" Tula giggled when Olun eyed the dark liquid apprehensively.

"When I asked you to come home," Genta muttered to Tula, "I meant *just* you."

Tula kissed his cheek in passing and continued preparing their breakfast the way she had done for Olun.

"Olun'll be our guest until she's ready to go," Tula tossed over her shoulder in a tone that kept Genta—and Olun, for that matter—from protesting.

And so, they ate in uncomfortable silence.

Genta was quite handsome for a mountain man, Olun begrudgingly admitted to herself as she watched him from the corner of her eye. From his high cheeks, chiseled jaw beneath his beard, to the lines of his eyes and the severe way he wore his dark hair back from his face. For someone who looked as he did, she could see why Tula had gone with him. He was like a sculpture cut from stone. But, what was it that Monta used to say? The tongue remembers not the sap, but the sour?

Whatever sweetness Tula claimed the man capable of, Olun would only remember how his words had hurt her.

Feeling her eyes on him, Genta looked up, and Olun dropped her head. She spooned another helping of porridge into her mouth as if she hadn't been staring at him for an immeasurable amount of time.

"Slow down," Tula said, her voice high with concern. "You'll choke!"

She reached quickly for the pot of tea close to the fire, but Genta intercepted her. He took his time filling the waiting cups, offering the first to Tula.

"Will you be resting today, my love?" Genta said to Tula, his tone soft and gentle. Olun realized she'd never heard Genta be anything but flat and angry. She really thought she *would* choke from the shock of it. She thumped herself in the chest to dislodge the lump of bread she'd used to lap up the porridge, and reached for one of the remaining cups of tea.

Genta pushed one toward her. "It's hot," he warned.

Olun nodded vigorously as she took the cup and averted her eyes, embarrassment warming her more than the tea.

"Me and Olun have plans." She heard the laughter in Tula's voice as she answered Genta. "We're going to make that old place more livable."

Genta grunted. "You are spending too much time coddling the girl. She needs to get used to things on her own, or she will never survive her Solitude."

And just like that, the sliver of brightness that she'd seen in Genta disappeared. Olun stared at him incredulously. *Coddling?* She'd never been coddled a day in her life! She knew how to take care of herself and could do it well. She never asked for Tula's help—only accepted it when it was offered! Olun glared at him. Should she remind him that it was he who'd brought her here in the first place? Now he spoke about her as if she were not sitting across from him. As if she were some child not worthy of conversing with!

Genta curled his lip. "Have you something to say?"

Tula sucked her teeth, disapproving of his tone.

"No," Olun gritted.

He held her glare steadily and took up his cup, the tea having cooled significantly during the conversation. "I am not a mind reader, and I do not like childish games," he said, and just like that, Genta went back to ignoring her existence.

***

Didan's home was indeed bare. The round, windowless hut sat up on a hill with no immediate neighbors, its walls worn and crumbled from the assault of wind each night. Moss grew between the cracks in the stone, and weeds snagged in the thatched roof. The yard was nothing but dirt and ash, and the fire pit, a simple hole. Coming upon it, the place indeed looked as if it were abandoned. Unlike Tula and Genta's home decorated with a low, painted stone wall. Other homes bore paintings along the sides; handprints of children, images of leaves, *ootingla,* or hammers—symbols that hinted at the people living there. Door flaps were made from tapestries, dyed and embroidered to give them character. Olun once thought these people living in the cold, shadowy mountains to be dull, but they were subtly beautiful in the way they cared for their homes.

Beside her, Tula surveyed the work cut out for them with excitement rather than dismay. "This's the best thing about havin' a home, ya?" she said, letting her desert tongue flavor her words. "Makin' it your very own—lookin' at it and seein' all the ways you can make it t'your likin'."

Olun cocked her head at the hut. It was plain and crypt-like, and obviously lacking in various ways compared to the two other homes she'd been in, but Olun had never lived in a home. She saw nothing of what it could be and knew nothing about how to make it her own. Her only possessions were the shreds of her ma's dress stuffed into an empty basket, ruined. Monta's cloak was only slightly better off.

"Genta says this used to be some kind of storage structure before Didan moved into it," she said. A slight breeze ruffled through her hair and shifted the hem of Tula's skirt, drawing Olun's attention to her swollen ankles. Olun frowned, concerned by them, but Tula didn't seem to notice.

"Storage?"

"Naleda didn't use to practice healing out of her home. She'd come here to treat the sick and wounded just like her teacher." Tula pointed back down the hill to a pleasant-looking home. It was the last home they'd passed, leaving the village proper. "Yadir only lives just down the hill. We passed her home on the way here."

They set about gathering the balls of brittle weeds that blew down from the mountain each night, collecting against the side of the home and getting stuck on the roof.

"Genta could fix up this wall or somethin'," Tula said, gesturing to the overly exposed property.

Olun shuddered. The man would be even less thrilled to hear that his beloved— *Bonded*—volunteered him for this task. He'd probably blame Olun for it, again.

"That's alright," Olun said quickly. "It's not my home t'begin with."

"It's fine," Tula said cheerily. They went inside, emptying the home of what little it held. Bedding and blankets were strung up to be beaten of dust and mites, and the candle nubs were added to Tula's basket to be made into new ones. Olun paddled the bedding while Tula picked the candle wicks from the wax. Sweat had drenched the front of Tulu's dress, Olun noticed, plastering her curly hair to her forehead. She didn't look so well, but still, she hummed to herself.

"Why is this place so empty?" she asked Tula, thinking about Didan. If this were his home, wouldn't he have certain feelings about them making changes? Especially if her living in it was only supposed to be temporary. Where was he to come back to, if he wasn't Elder?

"I don't know much," Tula gave a sullen sigh. "After his accident, Didan lived here until he recovered. Then, he left."

"Where'd he go?"

At Tula's silence, Olun peeked from behind the bedding to see her chewing her bottom lip. "I don't really know," she said. "He does this. Leave, I mean. It's common for Elders here t' be so . . . aloof. Didan comes and goes without a word, and no one ever knows where. Or asks."

The strikes to the bedding quickened along with the incensed beat of her heart. *Aloof.* Elder Kikyel was not aloof. She'd been part of Olun's everyday life as *more* than an Elder. She was her teacher, storyteller, grandma, friend. Elders *here,* it seemed, were none of that. *She needs to get used to things on her own, or she will never survive her Solitude . . .* was this what Genta had meant?

The repetitive motion and sound did little to quell her rising panic. Aloof. Solitude. Did he mean for her to be *lonely?* Olun wanted to get away from these people who were so different from her desert folk.

"What if I ran away?" Olun asked quietly. "I mean, *again.*" If no one cared of Didan's comings and goings, who would notice or really care if she left and didn't come back? She dragged her arm across her eyes to catch the sweat and pulled the bedding from the line.

Tula was slumped to her side, her eyes fluttering.

"Tula!" Olun shouted, rushing to her.

"Tula, what's wrong?" Olun lifted Tula's head, pushed the bedding beneath it, and fanned her with her hands. Tula's unfocused eyes scanned Olun's face in confusion.

"Dizzy," she moaned, her eyes scrunching closed. "Genta . . ."

"Tula, wake up!"

Olun tried to think—Tula's cheeks were flushed, her body feverish. With a pang of horror, Olun thought perhaps she'd brought the plague to the village! She pressed her ear to Tula's breast, listening for the telltale rattle and wheeze, and was relieved that it was not there. Tula was not sick with the Dry Sickness, but she *was* sick.

Olun scrambled for her waterskin and poured it on Tula's chest and hair to cool her. She quickly fixed an empty basket over her face to block the sun and jumped to her feet.

"I'll be back," she said. "I'm going t'get help!"

Like the evening of her attempted escape, Olun ran down the path to the nearest home.

"Help!" She shouted, leaping over the gate. "Please—Help!"

A young girl ran from the home followed by . . . Didan?

Olun skidded to a stop. One look at her face, and Didan was suddenly alert. He pulled her into the yard, glancing up the path she'd just come, a hand going to the sheath at his side. Olun jerked away from him as if he would harm her with it. It had been a weeks since he'd brought her to Naleda's after the echrol incident; she was sure he'd gone on his way. Olun glanced from the bedroll tied to the full pack slung over his shoulder down to the obvious traveling clothes he wore. He tucked a little pouch into his robe.

"What happened?" He demanded. "*Tell me?*"

Olun jumped, opening her mouth to explain, but no sound came. She could see his face distorting right before her eyes just like that night, and shrank further away. "I—I—"

"Take a breath," came a calming voice, drawing her attention from the shock of Didan.

The elderly woman from the bath caves hunched against the girl. Olun ran to them instead.

"T—Tula needs help!" she stammered. "Please—she's collapsed up there. *Help her!*"

The girl dashed past Olun and up the hill. The older woman, though slower in her age, was right behind her.

"Yadir and Jorre will help her," Didan said in what Olun believed was comfort. "Come and sit. When you are calmed, we will go back up together."

He held his hand out for her to take, but Olun could not bring herself to touch him. What else would she feel if she did? The scar on the back of her head itched with a memory she couldn't place, and she touched it, backing away from his outstretched hand.

"I have t'find Genta," she mumbled, turning on her heels without another glance his way. She didn't have time to spend waiting around. Tula asked for Genta, and she would find him.

Olun rounded the corner and onto the path that would take her to Tula's home when she saw Genta walking in the other direction. Sweat streaked the pale dust coating the bulbous muscles of his exposed arms and the back of his tunic was soaked down the spine.

"Genta!" she shouted, out of breath. He jerked around, frowning when his eyes settled on her.

"Come quick—Tula's collapsed!"

"Where?" he threw down the tools she hadn't realized he carried.

"My—the house—" There was no catching her breath, Genta dropped his tools and was off at a sprint.

The old woman and the girl, Yadir and Jorre, were sitting with Tula by the time they arrived. Tula was awake and taking the water that Yadir offered her while Jorre fanned her. Didan was nowhere in sight.

"We were talking, and I thought everything was fine," Olun babbled an explanation as Genta stooped briefly to lift his Bonded into his arms. "She didn't say nothing of how she was feeling, and I didn't think—"

Genta straight-armed Olun back when she tried to follow, the force of it sending her stumbling to the ground.

"Do *not* follow us," he said menacingly. "You are nothing but trouble."

"Genta!" Yadir admonished. But Genta was already striding away from them all, Tula cradled in his arms.

Olun hugged her knees tightly to her chest and watched them go. The way he looked at her—the bark of anger and loathing in his voice stung like slaps against her face. She buried her face in her arms, squeezing hard against the sting. She hadn't meant to cause anyone harm, least of all Tula.

"Do not take it to heart, child," the old woman said quickly in her crackly voice. "He gets like this when he is scared."

"Why would he be scared, grandmother?" Jorre asked the old woman in a whisper.

"It would seem that Tula is with child again," whispered Yadir in response.

The old woman put her arm around Olun in an attempt to comfort her, but Olun shrank away involuntarily. She didn't want this woman—or *anyone*—to touch her. Olun gathered the wicks and the wax nubs back into their baskets, snatching them from the girl when she tried to help. Olun wanted to be alone. She should get used to it, anyway, for it didn't matter if she stayed in the Zenika Mountains or returned to the desert.

Alone is what she was fated to be.

Alone didn't *hurt*.

As she dragged her bedding back into her dark hut, the person she thought of was not Tula, or even Monta, with her stern encouragement. It was Didan, packed and ready to leave everything behind. There was nothing for him here, just as there was nothing for her, either. Wherever he went, it was sure to be far from here.

If only she had the courage to go, too.

Chapter 10

"*You are dying,*" *a woman whispered in the darkness. Her cold breath was close to his ear. "Are you not afraid?"*

The clack-clacking of stone against stone echoed through the walls of her mind. Darkness, desperation. Fingertips that were nothing more than rotted nubs.

Clack-clack!

Olun panicked. *Help me!* She cried, clawing at the walls. *Let me out!*

"Do you want to see the Cave Stars?" a boy asked. Rough hands led her from the village.

"I'm so sorry that this was done to you . . ." a man said, his voice thick with sorrow, but the only sorrow the girl felt was for him as she watched him fight against the boulder—fight against the darkness. His wails of agony colliding with hers, stitching together to create a heavy tapestry of pain that flattened her into the ground.

"You're dying," a woman whispered in the darkness.

Clack-Clack!

". . . Olun?"

. . . Death was cold and dark. Death was . . . lonesome

"Wake up!"

Cold, strong hands gripped her shoulders tightly, jerking her forward and back. Olun clawed at the hands that threatened to pull her into the darkness for good. Their motions grew more erratic the harder she fought. She'd forever be in agony—forever full of regrets. The back of her hand connected with flesh before it was wrestled to her side.

"Bright Mother help me—Olun, *wake up!*" Genta bellowed into her ear. Olun snapped open her eyes and screamed at the sight of him crouched over her, lip welling with blood, his large hands securing her arms to her sides.

"Don't hurt me—" she whimpered. "Please!"

Surprised, Genta released her and backed away.

"Have you woken?" Genta asked carefully when she gathered herself.

"What?" Her throat was hoarse and sore. She touched it, shock growing as she followed the moisture up to her cheeks. Had she been crying in her sleep again.

"You did not answer when I knocked," Genta explained. "Nor when I called your name. What spirits have you screaming bloody murder each night?"

Disoriented, Olun squinted around the hut, relieved by each familiar item that grounded her to this reality. "I—" she began, but as the word left her mouth, so did the nightmare, leaving only the chill remembrance of cold. She shivered.

"I don't know," her voice cracked. "I don't know what's going on—I thought you were trying t'kill me."

Genta's brows lifted in momentary disbelief. "And why would I be trying to do that?"

Olun lowered her eyes. "Because I'm nothing but trouble," she mumbled.

Genta rose to his feet and looked down at her with an expression she didn't understand.

"Clean yourself up," he sighed. "I brought fresh water."

With that, he left, the door flap falling closed behind him.

Olun splashed her cheeks with the cold water Genta brought in and wondered why he was there. If it wasn't to scold her for yesterday, there was no other reason. He didn't seem like the type of man to let pity get the better of him.

She dried her face, slipped on her sandals, and stepped out into the front yard. When she rounded the house to the fire pit, she saw Genta stoking it to life and unwrapping strips of meat for roasting.

"What're you doing?" she asked dumbly.

"Making sure you do not starve," he grumbled. "*Or* sleep the day away. Sit."

Olun hesitated. Wasn't he angry with her? He'd been insulting, disinterested, and abrasive, and yet he acted as though he cared about her well-being. He was being, dare she think it, *kind*. Had he forgotten that just the other day he'd shoved her to the ground?

Genta sighed heavily. "I swear on the Dark Goddess's name, I will not kill you. *Sit*."

Olun hurried to the fire and sat. She watched him curiously while he stirred a pot of boiling porridge and removed cuts of bread from his basket. Like the way he carried himself, breakfast preparation was a serious affair. Genta's constant glower seemed to exude both annoyance and indifference, even as he passed her a bowl of food.

"What did you dream about?" he asked conversationally.

Startled by both his question and the affable way in which he asked, Olun found she couldn't answer. And when she could, she didn't quite know what to say. She picked at her food; if her morning terrors had brought him to her bedside as he'd said, she remembered nothing of it. They were like that. Vivid enough to send her heart racing and body thrashing. Real enough for the sensation to linger into waking, leaving only the wet of tears and pain of loss in her heart. But Olun could never recall *what* she cried about or feared.

She rubbed the scar at the back of her head absently. It was the same with her memories of this place. Recalling them was like staring into a shadow. The longer she looked, the more uneasy she felt.

"I'm sorry t'disappoint you," she said quietly. "But I'm no Elder. I don't know what I dreamed or if it'd be any use t'you."

"I did not ask to glean wisdom from you," he slurped from his bowl, his dismissiveness infuriating. "You are far from an Elder."

"Then why did you bring me here? You could have left me at the base of the mountain."

"I almost did," he said lightly. "But you have your duties, and I have mine."

"Duties," she said flatly. "You—*everyone* speaks like I just *know* what I'm doing. No one's told me what exactly my duties are. And it's not like I can just ask *your* Elder, now can I?"

Genta thought for a bit and nodded in agreement. "Yes, I suppose you have a point," he sighed. "Listen, every Chief has had an Elder to help him guide the village. That is a given. The Chief and his Doyens maintain the physical well-being of the village, and the Elder, its *spiritual* well-being. Do you understand? Oh, for the love of—*nod* if you have heard a single word I said."

Olun nodded vehemently, though she didn't understand. Spiritual well-being? She already knew *what* an Elder was. She just didn't know how to *be* one.

At the blank look on her face, Genta pinched the bridge of his nose. "What?"

"What did you mean by 'Solitude?'" she asked quietly.

"Every Elder the village has known lived the majority of their lives in minimalism and isolation. It makes it easier for them to take their Solitude."

Olun looked back toward the little hut she lived in. Tula had such great plans for this place for her. Why go through the trouble of making it hospitable if Olun would only leave it? She suddenly understood what Genta had said about coddling. Why make her care about Tula and the routine they'd managed together, if she would only leave it?

"But what is this 'Solitude' I must take?"

"Look, I do not know all the details," Genta said impatiently. "Only the Chief and his council of Doyens know exactly what that entails. And, since I am not yet either of those, I have no answers for you."

"But . . . your brother was Elder, ya?"

"He and I had different upbringings," Genta dismissed.

Olun stared at him, really trying to place him—or the boy he'd been—in her memories. The earliest one that she could recall was chasing the oombrak calves around their pens in what had to have been the Retryu's settlement. She'd been in her sixth year of life, the same age she would have been on her visit here.

"I don't remember you," she admitted sadly.

Genta was unperturbed. "I know."

Olun stirred her porridge absently. He was the eldest son of Monta's brother. She'd imagined that they'd shared meals around the campfire, perhaps even played together.

"We were friends, ya?"

"No," Genta said. "I had my own friends."

Olun stared down into her bowl, appetite lost. *They'd not even been friends.*

"If you are through, we can start our day."

Why bother . . .

Olun pushed her bowl aside. "About the other day . . ." She hazarded, "Tula's with child, ya? That's why she is sick?"

Genta eyed her carefully. "She is resting, like she should have been."

Olun couldn't help but flinch at the accusation in his words, but Genta didn't seem to notice. He gathered their bowls.

Genta sighed. "I did not come today to harm you, Olun. Tula is very unhappy with how I treat you, and I came to make amends. And to *thank* you for coming to her aid." He cleared his throat awkwardly and added, "I am grateful."

Olun could tell that Genta was not a man used to apologizing. Who knew a man as big and hot-tempered as Genta could be subdued by a woman half his size? *Remind me never to cross Tula,* Olun noted.

Genta came to his feet. "Now, shall we start our day? Apparently, I am to take you to get wax?"

Our day? Olun noticed for the first time that he wore a tailored, knee-length shirt and tapered trousers and not the stained, sleeveless tunic he labored in. "She wanted t'show me how t'make candles," Olun explained hesitantly. She was to spend the day with *him?*

Genta grunted and scraped the remnants of Olun's porridge into his bowl. "Very well, then," he said. "It is a simple enough thing; even children can do it."

Olun scowled and decided against responding. *Ma Bright, give me strength...*

***

Olun once thought traversing the desert's shifting sands and smooth silver dunes were challenging enough—challenges she had overcome young, as all desert nomads did. She was strong and resilient, able to walk miles and miles with a heavy pack on her back and little water. But, after following Genta up and down the sloping village all morning from one errand to the next, Olun was drenched in sweat. Her legs were so sore they were trembling by the time they made it to the grove where the hip-height bushes grew prickly, eyeball-sized fruit.

"Tula cannot stomach the smell of tallow candles," Genta explained, tossing Olun a sack. "The scent of wax fruit is softer and burns just as well."

Olun wiped the sweat from her brow and launched herself into the arduous task of harvesting the fruit, trying in vain to avoid the spikes of the bush. She knew Genta was in no mood if she asked for rest. He'd see her as an annoyance if she asked for the waterskin that hung at his waist. So she suffered the task in silence and without his help.

"Did they not teach you the proper way to greet people in the desert?" he asked abruptly. "Your rudeness this morning was an embarrassment."

"We speak when spoken to," she grumbled back, thinking of the villagers they'd encountered this morning. Like her outing with Tula, they'd only stared at her and whispered behind their hands. "*They* didn't speak t'*me*, either."

Genta grunted.

When she finished, though, and Genta turned to lead the way back down from the grove, Olun couldn't stay silent any longer.

"I know you must have other tasks t'attend today," she huffed, adjusting her grip on the sack of wax fruit so that its spines poking through the fibers didn't prick her. "I'll be fine on my own." *Besides,* she thought defiantly, *you don't want to coddle me, remember?*

Genta's silence was beginning to frustrate her. He didn't even turn to acknowledge that she'd spoken. If she slowed down a bit and let him pace further ahead, perhaps she could take a rest without his notice?

Olun doubted he even remembered she was there, lost in thought as he was.

Suddenly, the hard ground beneath her foot changed within a step, becoming so soft it crumbled away to encase her entire foot up to her ankle in loose dirt. Olun shrieked, falling to her hands and knees, the sack spilling its contents. Genta grabbed her arm and wrenched her free of the hole in an instant.

"Less daydreaming and pay attention to your surroundings," he scolded.

Olun glared at him, her body burning with such anger she shook with it. But Genta hardly seemed to notice.

"Looks like you stepped on a gacus burrow," he crouched before the hole and covered it with dirt.

Anger forgotten, Olun jumped back from it as if a creature far more terrible than the one from before would suddenly claw its way to the surface.

"A *what?*"

"Little scavengers," Genta nodded toward a shrub a little off the path where four pairs of eyes watched them from the shade. The long-bodied gacus clicked their teeth and chittered to each other, their bristle tails twitching.

"They burrow beneath the ground and raise colonies between rocks. They are quite abundant, and their pelts are a good lining for our boots in the colder seasons."

Her eyes widened at the sight of them, far more adorable than she'd ever thought a creature of the mountains could be. Nothing like the toothy snarl of an echrol.

"Are they friendly?" She crouched and held her hand out to them.

"They can be—stop encouraging them!" he snapped. "They are wild creatures that would sooner take a finger than let you *pet* them. I swear, it is like talking to a child."

Olun snatched her hand back and sprang to her feet. She glared at Genta, tired of his insults. Though his expression remained flat, there was a smugness to him. An arrogance that denoted a man who'd never been challenged. Or, at least, never *lost* a challenge.

Her eyes prickled with hot tears behind her angry glare. This situation did not warrant tears, but she was like her ma in this way—tears for sorrow, tears for joy, tears for anger. Tears for who-knows-why. Olun dashed them away with an angry roll of her eyes.

"Do not mistake my kindness for caring," Genta said gruffly. "Your tears have no power over me, so pick up the fruits before the gacus get to them."

Olun bit her lip so hard she could taste the bitterness of blood, willing herself to be as strong as Monta wished her to be. But she was overwhelmed into silence and rooted in place.

Genta crossed his arms and narrowed his eyes. He was not one for disobedience, either. "I will give you until the count of three."

Olun opened her mouth, then closed it again with a pop. *I am not a child!* She wanted to shout. She'd never felt as much rage and confusion in her entire life as she had in these past few weeks. It boiled beneath her skin. Pressure grew in her gut and stirred the bile in her throat. Yet she pushed it all down, the effort releasing yet another tear.

At the end of his count, Genta snatched up the sack and tossed it at her. Olun caught it with a flinch and threw it down to the ground. "Why are you being so—so *mean?*" she shouted finally.

Sure, he'd been impatient with her during breakfast, and his apology was the worst she'd ever heard, but Genta had still been kind at least. Civil. Yet, it seemed as the day wore on, the more he hated being seen with her. Anger and bitterness engulfed him.

"I—I haven't complained, not once, and I worked hard. And you're *angry*? What'd I even do?"

Genta massaged his eyes and flared his nostrils. "Is it so hard to believe that I do not want to spend my day fending off judgmental stares, gacus, and tantrums? There are other places I wish to be."

Like with Tula. The heat of her anger simmered slightly. "You wish t'be somewhere else—so do I."

"I do not want to hear it," Genta snapped. "This is taking far too long. Just grab your bag and let us get this over with."

"You hate me, ya?" Olun accused quietly, taking a deep breath to collect herself. Monta had always said that being emotional was no good to anyone. "Burden. Trouble. Obligation. So, take me back t'the desert and you'll never have t'see me again."

"Not this again—you want to go? Fine, I will not stop you, but I also will not be the one to save you *again*."

Olun gave a frustrated cry and hid her face in her hands. She tried so hard not to scream and sob like she wanted to. *He just didn't get it.*

"Oh, I was getting quite used to the intense emotions that you seem to throw at every whim," Genta chided, snatching away her hand so that she'd look up at him. "Do not hide now—*talk*!"

"I hate it here!" She pulled away from him. "It's dark *always!* I have never slept alone, but now I am forced to sleep *alone* in darkness—to *bathe* in darkness! And I hate Ma Bright and the Dark Lady, too!"

She was pacing now, her gacus audience growing silent from where they watched curiously from the rocks.

"Where I've known community, the openness of the desert, and its light my entire life, I'm trapped here—terrified t'leave 'cause of the echrol, and terrified because, if I *do* leave, the only thing for me is death! *Oh!* And t'be Elder, I must live, eat, and breathe alone! That's not living! There's no difference at all if I leave or stay. The outcome's the same, ya? Death out there, death here. So why is it so hard t'*die?*"

Tula had wanted her to let someone in. Olun had been so reserved with her despite their commonalities. Despite her growing affection for her, Olun couldn't bring herself to shatter the image Tula had of her. But Genta already hated her. He was the last person she ever thought she'd confide in, but she couldn't stop.

"And you treat me like an ignorant child without even knowing all the things I've seen, and all that I've been through. My *entire* life, I've seen my kinfolk die of the Sickness and starve in the worst of the summer—you've *no idea* what that feels like! You've no idea what it's like t'want t'trade your very life so that no one else has t'suffer and be afraid anymore—so that your little brother doesn't throw his life away! I've *tried* t'be strong, t'hold my tongue, t'be obedient t'whatever the Dark Lady wants of me—even though I don't want it for myself.

"I have t'be *aloof?* I have t'just *accept* this life? Maybe it would've been different if I hadn't had a family or wasn't raised t'know or want love and companionship. I'm going mad, locked in a stone tomb alone with dreams of what I lost and nightmares that I can never remember. I'm losing my mind—"

Before she knew it, she was screaming into her hands. Like the hot water spouts to the west, once the pressure had built, it was impossible to stop. Olun rocked herself and envisioned Monta's arms around her, the soft pillow of her bosom, and the muffled, rhythmic beat of her heart beneath. Only Monta knew how to console her when she grew too overwhelmed to speak. She knew, better than her own ma, how to help her work through her confusions. *"Let it out, and start again, my Olun."*

Genta said nothing as she cried herself out in the middle of the path. He did not try to touch her or offer words of sympathy or anger. He didn't scowl or roll his eyes or pace in his impatience. Genta allowed her the space to feel all that she was feeling. *Let it out, and start again.*

Eventually, he stooped to pick up the sack of wax fruit and un-corked his waterskin when she'd quieted. He gave it to her, and she drank numbly, the cool water doing nothing to dissolve the lump in her throat.

Start again.

CHAPTER 11

G ENTA SAID NOTHING FOR the remainder of the afternoon, though his attitude toward Olun had changed. He slowed his pace to match hers, shame replacing his impatience. He didn't look at her, though, or speak. Olun didn't expect an apology. She didn't expect anything from him at all as he went through the motions of showing her how to crack the hard outer shell of the fruit and scoop out the waxy coating within. She did as he did, going through the motions as well. This would be a useful skill to have for when they, too, would abandon her.

"You are not Tula," Genta said suddenly while he stirred the sticky wax shells until they dissolved. "She was agreeable to our ways. She never sulked or shunned us. Her arrival was a seamless one."

Something we agree on, Olun thought, but said aloud, "Tula chose t'be here. I didn't."

"Yes," Genta agreed. "And I have made the grave error in assuming that adapting to our ways would be as simple for you as it was for her."

She took up the spoon and stirred the lumps of wax. *There is nothing simple about this,* she thought.

"Babysitting, are we?" A young man called, trotting up to the crooked gate. He was tall and broad like all of the Ithoumi men Olun observed, but leaner. His curly hair was cut short, like his beard, which revealed a thin, half-moon scar denting his chin. Though his smirk was playful, he looked her up and down like a hunter assessing game. He wore a bow and quiver on his back and knives strapped to his chest and waist.

"Coming or going?" Genta asked, crossing the yard to clasp the man's hand in greeting.

"Going," he grinned. "Thought I would stop in and see Syndra, though."

"And you came *here?*"

The young man shrugged and looked past Genta to Olun. "So, this is her. Our new little troublemaker or something?" he said, ignoring Genta's question.

"Or something," Genta agreed.

"I had not the chance to get a good look at her, what with me being the hero who chased away the echrol and all." His grin was raffish, like Yuhi's. It was probably one he'd used many times to entice women into his arms and inevitably, his bed, Olun thought.

"They were right, though; she *is* all skin and bones. Is the Chief so worried about her blowing away that he assigned you to make sure she does not?"

"*Anyway,*" Genta shook his head in irritation. "Syndra is not here, Manuk. She should be working—like you."

"She is neither with your mother, at home, nor with the laborers," Manuk sighed dramatically. "But you know, *he* is back, and so that only means one thing."

"I doubt she is with him," Genta said, leaning against the wall and crossing his arms. "Didan does not keep *any* company."

Olun decided to focus on making sure the wax fruit melted down evenly while they chatted. She adjusted the iron crane, lifting the pot from the coals to lessen the heat, feigning disinterest in their conversation. This man, Manuk, was the first person courageous enough to strike up a conversation with them all day. She felt Manuk's curious eyes on her and tried not to make her discomfort too obvious.

"That has not given her pause before," he continued to Genta. "Now that *this* girl is Elder, he is free to do what—or *whom*—he wants."

"He may not be Elder anymore, but Didan wants no one. He is physically incapable, Manuk. Your fears are irrational."

"Fear?" Manuk snorted. "I am quite confident in *my* capabilities. I fear no one! Go ask Syndra how many times she has greeted the sun impaled by my—"

"Save your vulgarity for another time," Genta said, glancing at Olun's abashed face.

"Oh, an innocent, are we?" Manuk leaned against the wall as if he were leaning toward her. "Tell me, is it true that desert women take multiple lovers—sometimes at once? You are hardly a child anymore. It is unbelievable that *no one* has been between your legs."

Olun's flush deepened, and she turned her back toward him. Manuk burst with laughter.

"Elders are forbidden to take lovers," Genta reminded him.

"Yes, *our* Elders!" Manuk continued to chortle. "They must have different rules in the desert—is there something wrong with you or *down there*, I wonder?"

"Can you talk of nothing else?" Genta grumbled. "Even if Syndra were with my brother, Didan has not lived *here* for years."

Olun stared down into the pot, their voices fading out as she thought of Yuhi. Yuhi had no shortage of lovers. Yes, there were no restrictions on the number of lovers one could have, but she'd been waiting for *him* to be her first. *Elders are forbidden to take lovers.*

Had she known that this was to be her life, she would have wanted to experience the touch of a lover at least once.

"Hey, girl," Manuk called. "What abilities are you supposed to have, anyway?"

"Abilities?" Olun asked dumbly, looking over her shoulder. Both men watched her, Manuk with interest, Genta with his usual mask of indifference.

"Can you, like, open portals and see stars or whatever?"

Olun froze. *Stars?*

"Can you spirit yourself away like Didan supposedly can? Do you know how convenient it would be to take a shortcut through the In-Between! It would shorten my hunting trips by *days*!"

He's teasing me, Olun frowned and looked away. It was obvious she had no abilities. The only ability that she knew existed was that of an Elder's ability to commune with the goddesses and spirits. She hadn't even had that. Spirit herself away? Portals? *Yeah right.*

"So, you are saying you are lazy, is that it?" Genta chided him.

Manuk ignored him and leapt over the wall with ease.

"Pretty quiet, you are." He stood over Olun with his hands on his hips and nudged her with the toe of his boot. "She is feeble-minded; *that* is why you are babysitting?"

Olun stared up at Manuk whose mischief felt more like cruelty. She didn't like him.

"Manuk," Genta warned, the humor gone from his voice. He crossed the yard and pushed him back. "You are being a nuisance. Go look for your woman elsewhere."

"I am just having fun with her," he whined.

"Well, *stop*."

Manuk held his hands up in surrender as he backed away, but winked at Olun. "I would watch yourself," he said to her. "It is not every day your victim returns—he may be back to finish the job."

He who?

Manuk grinned at Olun's wide-eyed bewilderment.

"Keep your rumors to yourself," Genta snapped.

Olun looked to Genta. "What rumors? What's he talking about?"

"They say he bashed your head in and hid your body away," Manuk said before Genta could dismiss her question. "Who knows what *else* he did to you out there in that cave. Pity you have no memory—"

"Didan had nothing to do with that," Genta seethed. He jerked Olun to her feet and shoved her toward the hut. "Go inside."

Olun stumbled toward the door and planted her feet. *They say he bashed your head in and hid your body away . . . who knows what else he did to you out there in that cave . . .*

The scar on her head throbbed, and Olun wanted to touch it, but her arms would not raise. That man—Didan—was the cause of it?

"Just because Syndra *says* he had nothing to do with her own disappearance, does not mean he is innocent of *hers*," Manuk said with a shrug. "The girl deserves to know the truth. If Didan decides to linger, I mean, should she not be warned?"

"Warned of what? He is not dangerous."

"Not dangerous!" Manuk scoffed. He pointed to the scar on his chin. "The man cracked me in the face with a rock! He is not well—he has *never* been well! Is it really so hard to believe that he would harm a little girl?"

"You provoked him," Genta said flatly.

"Oh, did I, now?" The humor was long gone from Manuk, replaced only with bitterness. "Since when were you in the business of protecting that lout?"

Genta ignored Manuk's question, responding with a coolness that made Olun cower. "That *lout* is still my brother, Manuk, and you will neither look for him nor speak about him. And if I find that you have *approached* him, you will have more than a broken jaw and a scar to complain about."

"Well, if I catch him near Syndra—"

"You will do *what?*"

Olun stared between the two men, both like bull oombrak waiting to lock horns, and held her breath. None of her clan was as violent as it seemed these mountain folk were. *Brutes.* Sure, her people had a few arguments, and yes, a few heated disagreements had broken out at the Gathering, but none had come to blows. None of them bore any such aggression, passive or otherwise. Well, except Monta, who was ever ready with her threats of discipline. It made sense now. *She was born of a clan of brutes.*

Manuk was the first to back down, raising his hands again in surrender. But he grinned. "If we are getting what we deserve, as you say," he said lightly. "Then I think it quite fitting that you, of all people, ended up with a woman whose womb is drier than the desert she came from—"

Manuk barely had time to react before Genta had him on the ground with his face in the dirt. Olun screamed and clapped a hand over her mouth when he glared at her over his shoulder.

"I told you to go inside!"

Legs unfrozen, Olun spun on her heels and did as she was told.

Chapter 12

T HE MORNING LIGHT PEEKED through the window above where Olun lay on her pallet, gazing up at the pale blue sky. She pillowed her head on her hands as she watched the smear of clouds drift lazily above, the cool mountain breeze chilling her cheeks. Olun sighed with contentment. Though it wasn't quite the same as waking up surrounded by her kin beneath the vast expanse of the heavens, the window was better than nothing at all.

A week had passed since her day with Genta and, despite her reservations—or perhaps in spite of them—he'd grown friendlier to her. Well, "friendly" as only Genta could be. He acknowledged her presence when she visited and asked after her health and sleep. He took up the work on her home, making it more hospitable as Tula wanted. Neither of them spoke about Manuk or what he'd said about Tula and Didan, though her questions about the latter were never far from her thoughts.

Genta cut a window in the thatch of her ceiling, rigging it so that she only needed to push open a hatch with a rod to sleep beneath the night sky and wake to the sun. "I cannot return you to the life you once knew," he'd said. "But at least sleeping beneath the stars again will make this feel a little more like home."

It was the first time she'd hugged him—or anyone of the Ithoumi for that matter. Genta had rolled his eyes at the display, awkwardly patting her back while Tula chuckled at his discomfort.

"This is not so you can grow lazy," he'd told her sternly. "I expect you to take up a trade and really learn this village until the time comes for you to assume your duties."

As to the task he'd given her, Olun already knew what trade she wanted to take up. It had been in the back of her mind since her depression cleared. *I could heal a plague.* If she must stay in the Ithoumi village, she would learn the healing arts from Naleda, the Master Healer of the village. When Zafre and his council realized she had no spiritual abilities, she'd return to her people and rid them of their illness. Olun pulled back the door flap, ready to ask Naleda to take her as her student, and found Didan pacing just outside her yard.

"You will not harm her," he muttered angrily to no one Olun could see. "You will *not* harm her! Stay away—you will stay away this time."

He picked up one of the stones from the wall and threw it. With a gasp, Olun ducked back inside, a hand to her heart to stifle the panic thundering in her chest.

He was back, just as Manuk had said. He was back for *her.*

***

"I heard Didan is back, ya? Is that good?"

Olun poured hot water into Tula's cup and watched her mix in the powder Syndra had left her to alleviate nausea.

"If he's back, he won't come into the village," Tula hummed in thought. "I think he's seen Genta once or twice."

Olun had seen him more than that. He watched her home in the mornings. Other times, he examined Genta's work refurbishing the wall that enclosed the yard, even adding a stone or two. Sometimes he muttered to himself, growing angry with whoever it was that bothered him. He never came closer than the wall, and for that, Olun was thankful. She'd gotten in the habit of peeping outside, though, making sure he was good and gone before she ran down the path to Tula and Genta's.

"Genta doesn't think he's dangerous," Olun said, without looking at her.

"And, you do?"

"*Should* I?" She asked. Though Genta was adamant about protecting Didan from Manuk's slander, Olun couldn't help but think he was covering for Didan. Had he really done something to her all those years ago—something so horrible, she'd blocked it out? She fought the urge to touch her scar. Had he been responsible for taking away her memories? Didan had touched her twice before, and both times had brought nothing but pain. She may not remember her time in the village as a child, but her body did.

They stared at each other for a moment before Tula grimaced at the taste of her concoction and set it aside. "When I met him," she began, "he was still recovering from his accident. Genta tells me there was a cave-in and they had t'dig him out. He told me how much he blamed himself for what happened to Didan. That Didan wouldn't've been there when the cave fell if it hadn't been for him."

"So Genta defends him out of guilt?" It didn't matter what Didan did or didn't do, Olun realized, Genta would protect him no matter what. No wonder Manuk was so angry!

"He broke Manuk's jaw—I *heard*."

"Manuk? Yes, well, there are plenty of people who *wanted* to do it but held their fists because he's the nephew of a Doyen," she said with distaste. "He and Genta used to be friends growing up, but now even he can't stand him!"

Olun groaned. She knew next to nothing about these people and had not a clue about what to think about them. Perhaps it was just best to do as she'd been doing and stay away from everyone. *I expect you to take up a trade and really learn this village . . .* Olun groaned again.

"Honestly, Olun," Tula took her hand encouragingly. "Didan is harmless. And, he has no ties to his family or this village, so he'll be on his way soon enough."

Olun nodded, though she knew Tula was wrong. Even in the desert amongst the nomadic clans, she knew that sometimes the danger lies in an untethered soul.

She pondered this as she wandered the pebbly bank along the narrow stream that evening. Family was important to her people because, in a constantly changing world—lives uprooted and chasing the sun—the only constant was family. Family grounded them and kept them safe. A man who rejected his family didn't care about his own well-being and certainly wouldn't care about the well-being of others.

Olun plucked a smooth, iridescent stone from the lapping water to add to her growing collection. Such stones were nonexistent in the desert, even within the markets of the annual Gathering. *Perhaps it's different here in the Ithoumi Village,* she mused, absently examining the green and brown whorls of the stone. With everything so concentrated in the village, they had no need to hold on to family as tightly as the desert clans did. They had no idea what it meant to live *without*.

Movement caught her eye, and she looked up as Didan carefully made his way down the bank, spear in hand. Olun scrambled back from the bank and quickly threw herself behind a boulder before he noticed her. Heart pounding, she took deep breaths. It never occurred to her to see him anywhere else except early in the morning in front of her home. She never saw him in the village or at the bath caves or down by the stream where they washed clothes and scoured pots.

She peeked from her hiding place to see him scanning where she'd been, spear at the ready. Olun thought a feeble-minded and lame man such as him would cower at any signs of danger. And yet, he'd fought off that echrol back then and seemed ready to attack whatever came at him now, deficits aside. Didan was anything but harmless, and to think otherwise was a mistake.

After a while, he lifted the point of his spear and used it as a staff to aid his balance down the bank. Once at the water, he wedged it into place and began to undress. Stifling a gasp, Olun ducked back behind the boulder, heart hammering her chest. *He was bathing out here?* She didn't know why it embarrassed her; she'd seen bathers before. The warmth of embarrassment colored her cheeks even still. But morbid curiosity had her looking again.

Didan had waded out up to his waist. He cupped the cold water in his hands and splashed along his arms, drawing a wet cloth across his chest. He squeezed it at the back of his neck, and Olun watched the water run down his crooked spine, rough with the bumps and knots of keloid scars. The slope of his slanted shoulder bore the worst of the scarring, stretching in such a way Olun believed the shiny skin would tear altogether. When he turned, she saw that the right side of his chest was no different.

Olun had never seen a man who looked as he did. If he lived amongst the clans, he surely would have been ostracized by appearance alone. He would've been seen as damaged—cursed even. Her people did not have the skills to heal such wounds. Just the fact that he was alive when he should have been dead would have been enough for her people to shun him.

And yet, there was something striking about Didan that, once again, made Olun wonder about his story. What kind of man could endure all that trauma and survive? It shocked her to see the definition of muscle in his arms and chest as he wiped the water from his chin with the back of his arm, pushing his wild hair adorned with the pastiche of trinkets back from his face. Didan looked nothing like how she imagined beneath his billowing robes—not that she fantasized about his naked body, of course.

It wasn't until he began wading back to the bank, the recession of water revealing more and more of him, that she realized just what *else* she was about to see.

Olun gasped, jumped to her feet, and ran.

CHAPTER 13

OLUN'S ROUTINE PASSED IN a blur: Sweeping Naleda's apothecary, making bandages, repairing baskets, and cleaning linen. Naleda had agreed to take her as a student, but so far, there'd only been chores. It was just as well. She hadn't been able to focus since her last run-in with Didan.

In her thoughts, she picked him apart, wondering about his scars, speculating about his past—and hers. Wondering more and more about why she had such a strong reaction to his presence. Most importantly, she couldn't stop thinking about seeing him undressed. She groaned, not for the first time, disgusted with herself. If there was ever a man's body she wanted to remember, it should *not* be his. It was a morbid curiosity, she told herself, and nothing else.

When Tula sent Olun up to the mines to deliver Genta's midday meal, Olun was glad for the distraction. She took the path out of the west side of the village, climbing the steep incline and rocks expertly as if she'd always lived there. It'd been easy to learn the village's paths and dirt roads as if her body were operating on memories her mind could not fathom. Naleda told her on her very first night in the village that it had been Didan who'd found her after her accident. After she'd been missing and no one could find a trace of her—except him. Manuk had said that Didan was the cause—of both her disappearance and *re*appearance. Olun slowed to a stop and leaned against the rock wall, shaded by the cliff.

What if I wake up one day and my memories of the desert, like my time in the village, are no more . . .

Olun sighed and slid down the wall, resting her back against the stone. She closed her eyes and imagined the purple-desert sands. She imagined sinking her toes into granules warmed by the sun, and removing her head scarf to feel the dry breeze ruffle her hair. But no heat came. The stone grew frightfully cold, the chill penetrated through her to her scalp. Olun wrapped her arms around herself, bewildered by the change in temperature.

"What are memories truly worth?" The deep masculine voice was as soft as a whisper.

She snapped open her eyes. With horror, she found that she was no longer on the path but somewhere so dark she could not even see her own hand in front of her face. Her breath caught in her throat as, little by little, the darkness became alive with twinkling green stars. She'd been to this place before, perhaps in a dream—or from staring up into the night sky? Olun rose, pulling her eyes away from the stars to look around in the dim illumination of the light. *A cave?*

"Memories fester like old wounds, painful to the touch," lamented the man. *"To forget is but a blessing."* A silhouette detached from the blackness, and Olun screamed.

"Stay back!" Olun recoiled, catching her heel on a stone. She fell backward, arms cycling both to catch herself and ward him off. She hit the ground hard, but when she sat up—expecting to see the man standing over her—there was nothing but the wall she had leaned against in the afternoon light. Around her, rocks, shrubs, and the path.

Olun snatched up Genta's lunch and hurried the rest of the way to the mines, glancing fearfully about herself as she went. That man—she knew his voice. Though the darkness obscured his features, she was sure she *knew him*. But he was gone just like that place, the stars, her dreams, and memories. A dry sob slipped free, and she quickened her pace, anxious to be off the path.

By the time she made it to the mines, she was gasping for air, her chest tight from panic. Even the loud chuck of hammers, clink of chisels, and pop of splitting stones were dampened by the thunderous pound of her heart.

"Olun?" Genta parted from the group he stood with, taking her by the shoulder and steering her out of the way of passersby. Her limbs had already locked, and she found that she could not move on her own. "What is it? What happened?"

"I—I saw—I think I—" she sputtered, eyes darting frantically. What could she tell him? In one blink, she was somewhere else with a shadow man talking in her head, and in another, she was back on the path. She was just beginning to earn his acceptance, and this would surely cast doubts on her.

With trembling hands, Olun thrust the parcel into his arms. She turned, intending to run back to the village as quickly as she could, when a hand shot past Genta's to take hold of her wrist.

"You are hurt," Didan's voice was low as he stepped past his brother to examine her arm.

Olun looked down at her torn sleeve and the scrape on her elbow. Then she followed the hand back up to Didan's worried face. She hadn't noticed him—hadn't expected him to be there at all! His hands were coarse though gentle as he held her wrist, his fingers probing along her arm for other injuries.

Like the day she'd run into him when Tula collapsed, there was genuine concern in his attention. He stood so close to her that she could see the dark rims beneath his eyes and the patchy beard along the scars of his chin. Olun tried not to think about how she'd almost seen him fully naked—how she'd *seen* how damaged his body was—but failed miserably. An embarrassing heat crept up her neck. Didan caught her staring, brows furrowing beneath the curtain of his disheveled hair, and Olun looked away quickly.

"It—It's just a scrape," she said, pulling away from his grasp and stepping toward Genta.

"I didn't mean t'cause trouble. I just—Tula asked me t'bring you this, and the Shadow—" she stopped.

Clarity smoothed Genta's features. "You must have seen the shadow of a mawtiku. Their young should be taking flight by now."

Olun's eyes widened, and she shrank into Didan without thinking. "A *what?*"

Chuckles went around as the onlookers dispersed, having lost interest now that the mystery terror was identified.

"Creatures that live high up in the peaks with wings as long as a man is tall," Genta said.

"They are *harmless*," Didan emphasized, his hard eyes narrowing at his brother.

"Oh, simmer down. I was not trying to scare her," Genta scoffed.

"They are like bimi," Didan explained gently. "But larger and are able to fly."

Olun pictured the bubble-eyed bimi clumsily scratching at the dirt, then tried to picture them as tall as a man.

"You should stay," Genta sighed. "I can understand why you are shaken. I will take you back later."

"*I* will take her back," Didan interjected. "Or do you have a problem with that?"

He looked at Genta with an air of defiance as if he expected his brother to deny him. Olun glanced between the two curiously, wondering what had transpired before her arrival. Despite Genta defending Didan on more than one occasion, it was clear he still had his doubts about him. Should she have them, too?

Before Olun had the chance to speak, Genta spun on his heels, leaving her standing awkwardly beside Didan. She risked a glance at him, meeting his eye, and looking away as quickly as before.

Didan cleared his throat. "Let us find shade. Syndra can take a look at your foot."

"My foot?" She looked down at her sandals, torn and flapping at the heel. The stone that had snagged it had cut just enough of her heel to bleed, but not deep enough to bleed long. She hadn't felt it when it happened, though as Olun looked down at the damage, she felt its sting. Didan took her elbow, supporting her weight as she walked gingerly toward the spot he'd indicated.

It was hard to believe that the man Manuk had made him out to be, and the man Olun had asked Genta about, could be so gentle and considerate. The seemingly feeble-minded madman of whispers was actually more attuned than she realized.

She'd wanted to tell him she knew he watched her house, and that she heard him talking to himself. She wanted to tell him that she didn't know what he wanted from her or why he was back, but he needed to leave her alone. If he wanted his home back, she'd leave. If he wanted her to stop making changes to it, she'd ask Genta to stop. Even more, she wanted to tell him what she really saw back on the path—surely he of all people could tell her if she were going mad. But words failed her as he sat her down before him.

"Wait here," he said. Olun, uncomfortable with his attention and her own inability to speak, did as she was told while Didan briefly left her to inquire about Syndra's whereabouts.

She turned her attention to the tunnels, making up her mind to confront him when he came back. *What game is he playing at, acting this way with me?*

There were eight caves; the sounds of hammering echoed through each mouth. She knew from Tula that Genta was a stonecrafter, but she hadn't known what that meant. There were no stonecrafters in the desert. Men and women worked away at the pale, purple-gray rocks in the hot sun, expertly cutting them into the pieces they would use to build more homes, steps, walls, and other structures. Ootinglas pulled carts of dark rocks from the caves, led by dust-coated workers from others to sift through.

"Fire stone," Didan said when he returned, following her eyes to the black rocks. "They make our fires burn longer and brighter."

"Better than oombrak dung, I guess," she murmured, wrinkling her nose at the remembrance of the hard patties and pungent fumes of a desert fire. It was then Olun realized it hadn't even been a month since she'd smelled its scent. Weeks ago, she'd sat around such a fire and not given it a single thought.

Didan gave a soft chuckle. "Yes, far better than dung."

His chuckle was more of a rumble, or a growl. Nothing that could be identified as laughter, but Olun saw the glint in his eye and the way his tired face seemed to relax. *Was that a dimple?* Strangely, she relaxed, too, as if by instinct. Again, her need to confront him was pushed to the wayside, this time, in favor of curiosity.

"What else is in there?"

He gazed at the tunnels thoughtfully. "Ore to be melted into tools," Didan pointed to a burly woman swinging a hammer at her forge.

"Stone and mortar to construct new homes; minerals for my mother's medicines; porous stones for laundering and bathing with. The list is endless."

"You're joking," she said, voice going flat with disbelief. Olun knew the Ithoumi thrived in the mountains, but the mountains were so much more than she ever expected.

Didan quirked a small smile, and Olun tried not to react to the flutter in her chest; she wished she'd looked anywhere but at the dimple that had appeared in his cheek. She managed to tear her eyes from his face, heart beating fast, and searched for something more to say.

"I'd like t'see it with my own eyes." Would it look like the bath caves, with its many candles and pools?

Olun glanced up at Didan's prolonged silence. The ease left his face and he stared at her with those penetrating eyes that had frightened her the night of her ceremony. Olun regretted getting too comfortable with him; she took a step back and prepared to guard herself if he attempted to grab at her as he had that night.

"Stay out of the caves," he said soberly. "Death waits in them, for you *and* for me."

Olun's hand went to her scar, eyes wide, and her body trembling. *What did you do to me?* The question—the *demand*—was on the tip of her tongue.

"It is not bad," Didan said abruptly, and Olun realized Syndra was before them. "It should be cleaned nonetheless."

Syndra dropped her bag from her shoulders. Naleda's most senior pupil hardly wasted a glance on Olun when she'd begun her chores around the healer's apothecary. Olun had tried for days to get her attention. She'd gone missing, too. Olun wanted desperately to ask her what she remembered. But Syndra had ignored Olun's presence completely. Except for right now.

Olun stared at her in silent awe. While Tula's beauty was of a domestic nature—round cheeks, nurturing eyes, low curves—everything about Syndra was sharp and intimidating. Olun found herself wilting beneath her withering stare even more than she had beneath Genta's, her questions caught in her throat.

"What are *you* doing here?" she hissed at Olun.

"I—I brought Genta lunch," Olun stuttered, avoiding her eye and accidentally looking into Didan's. She was surprised to find comfort in them once again.

"She fell on her way here," Didan explained. "Could you take a look at her foot?"

"Oh no, Little Desert Girl has fallen," Syndra muttered. "Whatever shall we do?"

Regardless of her evident dislike of Olun—a dislike she didn't understand—Syndra knelt and took her foot into her lap.

"Look at those sandals, they are not fit for walking around anywhere," she admonished.

Olun touched them possessively. Her pa had made them for her. "They're all I have."

"Flimsy things," Syndra scoffed, jerking the lace to loosen it.

Olun hissed when Syndra peeled off her sandal and dumped water on her cut.

"Easy, Syndra," Didan said, noticing Olun's discomfort. It was enough to distract Olun from what Syndra did as she gaped up at Didan instead. He supervised Syndra's ministrations intently.

"She is not the first desert dweller to live in the mountains, Didan," Syndra said flatly as she wrapped her foot with linen. "It is insulting that, after avoiding me for so long, the only reason you would speak to me is to handle a little scratch. She has had worse."

"I am aware," he said mildly.

Olun glanced between the two of them, trying to keep her wincing to a minimum. Syndra finished and pushed Olun's foot from her lap.

"So, where are you staying?" She asked him lightly, wiping her hands.

"Syndra—"

"Look," she cut him off. "You do not have to tell me but—just stop running, okay? You no longer have to do that. You *have* a place, and I am here for you. Whatever you need."

"Are you done?" Didan asked abruptly, and Olun trembled at his change in tone.

"Yeah, whatever," She packed up her bag, not even bothering to look at the scrapes on Olun's hands and elbow, not that she needed it. Olun could have cleaned her heel and wrapped it on her own once she'd gotten back. Didan had made her look so incapable, Olun wondered if Syndra would report this back to Naleda.

Syndra gave Didan a hard stare and walked away without a glance Olun's way. Manuk waited for her at a distance, watching Didan with such abhorrence. It was a wonder how he hadn't run over to him. Perhaps he feared Genta more than he hated Didan, Olun guessed.

"Manuk," Didan nodded toward him by way of introduction.

"We met," she said, then added at the frown on his face. "He was looking for . . ."

She trailed off, unsure if she wanted to get into his business with Syndra and Manuk. Her life was already more complicated than it needed to be, and getting involved with the three of them would not help. Olun rose, gingerly testing her weight on her sore foot, jerking away when Didan took her elbow to steady her.

"I'm not delicate, ya?" she hissed, still very much aware of their surroundings and who might be watching. "Stop hovering."

Didan held up a single placating hand and backed away, but it was obvious she would need his help. She only wore one sandal, and already the hot, sharp gravel beneath her foot was starting to hurt. Didan was observant despite his partial blindness.

"I will be right back," he said, watching her timid steps. His limping gate was purposeful as he headed back amongst the stonecrafters now taking their mid-day break.

Clanks and chucks were replaced with the murmur of conversation and peals of laughter. But that wasn't the only thing Olun noticed. They glanced at Didan as he walked between them, moving out of his way or turning from him completely. Like the night of her ceremony, they whispered behind their hands or openly as if he couldn't hear. The pity in their eyes reminded her of the way her own people looked at her when Elder Kikyel announced her fate. It was a hopeless look, cold and unsympathetic. It was clear that whatever path he walked, he walked it hopelessly alone.

Olun didn't know why it bothered her so much, or why she suddenly wanted to protect him from their stares. Perhaps it was Didan's kindness today that suddenly made her want to defend him. Yes, she'd been the very one to stare at his deformity and dismiss him because of it. *Yes*, she found his stalking around her home and muttering creepy. He might even have had something to do with the scar on her head—who knew? *"You're a feeling child, Olun. It'll do you well t'trust those feelings,"* Elder Kikyel had told her many times.

But what if she had two *conflicting* feelings? Didan was terrifying yet comforting. When he touched her, she remembered pain . . . but also safety? Which should she trust?

The hair rose on the back of her neck, and a dull hum, like a magnetic pull of some unknown force, called her attention toward the tunnels.

"*Would you like to see the cave stars?*" asked a voice, too far away to discern its owner. Olun whirled around in panic, but once again, the hum of the tunnels called her back. Closer and closer she crept, hypnotized by its rhythm. No one seemed to notice her by the dark mouth, like jaws parting, the waft of air like a cool exhalation. The tunnel was alive. Or better yet, something lived *in there*, calling to her like many voices droning together in some indistinguishable chant. She'd heard this—*felt* this—before. It resonated within her, quickening the beat of her heart and causing cold sweats to dampen her face. She knew this place. This feeling. *There was no darkness, only the stars. No pain, only peace—*

A hand clamped around her wrist and dragged her back from the darkness.

"What do you think you are doing?" Didan hissed. "Did you not listen to what I said before?"

He held an empty sack in one hand, her wrist tightly in the other. There was panic in his disfigured face. True fear.

"I'm sorry, I didn't know I was moving." Olun stuttered, "Th—there's something in there!"

Didan was scaring her again; the hand clasped around her wrist trembled. She only felt pain and fear. Hatred.

"Let go of me," she whimpered.

Realizing what he was doing, Didan glanced around and quickly released her wrist. He stooped down in front of her abruptly, head bowed, and his messy hair falling forward to hide his face. After a while, he tore the sack he carried into strips, setting her torn sandal down for her to step into. When she did, he secured it around her foot and ankle with the strips.

"I am sorry," he murmured when he rose. "I will take you back now."

CHAPTER 14

D IDAN SAID NOTHING MORE about the caves as they navigated the path back to the village, the two of them limping in sequence. His face was unreadable and his mood swings were just as fickle as the wind, Olun thought glumly. A gentle breeze could end up a cyclone in mere moments, and a distant storm could be nothing more than a playful sweep of wind about the ankles. *Death waits for me and for you.* What a terrible thing to say—horrifying.

"Staring will not make me any less gruesome," Didan said brusquely, glancing down at her from the corner of his eye.

Olun looked away quickly. "I wasn't staring—" she cleared her throat awkwardly. "Naleda's going t'train me t'be a healer, so you can't have your house back yet."

She winced. *Why did I just say that?* She hadn't been this silly around Yuhi!

"Why is that?" Didan asked flatly.

Olun fidgeted with her sleeve. "I just told you, ya? I'm going t'be a healer instead of Elder. Elder Vasc made a mistake; there's nothing about me that says *'Elder,'* so after I learn what I can from Naleda, I'm going home. *My* home."

She had none of these vague abilities that were supposed to grant her favor with the goddesses; she was not made for Solitude, and she didn't think she could serve the Dark Lady of Death. It didn't matter what these people thought of Her; an exiled god is exiled for a reason.

"I do not approve of this situation *or* Vasc's decision," Didan said tightly. "I just wish Vasc's successor were *anyone* else but you. But being chosen is never a mistake."

"It was when they chose you," she said before she could stop herself. Didan looked away and his shoulders hunched, the fall of his hair hiding his face.

She hadn't been trying to be cruel or funny like Manuk. It was a truth that was spoken behind everyone's hand: Didan could not handle his role and went mad because of it. But regardless . . .

"I shouldn't've said that," Olun said quietly, slowing down so he could walk ahead of her.

Didan slowed, too. "Mistake . . ." he said, and Olun's guilt grew.

"All I mean is that some people just aren't made t'be Elder—like *me*. And like you."

"Regardless of that fact, here we are," Didan sighed. He walked on, and Olun followed, navigating the sloping path gingerly.

"They say you went mad. Manuk asked me if I'd started going mad, too," she said, unable to let the topic go. What if Manuk was right? What happened to her earlier that day, both on the way to the tunnels and at the tunnels themselves—what if she were going mad like Didan? The only thing they had in common, Olun realized suddenly, was the water they had to drink to become Elder . . .

"Manuk knows nothing. Here—watch out." Didan grabbed her arm before a stumble pitched her forward. His hand lingered against hers until Olun recoiled.

"I may not remember things, ya?" she said, wrapping her arms protectively about her. "But I remember—I *feel* like I remember—something horrible. I feel like I remember *you*."

Didan searched her face carefully from beneath his wild hair, and Olun lowered her eyes, afraid to meet his gaze.

"What *exactly* is the question you want to ask me?" Didan's eyes narrowed, and for an instant, he resembled Genta's ire. Olun wondered what he would have looked like without the scars. What kind of man was he, hidden behind the tangled mass of his hair that very much served as a wall keeping the outside world at bay?

"I heard that . . ." Olun swallowed hard. "Did you have anything t'do with what happened t'me as a child?"

She took a step back, ready to run to Genta if need be. How silly to confront a man who had the power—and rage—to break a man's jaw. A man whose moods were so unpredictable, he was laughing in one instant and squeezing the blood from her arm in the next?

"I have no idea what happened to you," Didan admitted solemnly, his crooked mouth going flat. "But I can say, with great shame, that it is because of my loneliness and negligence that you were hurt at all."

Loneliness. Negligence. This wasn't what she'd thought he'd say at all.

Didan cocked his head, brows furrowing. She thought he would say more until he shook himself free of whatever he wished to say.

"I am envious." He said instead. "The ability to forget is but a blessing."

The color drained from her face. "Where did you hear that?"

Didan looked down at her with such unreadable eyes that Olun almost reached out to touch him. *Almost.*

"I . . . I didn't see a mawtiku," she confessed. She wasn't sure what such a winged creature looked like, but she was certain she'd seen the shape of a man. "I saw—"

"The village is there," Didan pointed to the first house by the stream. "You should be fine to go back on your own now."

Olun took a hesitant step toward it and stopped. "You said I could talk to you," she turned back toward him. "Am I seeing these things—hearing them— because of the water from the ceremony? You told me not t'drink, but I did and now I'm losing my mind—"

"The water means nothing," Didan said abruptly, as if to calm her panicked thoughts. "It is symbolic. Before this village came to be, a man from the desert wandered through these mountains on the verge of death. It is said the Dark Goddess led him to a stream and, as he drank from it, he was restored. This man became our first Elder and this village sits near that same stream. Elders drink because it is a tradition centuries old." He finished tiredly.

"But none of this ever happened before I came here," she challenged.

Didan smirked. "I hear you have nightmares."

Olun opened her mouth to argue, then shut it again. How did he know about that? She'd had nightmares ever since childhood, but that had nothing to do with anything. She shook her head, continuing her inquiry. "Then why warn me not t'drink?"

"Because it still means something to *them*. Belief can be a dangerous thing, as you know." Didan nodded down the path indicating she should go, but she still had questions. Many, many questions.

"I see you each morning, watching my house, talking t'yourself . . ." She lowered her voice as she hazarded a guess. "You've seen it too."

"I do not *see* anything," Didan said tightly. "But I hear them."

You will leave her alone. Olun swallowed to wet her throat that had gone dry, and wondered at the nature of the words he'd spoken outside her door. "What do they say t'you?"

He moved past her, eyes faraway, and she wondered if he listened even now. Olun jumped when he turned back to her and clasped her hands. His slurred speech halted; he spoke as if he were unsure of just how much to say or who might be listening.

"Forget about the water, it is the mountains you should worry about. The mountains have their own stories—recorded in the stone and whispered in the wind. One can get seduced by their call. I have told them to leave you alone, Olun, but they will come. You must ignore them for your own sanity, and whatever you do, do not let them put you in Solitude."

It was the first time he'd said her name. There was tenderness in the way he'd said it, contrasting the seriousness of his warning. Her heart thawed, and somewhere, pushing to the forefront of her mind was a memory of a young boy.

"Who are they?" she breathed. "What *is* this Solitude?"

Zafre and Genta had mentioned it. Tula, too. No one would tell her.

"The council so staunchly holds to tradition," Didan continued, having not heard her question. "You may want to be a healer, but you are *their* Elder, and *they* control you. Be firm in what you want and do not let them turn your head."

CHAPTER 15

They came two days later.

Olun nearly tripped over the simple pair of leather shoes waiting for her in front of her door. They were sturdy with hard soles and thick straps that were not likely to tear. She slipped her foot into them hesitantly and was surprised to find that they were just her size and comfortable. Had Tula mentioned her broken sandals to Genta? She'd helped Olun mend her broken strap as best she could, after all. But even still, Didan crossed her mind.

"You know what Zafre said. And Hujak and Naleda will be furious we came without them—we are a *council!*"

"This is not about them."

Olun frowned, made curious by the approaching bickering. She rarely received visitors other than Tula and Genta, though the latter of whom's visits consisted of the manual labor of making the shack more hospitable. Old Yadir, her closest neighbor, looked in on her from time to time, too.

Doyens Helima and Zayeer climbed the path toward her, still wrapped in discussion. In the daylight, she saw how much the old pair resembled each other. Uncannily so. The only differentiating features were Zayeer's beard and Helima's modest bust. The pair sported matching braids and robes with identical embroidering along the neck and sleeves. It had been unfortunate that Olun hadn't spoken to the pair after the night of her ceremony. She'd seen them when Tula had shown her the crops and the herd of ootingla, but shied away from conversing with them. They were an interesting pair, but intimidating nonetheless.

"Good, you are up!" Helima smiled when she noticed Olun. "The Bright Goddess smiles on you!"

"You too," Olun responded, still getting used to the Ithoumi greeting. They were an interesting people, respectfully acknowledging Ma Bright even though they revered the Dark Lady.

"I'm sorry, I wasn't expecting visitors, or I'd have something t'offer."

"It is quite alright!" Helima chuckled, waving her hand. "These accommodations are only temporary, anyways."

Olun lowered her eyes to mask her gloom unsuccessfully.

"You have been here for litte over a month now, correct?" Zayeer said. "You understand the position we are in."

Olun nodded.

"And, Genta has told you what is expected of an Elder, correct?"

Again, Olun nodded.

"Good," Helima took over. "Have you considered what you will ask for when you take your Solitude?"

"No," Olun said automatically. Though she didn't know what was meant by 'ask for,' Didan's words were still fresh in her mind.

"No, you have not considered it?" Helima frowned.

No, I don't want to go. Olun remained silent.

The Doyens looked at each other in confusion. "You know, this must happen," Helima said.

"The longer you wait, the harder it will be," Zayeer added. "For you and all of us."

"What does it *mean* t'go into Solitude?" Olun blurted. "Everyone keeps saying it, but no one is telling me where I must go. What must I ask?"

"My dear," Helima took her hand. "Solitude is a sacred place that every Elder has visited since the first was entombed there."

Entombed?

"It is a place where an Elder can find clarity and converse with the Goddess freely. It is a doorway to Her home."

Olun shrank from the two. "I—I don't know what t'tell you," she apologized. "I'm not the—maybe you should wait for Elder Vasc t'come back, ya? He's *your* Elder, not me."

Zayeer scoffed. "Elder Vasc—that man has not been right in the head since he came back down from the Peak some forty years ago."

The woman elbowed him in the chest, and he wheezed.

"You are the Elder now," Helima said sweetly. "I know no one has been treating you like one, but they should. Vasc made his prediction, and just as he said, you are here. So you *must* learn to be what he says you are."

"You don't know that," Olun said flatly and ducked past the two to busy herself with her fire. Hadn't Didan said they would come? If she kept refusing, would they go away?

"I'm sorry t'disappoint you," Olun said, unable to meet their eyes, "But I can't talk t'the Goddesses. I've been trying my whole life, and Ma Bright don't talk t'me."

"'*Ma Bright?*'" Zayeer muttered, and again, Helima elbowed him into silence.

"Perhaps that will change when you take your Solitude," she suggested. "Once you speak to the right one."

They followed her around the yard.

"I told you this was a mistake," Zayeer resumed his muttering. "Vasc has gone senile. Like *you*, Helli."

"She *is not* a mistake! Elder Vasc knows what he is doing."

"Like he did with Didan?" Zayeer shook his head in dismay. "This one already said she is useless."

Helima took the firestone from Olun's anxious hands when she attempted to light the coals of her fire pit.

"You will do a wonderful job," she said, lighting the fire herself in two strikes of the stones. "I know Naleda has taken a liking to you, but playing with medicines is just busy work for you."

Olun blinked dumbly between them. They were not going away on their own. "Tell me what you want—*why* you want me t'go so badly."

"To be Elder, of course," Zayeer said.

Helima smiled and pulled Olun's hands into her lap. Olun stared down at their linked hands, the sudden urge to cry creeping up on her. There was a mixture of grief, hope, and anxiety all rolled into one, and Olun was sure it was coming from the older woman.

"You see, my brother," she said. "He has been sick for a long time. I just . . ." For a brief moment, Olun saw her face crumble.

"Oh no—" Olun disentangled their hands and dabbed at the woman's tears with her sleeve. "Please, don't cry."

But the woman took Olun's hand again and squeezed, and the mix of emotions returned. "Naleda does not know how long we have before he meets the Goddess, so, when you go into Solitude, you must ask Her to have patience with him in the Great After. Tell Her that he has been such a great man and brother and, if at all possible, for Her to reunite him with Creda."

Zayeer gave a strangled cry from behind them. He covered his face as he turned away, but Olun saw by the trembling of his shoulders that he was breaking just as his sister had.

"You *must* remember to ask Her this," Helima continued in earnest. "You see, my brother has always been by my side since the womb. We cared for each other, tending the farms, feeding the village. He never took a chance at the life he could have had with Creda. At least, in death, he should have a chance to spend the Great After with the woman he should have spent his life with."

Olun swallowed hard. Elder Kikyel used to sit with the sick, holding their hands as they whispered in her ear. Was this what they spoke about—last wishes? No wonder it couldn't wait. Olun gave Helima's hand an affirming squeeze; she knew what it meant to have a comfort in death, even if it was a simply holding ones hand and singing to them. It took away the wretchedness of dying and gave them dignity.

Satisfied, Helima smiled again and the hunch of her shoulders lifted. Olun could have sworn she became so much younger than before. Zayeer placed his hand on his sister's shoulder.

"You are an outsider to our ways and to our Goddess," he said to Olun. "But you must learn quickly. If I should go sooner rather than later, you must ask the Goddess to let my spirit linger just long enough for me to know my sister will be taken care of. Creda has waited this long; what is a bit longer?"

Again, Olun nodded mutely. She didn't know what to tell them that she hadn't already, but they believed in her. They believed that this Solitude would be the very place to awaken her abilities. And if it didn't? Their final wishes would never make it to the Dark Lady.

***

Sleep did not come easily to Olun that night, not with Helima and Zayeer running through her thoughts. She kept their visit to herself, though, hesitant about what would happen if others knew. It would be like an open invitation for the villagers to seek her out. She'd shown nothing of a promising Elder, but two of the village's most prominent people getting favors from her? Olun sucked her teeth and rolled to her back.

"To live," she sighed. "Did I ask for too much? *Not* t'be a sacrifice. Not t'die of the Sickness—not t'have my *people* die of the Sickness. No nightmares. A beloved. A family . . ."

Okay, maybe I was asking for a lot. Olun massaged her eyes with frustration and gazed up at the sky through the hatch. The stars blinked down at her, a sparse spattering of crystals against the velvet shawl of night. Death was terrifying. Not necessarily *dying*, though that was pretty scary, too. She'd buried the diseased bodies beneath the sand, never giving much thought as to what happened next. They were simply gone; the Dark Lady had done Her job in separating their spirits from their bodies and opening the door for them to walk on into their next life. What more was there? Zayeer didn't look sick, or move about like one caught on borrowed time. But both Helima and Zayeer were of an age where death was indeed close, and they were afraid of the "after." They shouldn't have trusted her.

With a frustrated sigh, Olun kicked off her blankets and sat up. She crossed her legs and drew herself up as straight as she could, lifting her face to the night sky. Elder Kikyel didn't have to go away to seek the guidance of the Gods; she traveled with the Rohta, with her people. Perhaps Olun didn't have to go away, either.

Hello?

No answer, as expected. Olun searched the stars, wondering how to direct her thoughts to the Dark Lady. She thought about Her, picturing what she thought She should look like—stringy black hair, thin frame, an arrogant face. She might have been pretty once. She had to have been if the Great God chose Her first to be His bride, as the story went. Olun tried again, closing her eyes to really focus.

I know it's been a bit since they dedicated me t'you, and this is my first request—if you don't count what I asked when I ran from the echrol. This time, I'm asking on behalf of others.

Olun waited, her body taunt and her keen ears listening.

Nothing changed. There was no response.

Most Revered Dark Lady, I have a petition—Will you listen? Useless. Burden. Trouble. Sacrifice. Mistake. She wanted to know if she was more than those things. Her nose burned the way it did when tears were close at hand. If the Dark Lady spoke to her now, she'd know for certain that she was needed—*wanted.* That she had a purpose.

I've no right t'ask you for anything, but please, please! Just this once, answer me!

"*I hear you, child,*" a deep voice rumbled.

For the briefest moment, the fog of her memory peeled back to reveal a dark chasm of nothingness. Her body remembered a finite darkness, blood pulsating in her ears in the silence. She felt a sharp pain in her skull, and a sticky warmth dampened her hair and face. A masculine voice purred in loops of familiar phrases, sounds, and words. Words filled with such anguish and pain that in her waking, it was as if she was the one suffering and crying them out.

Olun snapped open her eyes, hand trembling as she touched the scar on the back of her head and found a gaping wound.

"*I hear you, child, and I wait for you.*"

Olun screamed and tumbled out into the cool night air. Though she couldn't see him, she knew he was in her home—he had to be! This—this Shadow Man—he was everywhere! Her nightmares, the mines—her head! Oh, Great God, her head! She didn't dare touch it again, gaping and exposed.

She ran instead, sobbing, yet her frantic feet didn't take her down the path to old Yadir, or Tula and Genta, or even Naleda. Her mind wouldn't let her thoughts surface. Instead, it filled with whispers of unintelligible words. Hums and chimes of chants all fusing together.

"Stop—" she gasped, clutching her ears. "I'm sorry, I'm sorry, I'm sorry!"

Whatever she'd done—she only wanted it to stop. *Please stop!* The wide, paved path became dirt, grass, and an overgrowth of prickling brambles. Tough, wiry shrubs forced their way between the rocks, their waxy leaves covered in prickly fuzz that grasped at her clothes. The air grew colder the higher she climbed, the wind whistling over shelves of rock.

"Run to me, child . . ."

"Leave me alone!" Olun ran faster, the terrain growing steeper and rockier. The trail narrowed, but she didn't care. She needed to hide—to get away from the Shadow Man.

"Olun!" Hands were grabbing her, forcing her back into the shadows.

She fought them, kicking and clawing. "Let me go!" she shrieked until she was free.

And the ground disappeared beneath her feet.

Chapter 16

"YOU HAVE TO HELP me—Olun, *open your eyes!*"

The hand around her wrist was like a vice with fingers digging into her skin enough to bruise. It pulled her back from the mouth of the cave—from the tomb of her mind. Olun opened her eyes, her vision adjusting to the night, revealing the miniature scene of the village below. She screamed and grabbed at the arm, her only lifeline.

"Look at me, Olun!"

Her head snapped up to the man who held her dangling over the ledge, eyes going wide as she recognized Didan. He winced, but his urgent voice remained steady.

"I cannot hold you like this for long, so you *have* to help me. Can you do that?"

"Yes," she gasped.

"Feel around for a foothold."

She did as he said, knees scraping against the rocks until she found a hold.

"You are going to push up from there, and I am going to pull you, alright?"

His voice was soothing, as if they were sitting in the sun together, enjoying the day. Olun focused on that. She closed her eyes and pictured them sitting side by side, Didan's soft, placid voice lulling her to calm. She pushed up from her foothold, and with more strength than she expected, Didan jerked her up. With a squeak, she collapsed against him, clutching his cloak as if letting him go meant she'd fall back over the ledge, or worse.

"I have you," Didan said, dragging them both backward from the ledge. "You are safe."

Olun sobbed into his cloak, fear and relief gripping her heart with both hands. Despite the calm of his voice, Didan's heart beat rapidly, revealing his own panic. He patted her back and rubbed her shoulders, the soft murmurings of unintelligible words bringing her down from the terror of near death.

"My head," she sobbed. "It's *bleeding*—it—I can't—"

Didan sat up abruptly, and she felt his probing fingers part her hair carefully. Olun tensed for pain, but there was none. Perhaps she was still in shock.

"Were you injured?" Didan asked, though the urgency had left his body.

"No, I—" she froze. She'd been in her room. She'd been trying to reach the Dark Lady. The Shadow Man was there. Suddenly, Olun was aware that it all could have all been a nightmare.

Olun peeled her fingers from his cloak, pulling back just enough to touch the back of her head for herself. There was no wound. No blood. Not even the ghost of pain.

"I'm sorry," she whispered. She stared down at her trembling hand, free of blood, panic rising until she wanted to flee again. It didn't make any sense.

"Shhhh," he patted her back. "Take a breath, watch me."

Olun looked up at him, taking slow breaths and releasing them as he showed her until she calmed and the urge to cry subsided. She looked around. Behind him was a modest campfire, the remains of a meal, and a pallet of furs beneath a lean-to.

"This is where you live?" Olun asked abruptly.

"For now," Didan said.

"But—the echrol, and the mawtiku—"

"Mawtiku do not thrive below the clouds," he dismissed. "And they do not eat living flesh."

"But—"

Didan shifted beneath her, his scarred face mere inches from hers. It was then she realized she was with *Didan* of all people—in his *lap!* Olun rolled off of him, cheeks blazing with mortification. Whether he noticed her embarrassment or not, he gave no indication as he rose stiffly to his feet. He offered her his hand to help her stand, keeping his other hand to his chest.

Olun stood on her own, attention drawn to his arm. "I hurt you," she mumbled.

"It is fine," Didan gave an exaggerated stretch as proof, though his discomfort was easy to see.

He cocked his head and frowned. "What are you doing up here?"

Olun looked once more at the camp in front of her and hesitated a glance over her shoulder at the dark path that had almost taken her over the edge and down a sheer drop. She didn't exactly know why or how she'd ended up there with him. If he hadn't been camping there, she certainly would have died. She took a quick step away from the ledge, shivering.

Didan nodded toward the fire. "Come, warm yourself."

She followed him to the fire and sat as close as the heat would allow, drawing her knees beneath her chin. Didan stoked the coals, adding fodder to raise the flames higher. He settled across the fire from her, an arm draped casually over his bent knee, a stick toiling in the coals. He watched her, the glow of the flames illuminating his milky white eye and the shine of the keloid scars that pulled the corner.

"I will try another question," he said carefully. "What were you running from?"

Olun bit her lip. It wasn't a big secret, her night terrors. Not that she *could* hide it. She'd already disturbed the men who'd come with Genta to collect her from the desert. She'd unnerved Tula and struck Genta in the throes of one, too. In a way, Olun was glad for the separation her home allowed, for sleeping alone meant that she would no longer burden others with her fits.

"You already know of my nightmares," she mumbled, hiding her face in her knees. "I toss and turn. I scream and fight. Sometimes they make me cry—but they've never made me walk." *or run.*

Olun wasn't all that sure it was a nightmare. But then, how else could she explain the Shadow Man?

"What are they about?" Didan asked.

Olun shrugged. Voice muffled, she said, "I never remember."

Though that wasn't necessarily true anymore. She remembered feeling the flaps of skin on the back of her head slick with blood. She remembered the voice and what he'd said to *her* as if he were right there with her. If it were a dream, these things would have been long gone the moment Didan commanded her to open her eyes.

Olun sniffed and wiped her nose and eyes with her sleeve, composing herself as best she could.

"I should thank you, ya?" she said, staring into the fire rather than at him. He still watched. Olun could feel his eyes boring into her like a hot poker into wax.

"Thank me?" his voice rose with surprise.

"For—for the shoes," she stammered. "And for just now."

Didan was silent for a moment. "The shoes could have come from anyone," he muttered.

"But they came from *you*, ya?" she insisted, glancing up at him. She was sure they'd come from him. Any other person would have given them to her directly. And, they fit perfectly. He must have taken her measurement with the cloth strips when he'd tied her torn sandal to her foot. The realization made her stare across the flames to meet his eye in shock. Could this man really be as mad as the rumors said?

"At first, I thought you were threatening me at the ceremony . . . but you were trying t'warn me, ya? Same with the cave, too."

Olun thought the flashes of pain when he touched were violent memories of what he'd done. Then he'd grabbed her wrist to save her, and Olun had felt none of those things. Woven within the urgency and desperation of the situation was comfort. She felt jolts and flashes of panic, a cold wash of relief, and the breathlessness of joy deep in her lungs like a gasp of good news. When he'd held her after he'd pulled her to safety, that was exactly what she'd felt: *safe*. And not because she was no longer in danger of falling to her death, but because his arms were around her. She knew this embrace because she'd felt it long before.

"I feel things," she admitted. "My aunt used to say that I was too sensitive and Elder Kikyel that I was a 'feeling creature,' but I never understood what they meant. Sometimes I don't always know *what* I feel—or what they mean, or where they come from. I get so confused."

"What have these feelings told you about me?"

"A lot," she hesitated. "I don't understand it—but it feels like I should *trust* you. But you frighten me."

Didan smirked and looked away. "I frighten you."

"There's a lot that I don't remember . . ."

"And you still think I had something to do with that."

"No—" Olun was startled by how quickly she'd come to that conclusion. Whatever guilt he carried from the past, it was not because he'd harmed her. She knew that from their last encounter. He was *good*, but there was something lingering around the *both* of them that was bad.

"I mean, not *anymore*," she said. "But—I don't know. When I'm around you, sometimes I feel safe, and your presence is a comfort that I find myself missing when it's gone. But then, I feel pain and fear, and a suffocating sense that I shouldn't be here." Olun shook her head. "I don't know which feeling to trust, and no one I've asked about you or my time here can give me anything to help me remember."

The wind whistled through the rocks and reeds, making the fire jump. Olun shivered in its cold and rested her cheek against her knees, hunching her shoulders against the cold. Didan shuffled around the fire, removing his cloak to drape around her shoulders.

"You have been asking about me?" He seemed surprised by this.

"You're not around to ask, ya?" she muttered, blushing as she shrank back into the warmth of his cloak. *It's so easy to talk to him,* she thought with surprise of her own. Even through the nerves and apprehension, her thoughts seemed to just come out with him.

Didan thought for a moment, sitting down beside her. "There is not anything else I can say that you were not already told," he said. "We knew each other as children. Your Monta is my father's sister, so we were often in close proximity. I watched over you while she did her visiting."

"Syndra went missing, too."

Didan grunted. "I know even less about that," he thought for a moment, then shook his head. "I did not even know she was gone until she came back. She would not tell even me where she had been."

Silence fell between them. Olun bit her lip. Genta had made it clear that he'd not been her friend back then. Had Didan thought of her as a nuisance, too?

"Were we friends?"

"Yes."

Olun hid her smile in the fur of his cloak. She wasn't sure why this pleased her, but it did. But—

"Then why'd you treat me like a stranger when we first met—and then sneak around outside my door?"

"I seem to recall I asked you to go walking with me," Didan said dryly, and she shut her mouth with a pop.

The silence that stretched between them was not uncomfortable. Didan was nothing like she'd imagined him to be. She was expecting the angry man from the ceremony, the man muttering and swearing to himself as he paced in circles in front of her house. The dangerous brute that had busted Manuk's jaw—whether he deserved it or not. She'd been expecting to see this failure of an Elder, a man deserving of the punishments the Dark Lady had imposed. Perhaps he *was* all of these things and more for all she knew about him. But right now, she wasn't afraid. The idea of ever having been afraid of him was even silly.

"They came to see me, just like you said," Olun sighed.

"Which one?" Didan grimaced. "Hujak?"

"Helima and Zayeer."

Didan grunted in mild surprise.

"They tried t'convince me t'go. They asked me t'do something for them and . . . well, I tried. I wanted t'help them, but the goddesses don't listen t'me—I *told* them that."

"Olun." The light air that had settled between them shifted as Didan looked at her. "What did you do?"

Whether it was his sudden seriousness that made her anxious or the need to tell someone about her encounter and little experiment, Olun didn't know, but it came out in a rush.

"I thought, maybe I was wrong about everything, and Helima said maybe the goddess never spoke t'me because maybe I wasn't speaking to the *right* one. So, I directed my words to the Dark Lady and really tried t'make Her see that my questions were selfless this time—and *he* answered. The Shadow Man—I think he's from my nightmares. I heard him that day in the mines, too?"

Didan did not reply, and gradually, Olun found herself scooting closer to him, the chill of night cooling her damp cheeks and chattering her teeth.

"Despite what everyone may think," Didan said carefully. "Becoming an Elder is a curse we are taught to bear for the greater good of the village. We are kept at arm's length until they want our knowledge, but they know how much this burden can *ruin* us. They lock us away and pretend it does us good. They know nothing, and they do not care to know more."

"I don't want this," Olun said, voice trembling.

"I told you not to drink. I told you to ignore them," Didan was angry. "Not *speak* to them! If the life of an Elder is lonely, then *they* are a hundred times lonelier. They are bitter creatures full of longing for lives once lived—no good can ever come from conversing with them."

"They *who*?" Helima and Zayeer were insistent and aggrieved by their pending death, but they hadn't been bitter.

"The spirits!" he shouted.

Olun scrambled away from him, from the anger that made him tense.

Didan climbed to his feet and turned away. He took a breath and pinched the bridge of his nose to calm himself.

"I am . . . frustrated with Elder Vasc," he said quietly. "And my father and the village *and* what has happened to us both. I am sorry, Olun, I should not have yelled."

He moved away from the fire to sit looking out over the village. Nervously, Olun followed, sitting just out of reach if he should act out again.

"It feels like I'm being pulled in many different ways," she sighed. "I just want . . . all I want is t'save my family. Nothing more, nothing less."

"Is that really *all* you want?" Didan asked, glancing at her from the corner of his eye. "Or have you never truly had wants of your own?"

Olun frowned. What did he mean by that? Of course, she had wants of her own—didn't everyone *want* to protect their loved ones from certain doom?

"You know that sacrificing yourself will not save your people, Olun," Didan said quietly. "Just as you know that becoming a healer does not mean you can *save* them, either."

"You don't know that," she snapped.

"No, but I know you try to please people by becoming what they want you to become. You can only become who you *are*, Olun, not what they tell you."

"And who are *you*?" She demanded. "A madman who runs away? Who breaks jaws and hides away little girls? A cripple? A failed Elder?"

Didan smirked. "Yes," he said. "I am all of those things because I have spent my life not knowing who I am outside of it all."

She'd wanted to hurt him the way she was hurting, but all at once she felt guilt. It toiled in her gut while the cold fist of sorrow took hold of her heart. Did she feel horrible because of her scathing words, or was it the fact that Didan did not defend himself against them? Didan said nothing for a time.

"Belief is like a dagger; While one holds the handle in protection, the tip always aims toward another," he murmured.

"Belief brings people hope," Olun argued. "What are we without hope? How can we go on?"

"And what is the cost of such hopes and beliefs?" Didan didn't have to say it, but she knew he was referring to the circumstances surrounding her arrival in the village. The sudden urge to defend her people and their actions rose in her breast. What is one life compared to dozens if it could bring them hope for a future they believed they'd never see? Didan saw her retort on her face and held up a hand of surrender.

"Be my mother's apprentice and continue to be Tula's companion," he said, calmer than before. "You have what I did not: Aspirations. Giving up my life to be this conduit was all I had. My only worth. You are not like that."

"You had Genta and your parents, ya?" she said, accepting his surrender.

Didan shook his head. "They knew what I was," was all he said about that. "Perhaps these things you hold dear will prolong this curse a little while."

Olun rested her cheek against her knee and watched him. His features were very different from Genta's. There was a sadness to him; something so hopeless. She wondered who Didan was apart from his scars and who he could have been had he been allowed to live his life.

"Sleep," he said finally. "I will watch over you."

"What about you?" she begrudged a yawn. She glanced back at the narrow pallet and blushed at the thought of sharing it with him. She'd slept beside her family all her life and had shared her room with Tula. But she'd never slept beside a stranger before, let alone a man.

"I do not sleep much anymore," Didan said and leaned back on his elbows to look up at the moon.

"Because of the echrol or . . .?" *the shadows.*

"I do not fear the echrol," Didan said. "There are worse things to fear than creatures that hunt to survive."

"Like loneliness," she whispered.

"Sleep, Olun," Didan soothed. "I will be here when you wake."

CHAPTER 17

*W*HY HER? OLUN THOUGHT with dismay as she stood face to face with Syndra.

Naleda clapped her hands with an exaggerated burst of glee and pushed the two of them closer together.

"Syndra has been under my tutelage since she was a girl," she explained to Olun. "A prodigy—and I would expect nothing less! Her mother was my sister-student, both of us training under her grandmother—you have met Yadir. To be a village healer is in this girl's blood!"

It was quick, but Olun could have sworn she saw a flicker in Syndra's scowl at the mention of her ma.

Naleda wrapped her arms around Olun and Syndra's necks, pulling them both in even closer. "Syndra, it is only fitting that you should take Olun as a shadow. Learning how to teach is just as important as medicine, and Olun—if learning is what you wish to do with your time, then you will learn from Syndra. This young woman will surpass me one day."

Olun looked past Naleda's smiling face to Syndra's scowling one. Her dark eyes bore into Olun's like barbs. They'd always met in passing. In fact, that day at the mines was the first time she'd garnered even a word from Syndra.

Olun extended her hand in a show of good faith, a timid yet encouraging smile as she waited for the other woman to take it. Truth be told, she had no problems with the woman, but for reasons she could not fathom, Syndra had a problem with *her*.

Syndra sucked her teeth, annoyed, and ducked out of Naleda's arm. "Well, I cannot say 'no,' can I?" she said.

"No, you can*not*," Naleda said with an edge, halting all would-be arguments.

Olun trotted after Syndra, eager to start her learning but hesitant to start it with someone so against the idea of her. She didn't know what she'd done to offend the woman. It seemed as if everything she did touched Syndra's nerve. But still, this was her chance.

"Syndra?" Olun quickened her steps to match her brisk ones. "Y—you and I have something in common."

Syndra stopped and looked at her blankly.

"I've been meaning t'ask . . . do you remember what happened back then? I mean, when you went missing?"

"You and I are *nothing* alike," Syndra snarled, and that was the end of it.

***

Syndra was a deep well of knowledge, listening to ailments and answering concerns in passing. Trips to the mines to check for injuries and dust illnesses, making house calls, looking in on recovering villagers, and the elderly.

"I have an itch on my leg that's spreading; what should I do?"

"My sister has not joined with her Bonded in quite some time, and she is wondering if there is something she could take?"

"My son has a toothache, and nothing I've tried has worked!"

They were all ignorant of the way Syndra curled her lip before she turned to them with a bright smile, or how she rolled her eyes at their backs. There was a condescending undertone in the way she answered their concerns that none but Olun could hear. Nonetheless, Olun listened, telling herself that she was imagining such things. She didn't know Syndra well, if at all. And her question earlier had only made it worse.

A week came and went with Syndra frequently dodging her presence, pushing past her or tripping her when she couldn't. She treated Olun like a general nuisance and dismissed her to villagers— "Oh, she will not be here long enough to learn anything," and the more painful, "Her own Elder wanted her dead, why should I want her?"

"I don't know what I did t'that woman. It's maddening!" Olun vented to Tula and Genta one evening, all but willing to tear out her short hair rather than let her frustrated tears fall. They did anyway. Her hosts were used to it by now. Even still, Olun dashed them away, more upset than before. She hated crying. She never used to cry so much, but in this village, it seemed she couldn't stop!

"Syndra does not trust easily," Tula explained. "Didan, Genta, and Bana are closer to her than anyone in the village, aside from Zafre and Naleda."

"We grew up together," Genta nodded.

"Your ma's were students together, ya?" Olun remembered.

"Yes," Genta said. "But I was never Syndra's favorite brother."

"Has she gone to see him, then?" Tula asked curiously, refilling his cup of wine.

"If she could find him, she would not be so bitter," Genta grimaced. "Besides, Didan does not want to be found."

"I thought she was doing well with Manuk," Tula interjected. "It's surprising anyone could tolerate him."

Manuk. Olun had seen quite a bit of him since becoming Syndra's shadow. He doted on Syndra every chance he could, though what seemed to please Syndra most was his heckling of Olun. Anywhere from her appearance to her modest temperament was a target for his bullying. Syndra seemed to be extra affectionate toward him if he managed to bring Olun close to tears.

"Who knows with that woman?" Genta said, and to Olun, added, "Do not lose focus. She is a hard woman to understand, so do not take it personally."

Olun sipped from her cup. It was hard not to take Syndra's actions personally.

Early the next morning, Olun arrived well before Syndra and got to work making the kit they'd take on her rounds. The ointments Naleda had mixed the day before, oils, bandage rolls, and extra cloth. Around the corner, she could already hear the sounds of Naleda and her family waking. She glanced up, catching the sight of a drowsy Bana shuffling about. He lit the courtyard fire for his parents and lifted the yoke on to his broad shoulders.

"Bright Goddess smiles on you this morning, Olun," he yawned as he shuffled past her on his way to the stream for water.

"You too!" she said quickly, darting back and forth from Naleda's store room.

She'd just finished packing Syndra's kit the way she'd observed her do many times when the young woman passed through the gate.

"I—I prepared this for you," Olun said breathlessly, then fumbled around in her own pouch. "I also brought breakfast—"

Wordlessly, Syndra took the kit, her eyes never leaving Olun's as she upended it. Jars cracked, corks rolled, oils soiled cloth and bandages.

"Clean this up," Syndra folded the now-empty bag across her arm while Olun gaped down at the mess.

CHAPTER 18

D IDAN WASN'T ON THE ledge. The low flames in the fire pit and the cloak on his pallet welcomed her regardless. Like every visit, Olun wrapped herself in Didan's cloak to ward off the evening chill and watched the sun's slow dip beyond the peaks. It'd been all she could do not to blurt out to Tula and Genta that Didan still lived near the village and that she knew where because of her frequent evening rendezvous with him.

The truth of the matter was that her nightmares hadn't kept her up since that first night on the ledge with him. It'd been the first time since she could remember waking up rested. She closed her eyes and let the cool breeze finger through her hair. It had also been her first time waking up utterly embarrassed, having fallen asleep with her head pillowed by his thigh. Thankfully, he'd said nothing of it, returning her to her home at dawn without a word.

It was a curious thing, Didan's ability to chase the Shadow Man from her dreams. Or perhaps it was simply knowing he was there to watch over her that put her at ease enough to finally rest.

"Your face is swollen," Olun opened her eyes to find Didan standing in the fading sunlight, the long limp bodies of freshly dressed gacuses slung over his shoulder.

"Does it look bad?" she touched her face, self-conscious of the welts and swelling that puffed her lips and squinted her eyes. She'd almost forgotten.

"No, but it is . . . concerning," he frowned, coming closer to examine the extent of the damage. He took her chin between his fingers and lifted it gently to get a better look at the welts. He smelled of soap, and his shoulders were damp where his hair rested. He must have bathed after emptying the traps.

"I much prefer whatever caused your tears to what caused *this,*" he murmured. "Explain."

Olun sighed, warmth creeping into her still itchy cheeks and the tips of her ears. "Naleda and Jorre say I can't *use* medicinal plants if I don't know what they do."

It shouldn't have come as a surprise to Olun that Syndra's sister, Jorre, was just as talented. The girl, no older than thirteen, studied plants and herbs. She knew where they grew, how to harvest them, and how to dry them. She'd even started growing her own fungi. Perhaps the biggest difference between the sisters was their personalities. Where Syndra was hard and temperamental, Jorre was all giggles and excitable. Where Syndra was arrogant in her knowledge, Jorre was eager to learn and apply. Olun's knee had bounced restlessly while Jorre helped Naleda prepare her lesson on medicines—after Syndra had slipped her *again. "The best way to learn is by taste,"* Jorre had said with a wickedly gleeful grin.

Didan was gentle as he traced along the welts of her jawline and cupped her puffy cheek. Olun caught herself leaning into his caress, the intimacy of the action as surprising as it was *wanted*. She stepped back abruptly, breaking contact, and turned her attention to the skinned little bodies still strung over his shoulder.

"You—you caught dinner?" She took them to the fire to prepare for roasting, thankful for the task that helped calm her racing heart.

Wordlessly, Didan put away his snares and hung the pelts for drying. They moved about each other in their own individual tasks, sharing the space as effortlessly as if they'd always done so. Olun had gotten too comfortable in his presence—and he hers. Didan was pleasant company, listening to her daily adventures as a student healer, sometimes telling her bits about his own day and past travels.

Evenings where she'd come too exhausted and overwhelmed by Syndra and Manuk's bullying, he'd let her cry by the fire, sitting so close to her that their arms touched. Other times, they sat in comfortable silence, watching the sun set and the stars twinkle into existence.

Didan was the one person in the whole village who understood her struggles, more so than even Tula. He provided *answers* that no one else seemed to want to give—or even know *how* to give. He was familiar enough with the spirits to give her advice despite never truly expounding on the nature of his own interactions with them. She tried not to pry. Like her, there were some things that Didan was just not comfortable talking about.

"I could only get through eight of them," Olun recounted her lesson. "I can't imagine returning tomorrow to do eight more! Powders and oils—just little dabs on the tongue or lips. The leaves, Naleda rubbed here—" Olun slipped her arm from beneath the cloak to show Didan the redness on the inside of her forearm.

"It doesn't itch anymore, but you shoould've seen how panicked I was when my tongue went numb with the powder. Jorre had me rinse my mouth. But when the welts came, and my eyes puffed shut, Naleda reversed the symptoms before it got too hard to breathe!"

"I never liked those methods," Didan grumbled, flipping the meat and adding vegetables to a now boiling pot of water. "Drink lots of water and keep spitting, at least."

"It's not so bad, ya? She's right. Yuhi—my, um, friend in the Retryu—says the oombrak learn by taste just as well as sight. Besides, Naleda tells me that for everything toxic, there is always something t'neutralize it. It's amazing, ya?"

Didan nodded, amused by her enthusiasm. "I am glad you are liking your lessons, Olun."

She gingerly tore a morsel from the gacus rib cooling in front of her and popped it in her mouth while Didan rotated another.

"Yeah, well. It was a little embarrassing walking back home after with my face like this. It's hideous."

"It is *not*," he said with surprising conviction.

That wasn't what Manuk had said when he followed her through the village, barking with laughter. She wanted to tell Didan suddenly of all the nasty things Manuk had said—that her forehead was too large, her eyes too big, her limbs too scrawny, though she'd put on a healthier amount of weight since her arrival. Olun didn't have to be a swollen lump to know her looks were not preferred. After all, she'd deemed the Ithoumi less attractive compared to the desert nomads when she'd first seen them. Manuk had taken it to a whole other level entirely— "Making you Elder is a mercy; you are not worth looking at and definitely not worth wetting even the tip of a spear."

His crassness had embarrassed her but . . . it'd also made her look at herself differently. Maybe Yuhi never looked her way because he thought as Manuk did.

She told Didan none of this, of course.

The meat sizzled as Didan removed it from roasting to cool on a slab of stone, and he checked the simmering pot of sweetmeats, sweat glossing his scars. She'd spoken so inconsiderately about her looks. Welts and swelling were only temporary. Her embarrassment and upset over her unshapely features were nothing compared to what Didan had to live with.

"When Genta and I were children," he said conversationally, "we challenged ourselves to see how much of our mother's plants we could handle. She, of course, was unaware."

"I hope Naleda scolded you when she found out," Olun gasped. "Such a dangerous thing t'do, ya?"

Jorre had only placed just a little bit of the medicines on her lips and tongue. *Feel the sensations. Does it tingle? Is it cool or does it burn? What does it smell like?* She couldn't imagine willingly tormenting herself with those plants just for *fun*.

Didan flashed her a lopsided grin, and Olun thanked the goddesses for the camouflage of her irritated skin. His smile had her blushing like a silly girl!

"Genta and I were not very wise back then," Didan said. "Especially him. We were always fighting about one thing or another. Who was stronger, who was more tolerant, who was more . . . favorable. Anyway, Genta was the first to lose consciousness. My face only got swollen. It will not last. Here—"

He uncorked his waterskin and passed it to her, fingers skimming across hers.

"Why does father trust you so much? Weakling! You cannot even protect a little girl."

The tall, lanky boy who resembled Bana in many ways reached past the other boy to push the girl to the ground. She screamed and covered her head while he kicked dirt in her face.

"Leave her alone, Genta!"

Olun sipped the water, wincing at the twinge in her temple. *Was that a memory—of Genta?* She might have called him a bully once, but now that she'd gotten to know him, it wasn't the case. Genta was strict, and his way of caring was harsh at times. But cruel?

"Genta doesn't seem like the type t'do something like that," Olun murmured more to herself than to Didan.

"We have become different people, but some things still remain the same." There was an edge to his voice that gave Olun pause.

"I wish you'd tell me more about back then."

"There is nothing more to tell," he said shortly.

"There is always *more,*" she leaned toward him in earnest. "What was *Genta* like? Did he spend time with us, too? Was he—"

"Ask him yourself," Didan snapped, his easy smile replaced with a scowl. "If your memories have not returned, it is for the best."

Olun pouted and crossed her arms with a huff. She was beginning to get used to his mood swings, as irritating as they were.

"Stop sulking," he grumbled, but it only made her glare at him. "Let it go, Olun, you are being ridiculous."

"Ridiculous?" Her nostrils flared in anger.

If he thought her sulking was ridiculous, then his reaction was *just as* ridiculous! Her questions were simple. He wouldn't be acting like this if he were the one searching for lost memories, talking about '*it's for the best.*'

"I'm done talking t'you, I'm goin' home." The sun hadn't set completely; there would be just enough light to make it back before the echrols woke up to hunt.

Didan sighed incredulously and muttered something under his breath. When she stood, he pulled her back down and did something so unexpected that Olun had no time to react. He touched a thumb to her puffy, pouting lips, slowly tracing the path of the welts to the corner of her mouth. Olun held her breath, frozen as his caressing hand came to rest at the nape of her neck. Her lips parted in surprise, but no sound came. It wasn't until Didan drew closer, his face mere inches from hers, that she realized what he meant to do.

She covered her mouth abruptly. "Don't," she whispered, the word coming out just as suddenly as it formed.

Didan stopped, his bicolored eyes searching for hers, but Olun couldn't meet them. Her life was too messy—there was no telling what her future held, who or what she must become. Whether she was free to return to the desert or flee on her own, if she became an Ithoumi Elder by force or of her own volition. Didan was not part of any of it. Whatever they were to each other, they were not—*could not be*—this.

"Stay," he said, pulling back. "If only for a cool compress to soothe your skin."

Olun nodded mutely and, without a word, Didan rose to grab a cloth and some water for her face.

After dinner, they watched the last light of the sun fade over the village in silence. Olun shifted the damp cloth from her eye to her cheek and sighed. The swelling had diminished, and she was thankful that her skin no longer itched.

"My mother can be quite intense when it comes to her crafts and duties," Didan said, scratching his patchy beard absently as he sought a more neutral topic of conversation.

"I am surprised she has not told you already of the extent of her dedication: laboring for three days straight to bring Genta into this world, all while fulfilling her duties as Doyenne. Or how she had given birth to me while sheltering in a cave during a storm on her way back from trading her medicines with the Retryu."

"She might have mentioned it here and there," she mumbled, still thinking about what had almost occurred. She couldn't tell if she was shocked by the idea of the kiss, or if her shock was for *wanting* it to happen. She'd never even thought about kissing him until then. *It's not like I even feel the same way,* she thought with just as much confusion as she felt.

"She is a sensationalist with high standards." Didan shook his head with distaste. "She expects too much of her students. Be careful not to overdo it."

"I won't," she said, then glanced at him nervously. She pushed aside her errant thoughts before they could run amok and decided to broach a topic lingering heavily at the back of her mind.

"I've never been good at anything or been anyone's preference. The only thing I was ever used for was as a sacrifice, and you see what became of that. But you and Genta are right: I must find something to look toward and not lose focus of what's important."

"He gives good advice," Didan begrudged with mild irritation. "Surprisingly."

Olun glared at him but continued. "My Elder once asked me what the cost of life is. I know it hasn't been long since I became a student, but I think *this* is what I'm meant to do. My purpose. What if the cost of Life is not Death? What if it's tending to the *living?*

"If I can heal the body and treat the flesh, I can *save* people. I'll heal scars and end plagues like Naleda and Syndra, and I'll be wanted for what I *can* do, not for what I can't—or something with no guarantee. I'll help them *live!* Maybe not now, but I will. I'll make a difference to my clan someday. Maybe . . ." *Maybe I could lead them here and they'd never have to worry about drought or sickness ever again.*

"You cannot save everyone, Olun," Didan's voice went flat. "There are some scars that cannot be healed. Minds that cannot be mended, and bodies that cannot be restored. My mother knows this, and you should, too."

"She *healed* you," Olun blurted. Syndra had been right to say months ago that Naleda was near god-like. Looking at Didan now—he shouldn't be alive. A cave-in or whatever had happened to him had left him in pieces. Naleda *put him back together!* An Elder couldn't do that.

Didan poked at the fire, wiping his face of emotion. It went beyond simply self-preservation. He appeared as though he'd turned to stone. Olun reached for his hand, but Didan moved away almost knowingly.

"*Healing* and *saving* are two different things, just as *Life* and *living* are," he said in the level tone of a teacher to a student. "Having the means to heal is not the same as the act of healing. Just because the body has been healed, does not mean it has been *saved*. Suppose the only way to save someone is death? What, then, will you do?"

"I—I don't understand." Olun desperately searched his face, but he'd closed himself to her.

Hadn't she wanted that very thing? To save the people she loved with her own death? She'd wanted to end their suffering—end Oja's despair—but when Didan looked down at her, she saw that he hadn't meant *sacrifice*.

There were Truths that she understood: Old age was inevitable, and all men and women died. Yet, it wasn't until her arrival in the mountains that other truths were shown to be false. Scars were not the Dark Lady's spiteful doings; sickness and plagues *could* be cured, and here, in the exile prison of Death, Life *thrived!* And yet, even in a life full of abundance, there was still pain.

Olun reached for his hand again, and this time he did not pull away.

"I don't know what I'll do if . . ." she swallowed hard. "Didan, I *know* I won't sit by and watch another person I care about suffer. People'll do anything for the ones they love."

Didan closed his eyes, the tension in his body relaxing.

I'm here for you, Didan, she thought as she squeezed his hand. And, Didan squeezed back.

Chapter 19

T HE CHILD WAS INCONSOLABLE in his mother's lap as she bounced and rocked him. "He's been like this since yesterday," she told Syndra above the crying.

Olun rubbed the boy's leg, cooing to him in an attempt to soothe him into calm. And to see if her sensitivity to touch could be used in diagnosing his ailment. She'd been experimenting more and more with it lately. The boy was feverish, but anyone could have felt that. She tried again to feel what this child felt, but he was so restless, confused, angry, in pain—all things she didn't have to be sensitive to know.

"Has he taken water?" Syndra asked. "Used the bathroom? Eaten anything he should not have?"

"No," his mother said. "He will not eat or drink! Tell me—what is wrong with him!"

They brought him inside so that Syndra could examine his swollen abdomen.

"You packed my bag but did not think to carry it in here?" Syndra huffed and pointed Olun to the door. "Go get it, and then give me the pouch with the blue bead."

Olun quickly did as she was told, darting to the door where Syndra had left her kit. She rummaged through it and discovered the pouch she described buried deep inside. Olun frowned. She'd watched Syndra day after day—when she could—pack her kit. She'd taken mental notes of everything she put in it, and the items never changed. *Pouch with a blue bead?* When had Syndra packed it? But just as she'd said, the pouch with the blue bead threaded into its tie was right there.

"We are waiting, Desert Girl," Syndra called, and Olun brought the pouch to her.

She sat by the child's head, dabbing at his feverish face. His face was flushed, and he was out of breath. The poor boy.

"What is this?" Syndra asked abruptly, holding up a brown bulb from the pouch.

"Yellowroot," Olun answered, lips pursed as she searched her memories for its properties.

"How old is this child, Olun?"

She glanced at the woman and child again, the former of whom seemed just as confused by Syndra's questioning as Olun. "Four?"

"And lastly, what is it you think is wrong with this four-year-old child?"

"I . . ."

Syndra threw the bulb at Olun. "Are you trying to *kill* him?"

The woman gasped and yanked her son into her arms and away from Olun.

"No! Pouch with the blue bead, ya?" She said, desperate to recall the lesson. "*Yellowroot—not for people, but sometimes accidents happen, and it is ingested . . .*" Jorre had said. It was used to induce vomiting in *ootingla*. In a man, enough could cause sores on the throat and the belly to bleed. In children—Olun gasped.

Why would Syndra keep this?

Syndra grabbed her pack and produced a different pouch with *two* blue beads threaded through the ties, not one.

"You foolish girl!" Syndra scolded as she prepared a blend Olun recognized by scent as *ensa* root and redblossom milk.

"Instead of saving my people from constipation and stomach pain, I will be saving them from the poisons *you* sneak into my bag."

"Get out!" the woman cried. "Get out of my home—*Get out!*"

Syndra shouldered Olun out of the way.

Olun couldn't speak—couldn't *breathe!* It wasn't her fault. She tried to force out the words. To argue against this accusation, but the boy was more important than any point she wanted to make.

Wordlessly, she left Syndra to tend the woman and her constipated child.

The woman Olun had offended was Kaida, one of the village's loudest gossips, and word of her son's would-be poisoning spread through the village like the plague. If Naleda wouldn't pull Olun from shadowing her, Syndra would certainly make it so Olun wasn't *wanted.*

***

Olun rested her head against Tula's shoulder after dinner, the two of them watching Bana try to best Genta in a game of physical strength. After the day she'd had, watching the two of them was not as entertaining as the other times.

"I'm glad you could join us again," Tula said, resting her cheek against Olun's curly hair. "We've missed you around here."

Olun nodded. She'd missed Tula, too. Her days were so busy, and when she took her midday break to visit with her, she was too exhausted to do anything more than lie around. Then there was Didan. Olun tried not to think about him at his camp on the ledge, waiting for her to arrive. She'd have to tell him about her blunder that afternoon—or her speculations about Syndra, both of which she was too embarrassed to speak of. She'd made such a big deal about becoming a great healer, and she'd almost killed a child.

"You mustn't let such mistakes weigh you down," Tula said softly.

Olun groaned. "You heard?"

"*Everyone* heard," she sighed. "But you are still learning. Accidents and mistakes happen, that's why you are shadowing Syndra, ya?"

But it wasn't a mistake, Olun wanted to say. Syndra had purposefully told her to get the wrong supplement. Or—or she'd added those pouches to confuse her. And suddenly Olun felt silly. Excuses, excuses. It was crazy to think Syndra had intentionally endangered a child to embarrass her. *She* should have opened the pouch to check. *She* should have asked Syndra more questions. If it had been a test, Olun had failed it.

"Yeah," Olun said, blinking back her tears. "I'll do better next time." *If there even is a next time.*

"Indeed," Tula reclined against her cushion and rested a hand on the slight bump of her belly. Olun smiled despite her sour mood. News of Tula's condition had spread, and with it, questions about whether this time she and Genta would finally welcome a child. Olun knew their gossip made her friend anxious and downright angered Genta. *It's a good thing people are talking about me this time and not you.* Olun sighed. It felt good to see Tula so relaxed.

Bana landed on his back in the dirt. "You almost broke my arm!" he squealed, his adolescent voice cracking.

Genta beckoned him with a wave of his hand, and Bana scrambled to his feet, even more determined to best his brother. He charged with a cry, and the brothers locked arms again.

"Not so rough!" Tula called to them before remembering something. "Oh, Olun, when you see Syndra in the morning, will you give this back t'her?"

She twisted around and produced a little pouch with a blue bead.

***

The pouch was exactly like the other two. Small, its stitching large and simple. The blue beads were like the others, too. Decorative, yet somehow, very meaningful. Olun hadn't seen such beads around the village or the pouches among Naleda's supplies. *It could just be something of Syndra's own,* Olun thought. Jorre had her own bag stitched with motifs of flowers and plants, and colorful threads along the straps, after all.

"What is going on with Rhiya?" Bana asked.

Startled, Olun shoved the empty pouch back into her bag and faced him. "What?"

The boy nodded to the home she'd been leaning against.

"Oh! Syndra's inside."

"And why are you *not?*" he laughed, and Olun flushed with embarrassment.

Rhiya was yet another villager who had heard about the near poisoning of Kaida's son. The older woman would not let Olun set one foot beyond her threshold.

"I'm more helpful out here, apparently," she grumbled, eyeing the heavy sack he carried.

"Feed," he grinned. "I am one of the strongest *and* fastest, so I was tasked to deliver these sacks of feed, you see."

His chest puffed with pride.

"If you are so strong, you would not need my help," Manuk chastised, a similar sack slung over his shoulder.

"I did not ask *you*," Bana muttered, then smiled at Olun. "You, Tiny Desert Girl, need to toughen up and go in there. How else are you going to learn?"

Olun twisted her lips in irritation. *Good question.* Though having it come from a boy nearly five years her junior was a little infuriating.

"Thanks for the advice, now be on your way, ya?"

Bana laughed and adjusted his grip on the sack.

"Try not to kill anyone," Manuk winked.

She glared at him as he passed her on the narrow village street. Bana smiled encouragingly, giving her a thumbs up.

Syndra stepped out just then and looked between the three.

"Hey, Syn," Bana greeted her with a half-hug and a kiss on the cheek. She returned the greeting suspiciously.

"Got stuck helping the brat," Manuk shrugged. "Might as well make the shadow do it. Give us some time to ourselves for a bit, what do you think?"

Olun flinched when Manuk pretended to throw the sack at her. Syndra gave a bark of laughter, amused by the thought of Olun dragging a sack of feed down the street.

"Just you watch, Manuk," Bana chimed in. "One of these days, Olun will be carrying your sorry butt down the street! Show 'em your muscles, Tiny Desert Girl."

"What muscles?" she hissed, and Bana grabbed her arm and lifted it with a whistle.

"So strong. She can even carry the weight of your enormous ego!"

Olun laughed, surprised by the unexpected slight. She flexed what little muscle she had and said, "Genta always says, 'You put up with a lot, you gain a lot.'"

She actually felt better about herself. As the four of them walked down the sloping street, the steepness turning to a series of stone steps, Olun felt confident enough to talk to Syndra—at least while Bana was still there. He was still just a boy, but his laughter and jokes lifted her spirits. Of course, it had helped that he'd shut Manuk up.

"Syndra, I'd—"

A foot hooked around her ankle, pitching her forward. Olun stumbled, attempting to catch her balance, but her foot caught the edge of the stone step. She fell with a yelp of pain, tumbling down four more steps before coming to a stop.

"Olun!" Bana dropped the sack of feed and raced down the steps to where she lay. "Can you move?"

Bana looked back up the stairs. "Manuk!" he snarled. "How dare you! How *dare* you!"

Whimpering in pain and unable to move, Olun followed Bana's glare through the growing crowd of concerned onlookers, passed Manuk's wide-eyed look of shock to Syndra's unfazed gaze, her hard eyes cold and pitiless.

Chapter 20

DIDAN TAPPED AT OLUN'S door two days later, his lips pressing thin when she hobbled out.

"What are you doing here?" she gasped. Olun glanced past him, wary that someone might see despite the lack of close neighbors. Didan lifted her chin and took in the scab on it. He took notice of the way she held her arm close to her body, his scrutiny falling finally to her splinted ankle.

Olun shook her head free of his grasp and pulled him around back. *He* may not care who might see them together, but *she* did. Once out of view from the path, Didan planted his feet.

"Tell me *everything*."

And so she did. The mix-up with the pouches that nearly poisoned the child, Manuk's constant bullying and lewd comments, Syndra's evasions, and the villagers freezing her out, ending with her fall. Didan listened deep in thought, the two of them coming to sit against the finished wall. The sun was long gone by the time she'd finished.

"Manuk did this to you," Didan said darkly, and without her even saying. He seethed, his scarred face far more terrifying than before. Bana had been so sure Manuk was the one who caused her fall. And, though Manuk was guilty of many things, Olun felt it in her core that it hadn't been him.

"I—I think Syndra was the one who tripped me," she said, then dropped her head into her hands. "I don't know how I offended her! I try so hard—I don't want t'be a burden t'her but she hates me, and I don't know why!"

"I have known her to be temperamental and blunt, but never violent," Didan said carefully. "Syndra cares too much to do harm to others. Manuk is the likely culprit."

Olun deflated. *He doesn't believe me.*

"But I admit I have not kept up with those of my past," he said quickly, seeing her shift away from him. "It is surprising—"

"I'm *not* making it up!"

"I know," Didan said, reaching to thumb away her tears. "Whatever is going on with her, I am on *your* side, Olun. You are the one who has been hurt."

When she calmed, he sighed. "I would have come sooner, but I know how busy things have gotten for you. I only ran into Bana today."

"You were in the village t'day?"

"I needed supplies," he said shortly. He frowned at her splint, and moments later, he had her foot in his lap.

"What're you doing?" she gasped as he unwrapped it. She attempted to pull away, but he held her leg still. Didan sighed sullenly at the sight of it.

"It's not broken," Olun blurted out in an effort to convince him she was alright. It was better than it looked. But, despite the reduced swelling, the bruise circling her ankle and along the top of her foot was ugly even in the moonlight.

"Breaks are easier," he muttered and began kneading the tender flesh of her ankle, massaging along the tendon.

"Stop, you don't have t'do this. We're not—"

"Your ankle matters more to me at this moment than whatever you think our relationship is," Didan said sternly. "Sit still. *Please.*"

Olun sat back, and Didan continued his kneading. *So bossy,* she pouted, then, remembering the last time she'd done so, blushed. Didan stayed focused on her leg, working his way down her calf to her ankle, rubbing the arches of her foot, then her toes. His touches felt good. So, *so* good. Olun relaxed against the wall and closed her eyes.

"Have you soaked it?" He asked as he worked his way back up.

She nodded, eyes fluttering.

"Elevate," he continued. "Did my mother tell you that?"

She nodded again.

"I will fix you water for a cool soak when I am done. You are not to walk on it, understood?"

"Yeah," she moaned, and his hands stilled.

Olun snapped open her eyes and looked into his surprised face with horror. "I mean, '*okay,*" she said quickly.

She twisted away from him, cringing in embarrassment. It was hard not to notice his slight, satisfied smirk, but Didan resumed his massage as if nothing at all had happened.

Olun cleared her throat awkwardly and changed the subject. "You . . . you haven't seen her, have you? Syndra, I mean."

Didan shook his head. "Though it would seem that she and I should have a little chat."

"No!" Olun gasped, and he looked up curiously. "I mean, if you talk t'her about what I told you, you'll just make it worse. You don't live in the village—*I do.* I still have t'see her."

"Then maybe I should have a talk with *Manuk*, instead, about these vile things he has been saying to you," Didan seethed.

"Didan—" she pulled her foot from his lap. It was almost laughable to think someone like him would want to confront someone like Manuk. But Didan was serious.

"Just—*please*. Don't do or say anything. I'll talk t'her when I can. I have t'do some things on my own, ya?" She fidgeted with the hem of her dress anxiously, avoiding Didan's eye.

"Okay," he said finally, drawing her foot back into his lap. "Remember, I am on your side."

***

Syndra's bag was heavier today, though not because of its contents. Olun had been putting off talking to her all day, nervous about what to say and afraid of the consequences of speaking out of line. She'd resumed her shadowing as soon as her ankle could tolerate the exertion, but resumed it in silence. She'd made herself as unobtrusive as possible, sitting outside while Syndra amputated two of a man's fingers, black with infection. Olun had asked no questions afterward as she took away the soiled rags, disposed of the digits, and repacked Syndra's bag.

I'm a coward, Olun thought glumly, following the dirt path past tall crops of grain. Perhaps she should have let Didan confront her instead. He was less likely to wilt under Syndra's anger, and contrary to her first impressions, Didan could handle himself surprisingly well. Olun was never one to be the loudest nor the most difficult. She'd gone about her life holding her tongue and waiting to be acknowledged. She was a good girl, meek and dutiful, and yet . . . "*There's no fight in you,*" Monta had lamented often.

There'd been nothing Olun had *wanted* to fight for . . . until now.

Syndra stood in the way of her becoming a healer. Not only that—she stood in the way of saving her clan.

"It's not me I need t'stand up for," Olun told herself. "It's the Rohta."

Even still, her climb up the winding path to the mines where she knew Syndra impatiently waited for her was slow. She was thankful for the throb in her ankle, stopping to rest it and gather her thoughts. Olun had gone over what to say to Syndra since her chat with Didan, playing out various scenarios as her ankle healed.

"We fear what we do not understand . . ."

Olun scrambled to her feet, dread chilling her sweat.

". . . and we hate what we fear."

She hadn't heard the Shadow Man in weeks. She'd assumed it had been because of Didan. Or, at least what he'd said about focusing on her studies. Olun closed her eyes and took deep, steadying breaths to block him out. *Ignore him,* Didan had said. *Do not talk to him.* She picked up Syndra's bag. Biting back her discomfort, Olun started up the path when something cold and familiar washed over her. Like the first time in the mines, it pulled on the corners of her mind—inching memories closer to the forefront. He stroked her damp hair, setting the night alight with stars.

"I am patient," the disembodied voice said softly. *"I will wait for you."*

"Leave me *alone*!" Olun gasped, pushing the Shadow Man and the vision away.

She walked faster and faster, gritting back the pain in her ankle, when she saw Syndra and Manuk lost in heated discussion.

"I have stood by his side this long, and whether he is Elder or not, I will continue to be by his side!" Syndra jabbed her finger into Manuk's chest.

"Oh please, no one stands anywhere close to that man's side. Have you forgotten he *left* you along with everyone else? If he wanted you by his side, he would have taken you with him long ago—stop holding on to a fantasy."

"He will come when he needs me," Syndra growled, smacking away his hand when he grabbed her arm. "And he *will* need me."

"Syndra—"

"Your jealousy is childish, Manuk. Grow up."

"*My* jealousy?" Manuk said incredulously. He laughed. "*I* was not the one who terrorized the desert girl because he showed her more attention in two months than he has shown you in two years. *I* was not the one who tripped her that day because Bana was friendly with her. *Grow up?*"

He spun her around to face him. "Didan is not even *whole* anymore—he is a cripple who has lost his mind *and* the favor of the Goddesses. He has nothing to offer you, not even a home! You are too good for him, Syndra, you always have been. And *I* have always been by *your* side—I got my jaw broken defending you, and *still* you do not see me!"

"I have seen plenty of you," she snapped. "I let you into my bed, do I not? I let you have me whenever you want—you should be grateful! But instead, you whine and complain and want *more* from me."

Manuk clenched his fists and jaw, too shocked and enraged to respond.

"We had an arrangement, Manuk. If you keep changing the terms, then maybe you should find another woman willing to blow your tiny pipe."

Manuk's face darkened in anger, and he grabbed Syndra violently by her braid.

"Stop!" Olun shouted, rushing forward. Manuk released Syndra abruptly and backed away.

"Get a good earful, '*ya*?'" He mocked and threw his hands up as he stalked off toward the mines.

Syndra separated herself from Olun, stone-faced as usual. "He was going to hurt you," Olun explained. She didn't like Syndra, but she certainly didn't want to see her abused. "Are you alright?"

"And just what were you going to do?" Syndra spat. "Fight him?"

Olun flushed. "He shouldn't've put his hands on you," she mumbled.

"You should not speak on matters you do not understand."

What was there to understand? Syndra had been cruel, but that did not give him the right to hurt her. People shouldn't hurt others—especially lovers!

"Where is my bag?" Syndra demanded.

"Oh," Olun looked down at her hands, flustered and thoroughly uncomfortable by what she'd witnessed. "I'm sorry—I was distracted and—"

"I am neither Genta nor Bana, I do not care about your excuses or your tears," Syndra hissed. "Your uselessness and incompetence are insults—Now, *go get my bag!*"

"Yes—I'm sorry," Olun said quickly, then stopped. *No.* Syndra had humiliated, berated, and hurt her for long enough. She'd thought all this time that *maybe* it was something she'd done. Or Syndra was just being a tough teacher, forcing Olun to be more than she was. She'd even tried to defend her, and *that* did not dissolve her blatant loathing.

Olun turned to Syndra, fists clenched to keep them from shaking. "I'm not your pack animal, ya? Get your own bag."

Syndra was visibly taken aback for mere moments before her dark eyes burned with such rage that Olun took a step back. "What did you say to me, you dirty desert dweller?"

"I—I'm a healer, too, Syndra," Olun tried to be strong. She couldn't turn back now that she'd started. "Naleda has accepted me—she asked you to *teach* me, so—"

"All you desert dwellers know how to do is *take*," Syndra spat. "Our time, our resources, our knowledge, our men. Then you run away with little regard for who you hurt to get it."

"Running?" Olun couldn't deny that, in the beginning, she'd tried to run. She'd run from the village—and perhaps she was running from her responsibilities as Elder. But everything else? "Syndra, I don't know *what* you're talking about! If this is about Didan—"

Syndra threw her hands up. "Didan *and* Genta have gone through so much because of you, and you have no clue!"

"So this is because I have no memories?" Olun challenged. "Then *tell* me, Syndra! What did I do? Whatever was *so bad* that you blame me now for what I did as a *child*?"

They say he bashed your head in and hid your body. Olun glanced to where Manuk stood watching some distance away, arms crossed. Did Syndra blame her for the rumors that followed Didan?

"You are not a child, now," Syndra said bitterly. "And yet, you still latch onto Naleda, putting her in a challenging position with the other Doyens because of your wild fantasies of becoming a healer, and you worm your way into her family. Genta, Bana, Didan—you will *hurt* them. That is what desert dwellers do."

"You don't know a thing about me!" Olun shouted.

"No?" Syndra scoffed. "I know the only reason you came to Naleda is because you want to heal your clan. But even that is a lie. You take our compassion and faith only to run from our traditions and your own."

Olun's mouth went dry, and Syndra smirked.

"I knew it the moment you were brought here that you were not our Elder, but a plague upon all of us."

"My—my clan is dying," Olun had tried to salvage her courage as the discussion quickly disintegrated. "They sent me away so I could save them—what would you have me do, Syndra? I *can't* let them die!"

"Then you should die along with them," she said flatly.

Syndra's words hurt worse than any fall, the impact stealing her breath away and more than the stone steps.

"Now look at what you did," Manuk muttered, rejoining Syndra. "She is crying and *here*, of all places."

"*'You keep making her cry, Syndra.'*" Syndra mocked. "He is always coming to her defense, now you?"

Did she mean Didan? Olun froze. *He confronted her?*

"I am not defending her," Manuk hissed. "I am looking out for *you*, like always. People are coming."

Their commotion had drawn an audience. Dust-covered men and women watched with all the curiosity of beady-eyed gacus. Syndra stepped away from Olun, rolling her shoulders to compose herself. Olun wished she could do the same.

"What happened here?" Didan broke from the onlookers, glancing from Olun's tear-streaked face to Syndra and Manuk.

"Go climb back into whatever cave you came out of and mind your own business," Manuk said, stepping up to him.

Half a head taller than his rival, Didan peered down at Manuk through the curtain of his hair and clenched his fists.

"Going to hit me again?" Manuk taunted and tapped his jaw. "No more cheap shots this time!"

The grinding of Didan's teeth was audible. He moved Olun behind him with a sweep of his arm, and she thought with horror that the two of them would come to blows. She caught Didan's sleeve in fear, but it was Genta's interference that stopped all would-be fights from occurring.

"Disperse!" he growled, Zafre at his side.

"*I* was just making my rounds," Syndra argued. "I cannot help that your mother ladened me with this whelp—"

"Get over it," Genta snapped. "Your disruptions are becoming *our* disruption, and I will not have that here."

Zafre nodded his approval, chest puffing with pride in his eldest son.

"I will not have this kind of discourse in my village," Zafre added firmly. "Your squabbles end here. Are we clear?"

Zafre's words were final. The onlookers returned to their tasks with Zafre ushering them away. Around them, sounds of the mines started up again, hand-pushed carts moved rocks into piles, fire stone loaded onto wagons pulled by lazy ootingla. Hammers and chisels echoed from the caves.

Didan turned his back to Syndra and Manuk, hands on Olun's shoulders. "Are you alright?" he asked gravely, but Olun ducked under his arms.

"Syndra—I *am* part of this village, whether it is for a short time or not. And if you don't like it, I don't care. But I won't let you push me around anymore."

Syndra's nostrils flared, and her eyes flickered with rage. She looked past her to Didan. "Are you going to stand there and let her make me the villain?"

"This doesn't involve him," Olun said, stepping into Syndra's line of sight.

Her eyes fell on Olun once more, going as flat as her voice. "So be it."

She watched Syndra stride away from the mines toward the village, Manuk quick at her heels. Olun dragged her sleeve across her eyes, cursing her tears that fell even in times of triumph. She'd stood up to Syndra. She'd said what needed to be said, and though she'd probably doomed any and all future relationships with her senior, her words *were* necessary. The last thing Olun wanted was for her fear of Syndra to manifest into hatred.

"I am going to end this—I should have handled this long before," Didan murmured. He touched her arm to comfort her, but Olun recoiled.

"You made things worse," she accused. "I asked you *not* t'confront her on my behalf—why'd you do that?"

"I did nothing of the sort," Didan said with bewilderment, dropping his voice lest there be eavesdroppers. "What is said between us is *between us*."

"There's *nothing* between us!" she hissed.

"Olun," Didan tried once more, but didn't dare attempt to touch her again. "Let me take you home—or, we can meet tonight if you want. We can sort this out together."

Olun shook her head and walked away. Whatever had been growing between them, he'd ruined it before it could start.

Chapter 21

"You are doing it again," Genta mused. He'd kept his silence as he followed her from the mines for long enough.

"I don't know what you're talking about," Olun mumbled.

"Getting into trouble," Genta said. "A habit of yours, I understand."

"I didn't cause *that!*"

"You also did not hold your tongue *or* run away, either."

Olun spun around to face him. "Is that what I should've done? I thought you, of all people, would've appreciated how I stood up for myself."

Genta smiled and held his hands up in surrender. "I am not angry with you, Olun, stand down."

She turned away, cheeks hot with anger. "You don't need t'see me back, I'm fine on my own."

Truth be told, she feared running into Syndra and Manuk again just as much as she feared the Shadow Man. The adrenaline she'd had from her confrontation had left her drained. She didn't think she had the energy to encounter all three again. She'd been thankful, too, when Genta followed her back home instead of Didan.

Genta needn't know, though. She'd already worried him enough.

"Trust me, I am glad you do not need me," Genta smirked. "It is about time I checked on Tula. The baby has made her quite sick these past weeks, as you know."

Olun nodded.

"I saw Manuk get violent with Syndra," she said after a bit.

"The two of them have a . . . challenging relationship," Genta said grimly. "There is no separating them."

They didn't say anything further until they came across the bag she'd dropped. Neither Syndra nor Manuk had grabbed it in their descent. Olun hesitated, looking around for any signs of the Shadow Man. Genta looked around, too, his hand going to his hip where his large, curved knife hung as he scooped up the bag. Olun wanted to tell him about what was happening to her, but then she'd have to tell him about her visits with Didan and how he'd been helping her manage it. She didn't want to talk about Didan—or even *think* about him!

But Genta had other thoughts. "What is going on between you and my brother?" he asked abruptly.

Olun didn't look at him even as he shortened his stride to match her pace.

"Why was he there in the mines, again?" she asked him instead. "He doesn't like the caves, ya?"

Genta peered at her from the corner of his eye but answered her question. "We had business, and he would rather meet me here than in my home."

She'd known Genta to be a serious man, but the malaise in his voice gave her pause. She didn't believe he'd meant to let her see such an emotion, because just as quickly as she'd heard it and seen the fall of his face, it was scrubbed away completely.

"What happened between you two?" Olun wondered out loud.

"What do you mean?" He said neutrally.

"I mean . . ." The way Didan talked about Genta was not like the way Bana talked about him. And Genta?

"You aren't close, so I thought something must've happened," she mumbled.

"My business with my brother is none of yours," Genta said tightly.

She'd never asked Didan about his reaction to his brother, but she'd felt it. Loss and regret. Frustration and shame. Olun touched Genta's wrist and felt those same emotions and more.

Genta sighed and patted Olun's hand, unaware that she could feel his melancholy.

"It is rare that he stays close to the village," Genta said. "Rarer are his visits to me. You are right, we are not close. But it seems you are changing that."

"*Me?*"

"He turned his back on Elder Vasc and the village after his accident. Then you appear again after what, fourteen years? And suddenly this is the most I have seen of him."

Olun blushed.

"He checks whether or not I am looking after you," Genta twisted his lips sardonically. "Asks me if you are eating and sleeping well, if you are unhappy, how your studies are. Today? He pulled me aside, furious, and demanded to know why I had not taken your fall serious-ly—despite the he-said/she-said from Bana and Syndra, demanding to know what I was going to do about this hazing."

Genta gave a bark of humorless laughter. "And here I am, escorting you home because my brother *commanded* me to do so—so I ask again: What is going on between you and Didan?"

Olun could only stare up at him in shock. *Didan had been going to Genta?* Not only that, but he'd been concerned enough about her to set aside whatever issues he had with him. Olun didn't know *how* to feel about this information. She didn't know how to feel about *him*.

Genta walked her up to her gate but held it closed. "Your silence is telling, Olun. As much as I appreciate the excuse to see my brother, you must stop seeing him."

"Because I'm supposed t'be Elder?" Olun rolled her eyes.

"*Because* it is concerning," Genta said gravely. "If you are looking for a friend, you should look elsewhere."

A chill crept up her spine. "You said Didan wasn't dangerous."

"Didan is not a man one would call . . . stable," Genta said carefully. "He may be here one day, then never to be seen for months at a time. His interest in you will fade along with his lucidity. You are better off focusing on the people of this village, and if you are to be our Elder, prepare for that."

Olun lowered her gaze, trying not to let him see her hurt. Genta waited, hand still barring her from her home.

"Nothing's going on between us," she assured him, and, satisfied, Genta let her pass.

***

Olun hesitated at the sharp corner to Didan's camp that evening, wringing her hands nervously. She wouldn't stay. No, today had opened her eyes to many things—Syndra's upsets, Genta's warnings. *You keep making her cry, Syndra.* Didan had gone to her even when she'd asked him *not* to. She didn't need him to defend her or come to her rescue, but he'd been doing it all along. No wonder Syndra hated her and Genta babied her.

She took a deep breath, pacing to work herself up to what she needed to say. *I can't see you anymore.* What were they even hoping for with this friendship? Didan would leave, as Genta said, bored with whatever this was. Is that what he'd done with Syndra? Olun shook her head. *That doesn't matter.* Genta was right. Whether she was Elder or not, she couldn't focus on him.

But why was it so difficult?

"Graceful Ma Bright," Olun whispered for strength and rounded the corner.

Didan stared listlessly into the fire, dark blood smeared across his face and down the front of his shirt.

"What happened t'you?" Olun cried, throwing herself down beside him. She patted down his chest searching for a wound, but saw only the trickle from his nose.

Didan shrugged her off and lifted a rag to staunch the bleeding. "Go back to the village, Olun," he said with effort.

"But—Didan, you're *bleeding*!"

"So I am."

"Are you hurt?" She pushed back his hair to try to see him clearly, and attempted to remove the rag. Had he broken his nose? She'd seen Naleda reset a nose before when two of the herder boys had gotten into it. She could do it, but he'd be in so much pain. Olun didn't think she could handle hurting him—

"I'll get Naleda—"

"Olun!" Didan snapped, shoving her away from him so hard, she fell to her back. "*Go home.*"

Olun sat up, eyes wide in shock and fear. He'd never pushed her—never raised his voice at her with such hostility. He was a different man from even his moody self. *Didan is not a man one would call . . . stable.*

Didan closed his eyes, the veins of his temple pulsing through the skin. "I am sorry, do not cry," he rasped. "I will not be much for conversation tonight, so please, just go back home while there is still light."

Olun hesitated, crawling closer to him, desperate to know what happened. "It's alright," she soothed. "Let me help—"

Didan snapped open his eyes and glowered at her. "I said *go*!" he barked.

Olun jumped to her feet and ran.

Chapter 22

*T*HE BLACK ROCKS WERE *jagged, and the rushing water, like a warning hiss of a serpent. But it was beautiful. The water, so inky in the dark of the moonless night, like soft hair flowing through the tines of a crown. The Dark Lady's crown. The mountain range, her stone palace.*

"Do not be afraid." Her voice was serene. Louder than the rushing water yet softer than a whisper. It was cold in her ear like mountain air. But the words were not for her. Manuk rose from the water, reaching up to grasp the delicate hand extended to him.

"Let me show you peace," She said.

Manuk hesitated briefly and followed. "Where are we going?"

"Somewhere your journey can continue."

Olun watched as they walked along the stream and came to the mouth of a large cave. Manuk looked sad as he stared at his shaking hands in disbelief and heartbreak. "I thought things would be different . . . she would be different with me. Did I not love her enough?"

"Such woes are no use to you now," She said indifferently.

Manuk hesitated, his voice thick with sorrow. "It is over, then?"

"No, "She ushered Manuk forward, hand on his shoulder, and Olun followed unnoticed. "This is the beginning. There is beauty in death just as there is in life. Do not be afraid."

Manuk took one step, then another until he disappeared completely within the cave. The woman turned suddenly, her body a blur of smoke and her hair like black clouds shrouding her features, except her eyes. They glowed brighter than any star . . .

. . . and they stared at Olun.

***

Olun bolted upright in her bed. Gone was the moonlight and the chill of night; the spray of the rushing stream and the deep inhalation of the cave drawing her in. Gone were those eyes. She massaged her own, waiting for the dream to fade as it often did upon waking. But the dream persisted as she dressed in her simple tunic and tailored sloppily trousers. Olun didn't bother with her fire; she wasn't hungry. Something about the dream had stirred her belly to nausea and set her heart racing. Something was terribly wrong.

Grandma Yadir's home was quiet when Olun trotted down to it and knocked against the stone. *Manuk had to be here.* He often sought Syndra before he left on his hunts and as soon as he returned. Many mornings, Olun had risen early to see Manuk leaving the home. Grandma Yadir's bleary eyes squinted into the morning as she drew back the door flap.

"I'm sorry t'bother you, is Manuk—" Olun paused. What excuse would she give to ask about her granddaughter's lover? "Is Syndra here?" She asked instead.

Grandma Yadir shook her head tiredly. "Syndra and Jorre took off not long before you came."

"Thanks!" She called over her shoulder with a hurried wave. But on the path to the village, Olun dragged her feet, worried about what she'd be walking into. "It was *just* a dream," she told herself earnestly. "The mind works in mysterious ways."

Besides, Manuk was a merciless bully. Not only that, she'd witnessed him try to hurt his lover and incite violence against Didan a few days prior. Dreaming of his death was normal, wasn't it?

"But . . . he was so sad," Olun mumbled. And there'd been no triumph in the scene. No courage over conquered bullies. No, it had been as if she were there with them, appearing just after whatever horrible thing had happened to him. Following them along the stream and through the dark to stand at the cave where he disappeared.

Olun let herself quietly into Tula's and Genta's yard. Genta laced his boots, wearing travel leathers instead of the sleeveless tunic that allowed him to swing his hammer unrestrained.

"Where're you going?" Olun asked.

"Manuk did not return yesterday," he grunted without looking at her.

Olun froze where she stood and managed a nervous chuckle. "He couldn't be just late, ya?"

"Manuk is many things but tardy is not one of them."

Olun took her breakfast with Tula without tasting it. She went through the motions of her duties with Naleda, glancing at Syndra when she crossed her path for any appearance of distraught. Perhaps Manuk really was just tardy. A man couldn't be punctual his whole life, could he? Maybe he tripped, or lost his catch? Syndra did not seem alarmed by his absence or even concerned as the day wore on and nothing of her lover turned up. But the amount of men and women joining in the search increased throughout the day. She'd even overheard Jorre and Bana conspiring to join the search.

When evening fell and Manuk still had not been found, Olun grabbed Syndra's sleeve.

"Are you alright?" She asked her.

Syndra's frown was one of confusion rather than her usual annoyance.

"About Manuk," Olun elaborated. "I know your relationship with him is—strained—but I just wanted t'make sure you're okay."

Syndra brushed her away and snorted. "You and I are not friends," she said. "Save your concern."

"We *could* be friends," Olun mumbled, the two of them following the path that would take them to their prospective homes. "I don't know why you won't let me be."

She said nothing and Olun let out a sigh of discontent. Syndra's friendship wasn't what she was there for, anyway.

"I don't think they're going to find him," Olun said. Syndra stopped abruptly and swung around to face her. Her eyes narrowed and her lips parted in a question she would not allow herself to utter.

"I just—I just *think* you should prepare yourself for the possibility that he won't come back."

"What makes you so sure?" Syndra managed to say, her voice low.

"I had this dream and—" Olun didn't know why, of all people, she was telling Syndra this. Perhaps it was some desperate way to make Syndra see that she was harmless. That, whatever fears or hatred she'd come to regarding Olun, maybe those could be lifted and they could finally be amicable toward each other. "—I know it sounds silly, but it makes me think that maybe something happened to him."

"A dream? What, like a vision?" Syndra shifted from foot to foot, her lip caught between her teeth. "What else have you seen?"

Olun was caught of guard by her anxiousness and shook her head profusely. "Nothing!" She didn't have visions. She didn't really know what happened to Manuk, either, just that he was gone. The last thing she wanted to do was give Syndra hope. Or bring her despair. More selfishly, Olun didn't want to give the Doyens any reason to double down on their decision to cast her as Elder.

"It was *just* a dream. I don't normally remember them, so . . ."

Syndra rolled her eyes. "Then why are you telling me about 'just a dream?' Go tell it to another desert dweller." And, just like that, she was back to her usual self. Syndra resumed walking and Olun gritted her teeth as she followed.

"Has anyone gone missing—after you, I mean?" Olun called after her and this time, when Syndra turned, her fists were clenched and her face was image of rage—eyes wide, nostrils flared, and teeth bared. Olun cycled backward and out of her reach.

"Why are you bringing *that* up?"

"Because Manuk is *missing*," Olun all but shouted.

"You do not know that!"

"But what if I'm right? Syndra, what if what happened to him was the same that happened to you and me?" the itch of her scar made Olun wondered what scars Syndra hid, too.

"Nothing *happened* to me," she hissed.

"But—"

"Zenika strike you and your annoying tongue!" She put her hands on her hips and scowled. "Why are you so interested in Manuk? What, do you miss his attention? Have you grown fond of yet another thing that is mine?"

"No, I—"

"Then stay out of it! Do not pretend to care about the affairs of this village. Do not pretend to care for *me.*"

***

Manuk's body lay on a raised pallet in the middle of the village three days later, cocooned from head to toe in plain linen. Mourners approached his body to rest their hands upon him in respect. When he'd gone missing, the search for him lasted three days, fanning far into the mountains and deep into the ravines. Hujak insisted his nephew was skilled enough not to fall prey to an echrol. He insisted Manuk must have been injured somewhere, too far to call for help. No one dared to think of finding his body battered by the stream, caught like debris against the sharp tines of rocks, except for Olun. She hadn't been surprised when they found his body right where she'd said they would . . .

They carried him away just before the fall of evening. Olun had not been fond of the man, but she'd never wish such a fate upon him. The quiet procession followed to the edge of the village. His ma sobbed over his body, and his pa, uncle, and the other hunters pointed their spear tips to the ground in mourning. Zafre, a boisterously jovial man, wept as if he'd lost his own son. Syndra was the only face not among them.

"Where are they taking him?" she whispered to Tula. "Up into the clouds," Tula said wistfully. "We can only do so much for the body. The mawtiku will cleanse it and, in a few days, there will only be bones."

"You mean, they'll *eat* him?" Olun gaped at her, voice rising shrill enough to draw attention. "That's barbaric!"

"Shhh," she hissed, nodding her apologies to those who'd heard. "It's not like the desert, Olun. The mawtiku'll eat Manuk's body, yes, but the creatures belong to the Goddess and through them, he'll be returned to the mountain."

"But he'll be *eaten*, Tula—how is that okay?"

"Because we can carry them with us always," Tula pulled a necklace from her neckline and held it up for Olun to see.

It dawned on Olun that the off-white beads threaded through the twine were not the bones of animals. "Oh, Tula," she took her friend's hand.

"The button Genta wears in his sash belonged to his great-grandpa. The comb Naleda uses to secure her hair is even older than that," she said. "Manuk's loved ones will carry a piece of him always."

If she didn't think about how the mawtiku factored into the process, it was actually quite beautiful. The Rohta didn't keep such tokens and, as far as she knew, neither did the other three clans. Olun wished she'd had more of her family to remember them by.

"I shouldn't have called it . . . barbaric," she said, giving Tula's hand an apologetic squeeze. Just then, she caught sight of the Doyens and turned away.

"I'll see you later, ya?" she told Tula, quickly. The Doyens had interrogated her profusely when she'd led them to Manuk's body. "*How did you know?*" — "*What happened to him?*" — "*Did the Goddess send you there?*" — "*Why has this happened?*" And worse— "*Didan was seen quarreling with Manuk, has he anything to do with this?*"

Olun had no answers for them then and none now. What she'd seen hadn't been something she'd *sought*, and she honestly had no idea about Didan. She didn't want to think about him or whose blood had stained his clothes that evening.

She'd only just made it down the steep stairs of the plateau and onto the empty street when she saw Didan, of all people, turn down another narrow path. Her heart fluttered, and a knot formed in her throat. She hadn't seen him since that evening a week ago. Olun had just assumed he'd packed up and gone—he hadn't even come to Manuk's funeral. Olun fought the urge to run to him and bombard him with as many questions as the Doyens had done with her. Had he gone to look for Manuk after that afternoon at the mines? He'd told her he wouldn't confront Syndra or Manuk on her behalf, but he'd been ready to come to blows with the man right before her very eyes!

No, she'd tell him to leave the village—they all suspected him of something. If he stayed, there was no telling what they'd do to him!

Instead, she followed Didan through the village and up the path that led to her home. Was he looking for her? She'd almost called out to him when he quietly let himself into Grandma Yadir's yard. Olun stopped at a distance, but even she could see Syndra step out into the fading light and throw her arms around his neck. Didan held her close. It was an intimate picture, one that could have been of secret lovers rather than childhood friends. Olun backed away as the pair went inside, swallowing hard as the lump fell to the pit of her stomach. There would be no mourning Manuk between the two of them tonight.

CHAPTER 23

S YNDRA HARDLY LEFT HER home since Manuk's funeral. Jorre told them that all she did was lie in bed and stare at the wall. "She does not speak to me, or Grandmother, but at least she still eats," Jorre said.

"Eating is good," Naleda agreed. "We cannot heal if we do not eat."

Olun couldn't help but feel for Syndra. Loss was loss, and pain was pain no matter how one chooses to deal with it. She'd known people to shout and curse the Dark Lady, and others who simply wept in silence. There were people who masked their sorrows with recklessness and others who hid their pain with passion. Syndra pretended nothing at all fazed her, but even the best pretender could not hide grief.

Jorre and Naleda picked up the slack in Syndra's absence, and Olun tried her best to support them. But every evening as she passed Grandma Yadir's home, Olun hoped upon hope that she would not see Didan there. *What did it matter if Syndra chose Didan to take away her pain, or that he was willing?* She'd rejected him again and again. It was only a matter of time before he moved on.

Olun had reminded herself yet again that she'd washed her hands of him when he'd sent her away. Didan meant nothing—Syndra could do whatever she wanted with him. But then why had she lost her appetite? Why did that scene of him with her replay over and over, re-placing her nightmares? She almost preferred her nightmares, because at least she never remembered them upon waking.

Why do I feel so wretched whenever I think of him?

Tula noticed her change almost immediately, placing the back of her hand against Olun's forehead when Olun sat down beside her for breakfast.

"What's wrong? Are your night terrors back?" she asked.

Genta passed her a bowl, but Olun set it aside with disinterest.

"This is the second day you have turned away food," he said sternly. "Why come to breakfast if you do not eat?"

Tula reprimanded him with a swat on the arm and felt Olun's cheeks for fever. "You don't look well."

"I'm *not* well," she all but wailed, and rattled off her symptoms. How she couldn't sleep, how her heart hurt, and she wanted to weep. How food tasted like sand, and the small joys of the day felt like heavy weights upon her chest—burdensome and uncomfortable.

"I don't know what's wrong with me," she sniffed. "I can't think of a single remedy t'make this stop."

Tula rubbed her back. "Oh, Olun, there is no remedy for heartache."

Heartache? Olun pulled back from her, looking for the humor in her eyes or the eager smile that gave away all of her jokes. Tula's eyes were sincere, and her smile, kind.

"It happens sometimes when you hold someone dear in your heart. It feels as if the whole world is ending, and your heart breaks."

Olun shook her head. "This isn't about my family, Tula."

She knew what heartache was. She'd felt as if her very world was collapsing around her when she'd left her family. It still hurts to think about them, but far less than before.

"I know," said Tula. "You're in love."

Love? Olun stared at her friend in horror. She felt Genta's narrowed eyes on her, waiting to hear who it was who'd gotten too involved with an Elder.

"I have to do inventory." Olun jumped to her feet. She didn't look at either of them as she grabbed her bag and hurried to the gate.

"This business with Manuk is not over," Genta called after her, but Olun was already trotting off down the street. "Be back for dinner—and stay close to the village!"

*****

Bundles of herbs hung from the rafters in the drying room while leaves, petals, and fungi dehydrated in baskets of sand. With Jorre picking up Syndra's schedule, it fell on Olun to maintain their plants. Olun walked down the rows, taking mental note of the bundles, baskets, and jars and their contents, thankful for the distraction the task provided.

Me, in love with Didan? Olun scoffed.

She thought of Yuhi's flirtatious grin and how she'd not been alone in vying for his attention. How she'd heard Yuhi had taken *another* giggling girl to bed, or how when the annual Gathering concluded and he'd still not asked her to be his beloved. She'd been upset, yes. Frustrated and a little hurt, but this was different. She'd never felt like this before—and for *him?* Didan was kind one moment and hurtful the next—unstable, as Genta'd said. The last thing she wanted to do was turn into Syndra, who grieved a man who'd attempted to physically harm her.

How could love make someone feel like that? If *this* was love, why would *anyone* want it?

"It's not like I even *know* him," she mumbled, examining a particularly small bundle of herbs. She'd known him once, as a child. Even if she could remember the boy from back then, he was a man now. Didan wasn't handsome like Yuhi or strongly built like Genta. He hardly laughed and rarely joked. He wasn't exactly a man with women lining up to share his bed— aside from Syndra, that is. But he'd known Syndra all his life. They had a special bond. Even amongst the desert clans, regardless of how many lovers one takes, one never forgets their *first*. Had Syndra been his—

—*Stop thinking!* Olun scolded herself. *Not about Syndra, or* him. *Stop.*

If she should think of anything, it should be about her training. More importantly, Monta and Oja.

Olun teased a dry sprig from the sparse bundle of blue nettle and strode out of the drying hut. They didn't grow too far away from the village. Blue nettle was important in Naleda's medicines. It was a wonder how the depleted supply had gone unnoticed for so long.

"I just do not believe it a coincidence, Zafre,"

Olun ducked back inside as the voices neared. *Hujak,* she stifled a groan. She'd been avoiding him, Helima, and Zayeer since the funeral.

"Manuk and Didan were *seen* fighting in the mines—"

"There was an argument, that was all," Zafre interjected.

"—and my nephew suddenly goes missing afterward? You saw the body the same as I. Do you honestly believe the current was responsible for crushing his *skull*? Ask Naleda where she has seen such a wound before. She will tell you plainly."

"I hear you," said Zafre. "Really, I do. I am sorry about what happened to Manuk, but coincidences *do* happen just as accidents occur. Let us talk inside."

Their voices grew more distant, and Olun peeked outside just in time to see the door flap fall to Zafre's home. She gathered her basket and the blue nettle sprig and hurried off.

So, he still thinks Didan responsible for Manuk's death? Did Genta think so, too?

Part of her wanted to look for Didan to warn him of these dangerous speculations. *Murder?* But what if they weren't wrong about him? She touched the scar on her head, rubbing the puckered skin.

"Ask Naleda where she has seen such a wound before . . ."

"They say he bashed your skull in and hid your body . . ."

"Who *is* this man?" Olun mumbled as she stared absently up the path.

The air around her cooled, and darkness crept along the margins of her sight, slowly consuming her. Like before, her body tingled, the hair standing on end as the chorus of whispers pulled her toward something buried too deep to find.

"Olun?"

She looked up, the encroaching blackness dissipating, to see Didan closing the gate to Grandma Yadir's yard. He was more disheveled than usual. Haggard, as if he hadn't slept in days. Syndra stood in her doorway, arms crossed, and her thick hair, which she normally wore in a tight braid, flowed loose over her shoulder. *Of course, they'd be together.* Olun's hands tightened around the basket, upset by the thought.

She lowered her eyes and hurried by, feeling as if the air had been sucked from her lungs.

"Olun—" Didan caught her arm, but she brushed his hand away and walked faster.

He did not try to grab her again as he followed her up the hill to her home and waited against the wall while she went inside.

Think, Olun, she pinched the bridge of her nose. She hadn't planned to go home, but she couldn't exactly run the other way, either. She looked up through the window hatch to the blue afternoon sky. Would he go away if she stayed put? Something told her he would wait for her, even if it took the rest of the day and night for her to emerge.

Olun sighed and pulled her harvesting knife from her pocket, dropping it into her basket. Her excuse for going home, not that she needed one.

"We need to talk," Didan said when she emerged.

"No, we don't," she mumbled as she tried to push past him. Didan took the basket from her arms, keeping it away from her when she tried to take it back.

"We *do*," he said firmly and paused as if he were trying to work out where to start. "What happened that day—and what you saw on the ledge that night—"

"I'm sure you told Syndra all about it, ya?" The words came out before she had time to stop it. They tasted as bitter as she felt.

Didan scoffed. "I can assure you, you were never a topic."

Olun flinched despite herself and pushed past him.

"No, that is not what I meant—Olun, stop."

She did, but not because he told her to. No matter how horrible she felt, he still needed to know what people were saying about him.

"Look, Didan, it's really none of my business who you confide in or whose bed you share," she looked down at her feet—to the sturdy shoes he'd made her. "But they think you did something bad—"

"Wait," he said, bewildered. "You think I have been *sharing* Syndra's bed?"

Olun looked up in time to see him smile. She bristled in annoyance and embarrassment. *What was so funny?*

"It's a normal thing for people t'do," she faltered. "I don't see why it's so funny—you've been together before."

"I was in training, Olun; it was not appropriate."

"You're not training now," she argued. "You're not even Elder, so you could—"

I've lost my mind! She turned away from him, shocked by her own actions. He'd said they hadn't shared a bed, so why was she arguing back? Even if he *had*, what difference would it make to her?

Didan caught her sleeve.

"When we were children," he explained carefully, "Syndra lost her mother. Her father left not long after. I was there for her in those dark moments just as I am here for her now. She has done so much for me, Olun. She cared for me during my recovery—and was the only one to do so at that! It is thanks to her that I am half of what I am today. So, whatever amorous liaisons you believe her and me to be having are not real. It is nothing more than a friend comforting a grieving friend."

Olun stared at the hand that now circled her wrist, waiting for the lie.

"She has feelings for you . . ." she trailed.

"And I do not share those feelings," Didan murmured, stepping closer. "I am not a man so easily seduced to intimacy."

All at once, Olun was ashamed of her behavior. All of this jealousy—and *heartache*—confused her and made her act in ways she'd never acted before. She'd let herself lose focus. If Monta could see her now . . .

Olun sighed and stepped back from him. When it was clear she understood his sincerity and that she wouldn't run again, Didan released her.

"What happened that night you were bloody?" she asked, eyes still low.

"I am ashamed of what happened," Didan said. "I am deeply sorry I hurt you."

Olun closed her eyes and took a deep breath. "Did you and Manuk fight that day?" she asked, looking up and meeting his eye.

Didan frowned, caught off guard by her question. He stared at her. Olun couldn't tell if he attempted to discern the meaning behind her question or to figure out what exactly to tell her. But when he spoke, it was slow and careful.

"You asked me once if I had anything to do with your disappearance. Are you asking now if I was responsible for Manuk's?"

"I'm not saying it was on purpose," she said quickly and tried to explain. "You said there's nothing between you and Syndra—and I believe you—but I don't think Manuk ever did. He must have confronted you and then you—"

"I did not kill Manuk, Olun," Didan said darkly, a look of utter betrayal on his face.

"You were covered in blood, Didan," said Olun in dismay. "And, did you know he attacked Syndra? You were angry that day—and—people are starting to say Manuk's death was no accident. Even Genta believes—"

"Oh, *Genta* believes?" Didan gave another humorless laugh. "My brother believes that if the sun and moon are not revolving around his head, it is because *I* have had something to do with it, or have you forgotten what I told you about 'belief?'" he scoffed. "Of course, I would be the monster in his tale—but *yours*? I know I may look the part, but do you honestly believe I am a monster?"

"I don't know!" Olun cried. "I don't know *you*, Didan! You've never told me why you aren't Elder anymore. What happened two years ago when you broke Manuk's jaw? You say I went missing for days and then you found me—*how?*"

"How did *you* discover Manuk's body?" Didan tossed back. "Did *you* put him there?"

Olun shut her mouth. Frustrated tears welled in her eyes. *Why must I always cry?* Of course, he wasn't going to tell her what she asked. He always made it so difficult!

"I just thought you should know what they think," she said finally.

"I do not care what *they* think," Didan hissed, and Olun turned away.

He didn't stop her from walking away this time, but followed at a distance as she made her way toward the outskirts of the village. The ootingla belched on their cuds and watched them from the rocks. Somewhere, Bana and the other boys made sure the rest of the herd didn't stray too far from the pasture.

It wasn't until Olun patted herself down for her harvesting knife that she realized she'd tossed it in the basket Didan still held.

"Olun," Didan said quietly. "The blood you saw did not come from a fight. It happens to me sometimes. A lasting effect of my accident."

Olun felt that she should turn, but something in her told her that this confession was hard on him. If she looked at him now, he might never tell her.

"It happens when I am overwhelmed or—or angry. The pressure builds and builds. At its worst, my head feels as if someone is taking a hammer to it. I cannot see, I cannot move, I am simply at its mercy.

Agony. *That* is what you saw, Olun. Me suffering, and I am afraid it will get worse."

Olun dabbed at her cheeks and faced him. "Does Naleda know?"

"I would not dare burden her," Didan said, his hair falling into his face. "My mother has done enough."

"She could help, Didan," Olun approached him. "*We* could help you."

"Syndra and her grandmother know. Yadir has been helping me manage the pain with meditation and Syndra . . . she knows her medicines."

Olun nodded, finally understanding, but Didan wasn't finished.

"As for two years ago, I had no idea about Manuk's violence toward Syndra, but I suspected. I confronted him, and when he grew jealous and attacked me, I hit him once, defending myself with what I had."

Olun swallowed and nodded again.

"And . . ." Didan paused, taking a deep breath before continuing. "I found you that day, Olun, because that voice told me where to look. Unfortunately, why I am no longer Elder is a little harder to put into words. You have to understand, much of my life was spent in isolation. I am not used to sharing such things with anyone, so *please*, give me time. I promise, I will do better."

Olun was touched by his confession and even more so that he wanted to share himself with her. This was what she wanted—honesty. No secrets. But instead of relief from her heartbreak, Olun only felt worse.

She wanted things to remain as they were between them. Innocent. Amicable. What had grown between them was neither of those. She didn't want to care, but it was hard not to when he spoke to her like this, and when his fingers brushed against hers as he handed back her basket. He stirred emotions inside of her that were definitely *not* innocent.

Olun turned her attention to the bushes, pulling the harvesting knife Genta had gifted her with from its sheath. She didn't know what to make of his confession—*all* of it. What did he possibly hope for by telling her?

"I do not think this is what you think it is," Didan looked over Olun's shoulder, oblivious to her turmoil. He crouched beside her and took the cut herb and compared it to the one Olun had brought with her.

"Similar, but different," he said, holding up the dried sprig. "I recognize the smell. This is *night aster.*"

Olun gave it a sniff, and the faint scent was dizzyingly sweet. *Of course!* This had been the very plant to make her tongue numb during her lessons with Naleda and Jorre. *Night aster* was a sedative. A little bit could numb pain, and a few drops more would have a sleeping effect. More than that could cause death. Why was so much of it missing? Olun stared at the sprig and tried to recall the past few weeks. There had just been Syndra's finger amputation—had she missed something? She'd been so tired. So *distracted.*

"Come," Didan rose and extended a hand to her. "I will take you to where it grows."

Olun looked up at Didan and took his hand without another thought.

CHAPTER 24

GENTA PACED HIS FRONT yard in the fading evening light. Behind him, the fire was low, and the food Tula had prepared was untouched.

"Thank the Goddess!" Tula clasped her hands together, the first to notice Olun when she entered. She threw her arms around Olun's neck and hugged her close.

"I worried about you all day—no one had seen you since this morning."

"Where were you?" Genta demanded, striding up to Olun as if he would shake the answer from her. "I *told* you to stay in the village!"

"I had t'do some harvesting," she stammered, bewildered by his outburst. "I'm sorry I was late, ya, I got sidetracked. But I wasn't alone—"

"Do you *want* people to worry?" Genta threw his hands up, too exasperated to hear a single word she'd said. "If you are back to your attention-seeking ways, I will have *none of it*!"

Olun flinched away from him and cowered into Tula's arms. Yes, she'd been late—and yes, she'd gone outside of the village, but it wasn't as if she'd been in danger. He hadn't been this angry with her since the echrol incident.

"Calm yourself," Didan warned Genta. "She was not alone."

Neither Tula nor Genta noticed him before, but Didan's presence seemed to enrage Genta even more.

"And that makes it better?" he roared. "She is not your responsibility! I have been patient. I have been looking after her, keeping her fed and safe at the expense of my Bonded's health and my own sanity! I have had to put up with *you* inserting yourself where you do not belong on top of it all!"

"Genta, *please.*" Tula hugged Olun tighter, apologetic and fearful all at once. Didan straightened his back as best he could and moved the two of them behind him and out of Genta's rage.

"I am trying to do my duty to protect her—why must you insist on making it harder on me?" Genta growled.

"Because it has *always* been about you, has it not?" Didan said coldly. "Everything I have ever done has been to slight you. One word out of line—one foot set outside of what you are comfortable with. It is all about you and what *you* want."

Genta seethed. "I am keeping her safe. *You* may have little regard for life, but I will sooner spit in the face of the Dark Goddess than let Olun become what you are."

Didan caught Genta by surprise with a blow to the chin. Genta recovered quickly and grappled Didan to the ground. Olun felt as if she were in a dream, fighting her way through the haze of her memory where two boys rolled on the ground in a barrage of fists. They were hurting each other—*bleeding*—and all she could do was stand and watch them, just as she did now. But Tula's scream jolted her back to present.

"Tula, *stay back!*" Olun shouted, catching her around the waist and towing her to a safe distance.

Didan was a lot stronger than Olun had imagined, his limp not hindering him in the slightest, nor did his crooked back and shoulders become a disadvantage. He knew Genta's strikes well enough to avoid the worst of them as if he'd done it many times before.

"Stop it!" Tula screamed.

She struggled against Olun's tight embrace. It was all she could do to keep Tula out of harm's way. Their fight and Tula's cries had drawn onlookers. Willa, their neighbor, took hold of Tula, and three men from the crowd rushed to pry the men apart. Genta let them pull him back, his hair disheveled from its usual neatness, as he wiped the blood from his lip with the back of his arm. Didan struggled against his captors, just as battered.

"I have done you favor after favor," Genta shook off the men who held him back and pointed a finger at Didan. "And you still behave like some untamable beast!"

"Look at what you have done to me!" Didan cried, struggling harder against the arms that restrained him. "You have done me no favors—"

"Didan, stop," Olun rushed to him, a steadying hand against his chest. *"Please!"*

He paused to glare down at her, but Olun planted her feet and lifted her chin defiantly in response. She trembled uncontrollably, however. With such rage in his body, he could strike her away at any moment. But his rage was not as blinding as she'd thought. He saw the tremble of her lip and felt her shaking hands, and his angry glare morphed into horror.

Then, shame.

"Let me go," he whispered to the men, dropping his fists and going lax.

When they did, he turned from her and left them all without a word.

"Let him go!" Genta called to the men who had started out after Didan. "Just leave him be!"

He strode back toward the fire and plopped himself down onto a cushion. Tula was at his side in an instant, dabbing the blood from his lip and nose with a cloth. There will be a bruise there, Olun thought as she watched Genta flex his jaw gingerly.

He caught her watching him and glared. "What a foolish thing to do," he snapped.

"Because I like causing trouble, ya?" Olun snapped back. Maybe it was the adrenaline still coursing through her veins or the shock of what just occurred, but Olun found herself angry with him.

"Eat without me," she turned, wanting to go after Didan. He may have gotten in a few good strikes, but Genta was larger and well-equipped. The man broke apart boulders, for pity's sake!

It dawned on her. "You weren't trying to hurt him," she gasped. "You didn't *want* to hurt him."

"He is still my brother, Olun." Genta's voice was ice, as if the thought of being related to Didan was a pall over him.

Tula shifted the cloth to her other hand, wincing as she touched the bump of her belly. The small action drew Genta's attention, and he turned his worried gaze to her.

"Just nerves," she said shakily, and Genta took the cloth from her.

"I am sorry you had to see that," he said softly. "My brother is not suited for public appearances—"

"Stop *doing* that!" Olun stamped her foot. "You were happy that he was back—thankful that he's coming t'you. Why do you keep belittling him?"

"Because he is acting like a child," Genta said. "Just as you are now."

Olun threw her hands up. "Didan is right—it's everyone else who is a problem *but* you, ya?"

"I am trying to keep you safe," Genta said between clenched teeth.

"I don't need you to do that—I've never asked you to do it."

"You did not have to ask, I was *told!*" He leaned forward on his knees. "Do you think I brought you here out of the goodness of my heart? I have little faith in the Dark Goddess. The spirits do not protect us. *But* I could not bear to see Tula's heartbreak after our last loss—and the only way to see my Bonded happy, Vasc said, was if I retrieved *you*. If I protected *you*. If I made sure that you did not go down the path of madness as Didan had before."

He pushed himself to his feet and glared down at Olun. "*That* is the truth of it."

Both Olun and Tula stared at him in shock. All this time, she'd come to think of Genta as the brother she'd never had. Stern and protective. Fiercely loving and unwaveringly loyal. He'd been none of those. At least, not to her. After all this time, he still saw her as—no, she *was*—a burden thrust upon him.

"So that is the truth of it," Olun repeated slowly. She picked up the basket of *night aster* she and Didan had spent the afternoon collecting.

"Where are you going?" Tula asked quickly, following her to the gate. She tugged her to a halt, but Olun couldn't meet her eye. *Had she known all along?* Thinking back on it, it'd been so obvious. Her excuses were as transparent as they come.

"Olun, my *sister,*" she took Olun's face in her hands. "He didn't mean it, ya? He says things but—please, don't listen to him."

"You will stay away from Didan," Genta said, coming toward them. "You will stay in your home, even if I have to guard your door—"

"My friend among the Retryu used to say," Olun said carefully, though her heart was breaking anew. "'*No beast is born a beast; bad men create beasts.*' You have created a beast of Didan, what will you create of me?"

Genta froze, stunned into silence.

Olun pushed her basket into his chest, strode out of their yard, and down the dirt street.

CHAPTER 25

DIDAN STARED OUT OVER the village. The coals in the firepit were cold, and his camp, dark. He didn't turn when Olun approached, but lifted his face to the breeze that blew down from the peaks. He was so close to the edge. Olun took a hesitant step toward him.

"Let's start a fire, ya?" she said, hopeful that he'd hear the worry in her voice. "It's cold—"

"Go back to the village, Olun," Didan said without turning. "I do not care to talk tonight."

"Then we won't talk," she said softly, coming to stand beside him.

She glanced up at him; his tall frame loomed like a shadow, and his long, messy hair hid his face. Was he hurt? She wanted to brush back his hair and dab away the wounds he hid from her. Olun looked out over the village, her nails biting into her palms.

She couldn't imagine what it must have been like growing up with someone like Genta. Growing up how Didan had—not as a *child*, but shouldering the burdens of the living and dead. Had Didan even once felt part of the village? Had he ever felt part of a family?

Her own family wasn't perfect; her ma had a weak constitution and was not always able to parent her—that was where Monta came in.

Her aunt was strict, instilling in Olun loyalty and honesty even as she *lied* to her face for nearly twenty years. Her entire clan saw her life as both valuable and worthless—valuable enough to sacrifice to the Dark Lady yet not worth fighting for. Had Didan felt this way, too?

"Fear is a great and terrible thing . . ."

The words came to Olun like a trickle of cool water down her back. She shuddered but the words grew, expanding to the corner of her eyes and deepening the shadows of night around her. Olun grabbed Didan's arm without thinking, forcing back the terrors that sought to pull her in.

"Your pity is insulting," he hissed, misinterpreting her action. He disentangled himself from her grip and moved away from her.

"Pity?" she said, caught off guard. "I—I *worry* about you. What Genta said was unfair and just *mean*. You shouldn't be alone right now."

At this, Didan turned. He studied her carefully, his expression shifting from disbelief to contempt. He scoffed.

"I am an uncontrollable animal," Didan said. "A madman. You do not worry about *me*, you worry that you will lose one so much more *pathetic* than yourself."

"Don't tell me what I should feel!" She shouted. "I can't stand it when Genta tells me what t'do. I won't have *you* tell me my own heart."

"Then tell me what is in your heart, Olun?" Didan challenged.

"I don't know!" she said, and that was the truth. She'd known nothing when she'd come to the mountains—she was making it up as she went! Living in the desert had been easy; she understood her place, knew what was expected of her, had seen it in her clan members. Those who had not died, that is. And even death—suffering from the Dry Sickness—was all part of desert life. No one had to *tell* her who and what to be. She just *was*. But here?

Elder. Healer. Sacrifice. Savior.

Olun of the Desert . . . or of the Mountains?

She'd never seen any of this coming, especially him. She didn't know how she felt about Didan because she was still trying to figure out who *she* was.

"Let me remind you," Didan said and pointed back the way she'd come. "There is *nothing* between us. *Go.*"

Why was he trying to push her away?

"You're in pain, I know it," she said. "You and Genta are a lot alike, lashing out like this when you're scared and hurt—"

"Genta, Genta, *Genta*—Enough!" Didan turned his back to her. "I forget how fond you are of him. Perhaps you are more comfortable being with *him*."

"That's not fair!" Olun spun him around but Didan caught both of her wrists and forced her back against the wall.

"Is it?" he challenged, trapping her with his arms on either side of her. "I am the madman of the mountain. The feral beast! Was it not you who accused me of inflicting that scar on your head? Was it not you who believed me a murderer? *You* who accused me of taking advantage of my friend's grief to bed her? Of deserving these scars—*Look at me!*" he demanded.

Olun lifted her chin to him, keeping her eyes low for a moment longer before flicking them up to meet his. In one swipe, he brushed his hair back from his face until she looked into both of his eyes. Though the sun had set and the last shreds of light disappeared beyond the dark mountain tops, she saw his eyes clearly; one, an orb of black, and the other, milky white and sunken in its socket, surrounded by jagged, puckered scars.

"If I did not look like this," he murmured, "Would those thoughts have ever crossed your mind?"

Olun opened her mouth to negate his words, but the lie caught in her throat. She looked away, ashamed, and searched for the right words to assuage his doubts. There were none.

Didan dropped his arms and backed away from her, sneering. "Not fair, indeed."

He returned to the ledge, his back to her.

This wasn't the man she'd gotten to know over these past few months. Didan had every reason to become heartless, but he wasn't. He had every reason to *hate*—but he didn't. Despite his callous words, there was not an ounce of hatred in his body, not for her or Genta. Olun knew, because when she'd grabbed him, he shook with nothing but *fear.*

"You are not a monster," she whispered. "Please don't become one now."

Didan said nothing for a time, then he let loose a doleful sigh. "I am in so much pain—I am so tired of *being* in pain."

Am I to set him free?

Once again, Olun found her way to his side and slipped her hand into his. Didan didn't pull away. *It had been his pain all along.* When he touched her at the ceremony and in the mines, she'd believed the pain she felt had been memories—*her* memories. But they weren't. They'd come from Didan and his past. *His* fear, *his* pain, and *his* darkness. She felt it all now as she held him, but she didn't let go. He'd suppressed so much for so long; had he never allowed himself to break?

"My body, my mind . . . it all hurts." Didan closed his eyes and swayed with the breeze. "I started coming up here to this ledge because I sought to end the pain."

Suppose the only way to save someone is death . . . Olun went cold. It took her a moment to palm the tears from her cheeks.

"Didan," she called his name shakily, eying the ledge. She took a breath and continued indignantly. "I'm *glad* I don't remember you. I can't compare you t'the past. I don't know the boy you were before—but I know the man standing with me now. *He* is real t'me. You matter so much more than you think."

Despite Genta's harsh words, Didan mattered to him. Why else would Genta have been so furious with her for putting his brother in danger the day she tried to run away? Why would he defend him from her biases and Manuk's vendetta? Why would he tell her that he was grateful for the circumstances that brought Didan back into his life?

"Your brothers care about you, Didan," Olun said softly. "Your ma, too. And *I* care about you."

Sorrow, like the rush of a cold stream, washed over her. She let herself feel this—let herself tremble as he did. Didan shook like the ground before a geyser's release. He curled his fingers around her hand and squeezed as if she were his only lifeline in the dark, and she held on to him as if she were just that.

They stood side-by-side in silence for a time, with Didan's shoulders shaking with sobs he could no longer contain. *Good.* Whenever he was with her, he'd tried to maintain a sense of control. Guarded and careful. His mood swings and bursts of emotion were simply effects of years' worth of control slipping.

"I'm here," she whispered.

His shaking increased until the hand that gripped hers tightened so suddenly that she yelped in pain. Didan slumped, and Olun jerked him onto her; it was all she could do to keep his body from falling forward and off the ledge.

The two of them fell to the ground. "Didan!" she cried, rolling him to his back.

His eyes were wide and frantic, his breath quick. He squeezed her hand even tighter, his body tensing in agony.

"Ah—" he gave a strangled cry, slapping the heel of his palm against his forehead.

"I'm here," she said, but Didan groaned in pain, gripping his head desperately. She'd stay with him and get him through this. He'd endured so much on his own; she wouldn't let him go through this another night by himself.

"Don't let go of me, ya?" she soothed again, the bones of her hand he grasped grinding. She wouldn't leave him. He nodded, breath hitching before his hand fell away from his face and his eyes rolled back in his head.

"Didan!" Olun shrieked, touching his face to get him to look back at her. His skin was hot, and she looked around for something to cool him. A waterskin that he'd brought or— *something*. There was nothing. He tensed again, this time, his entire body going rigid like a board, and his head tossed from side to side.

Naleda had not prepared her for this. Olun didn't know what to do or how to help him. His thrashing drew blood on the side of his head, and his nose gushed with more. Olun turned him to his side before he choked and cushioned his head with her lap and held him steady. Minutes seemed like hours before his convulsions stilled, his body going limp in her lap.

"Didan?" Olun placed an ear to his chest; his heart beat slowly, his breath shallow.

"Help!" she cried as loud as she could. She saw the firelight in the village below—little pinpricks that felt just as far away as the stars above. They would not hear her. An echrol was more likely to find her than anyone in the village.

Didan shivered, his sweat drying in the cool night air.

Fire. I need fire! Olun gently took his head from her lap and took hold of his cloak. Her hand ached terribly, and she had trouble closing it, but she managed to get enough of a grip on him to drag Didan closer toward the dead fire. She scurried over to his bag without pause, upending it in her search for striking stones. Olun found them and returned to the fire pit, striking them desperately for a spark. Nothing happened. She needed light—*he* needed warmth! How could they *not* work?

She tried again and again, desperate tears flowing harder with every false strike until the stones were wet. Her hands were wet, too, covered in her own tears and Didan's blood. Olun threw the stones with a cry of frustration and crawled over to his pallet, stripping it of covers and skins.

What should I do? Think, Olun. She couldn't leave him for help—he could convulse again. She couldn't yell and make noise, either. She had no fire *or* a healer's kit—but perhaps she had something more. The Dark Lady would not answer, but Olun knew who would.

"Hear me, *please*," she whispered, closing her eyes tightly.

"*I hear you, child,*" said the Shadow Man, his somber timbre vibrating through her mind.

Though she feared the Shadow Man, Olun feared losing Didan more.

"Tell me how to help him," she demanded.

"*Pain cannot be helped—*"

"It *can!*" Olun protested. Naleda was right, they were healers, not gods—but what was the Shadow Man? He *had* to have some kind of power.

"*You cannot take away pain,*" the Shadow Man said patiently. "*It is part of life. You may dull it, cover it, manage it.*"

Olun looked back at Didan, tears brimming anew. She knew all of this and had time for none of it!

"*Please*, just help him," she whimpered.

"*Pain cannot be helped,*" said the Shadow Man softly, as if moved by her tears. "*But it can be shared. Suffering can be shared. He who suffers alone truly dies a painful death.*"

Didan gagged, blood from his nose flowing into his mouth. Olun quickly returned to him and rolled him to his side as he went into another round of convulsions. When he stilled, she wrapped his cloak more securely around him and covered him with the skins from his pallet. She ripped the hem of her skirts and dabbed away the blood from his nose, lips, and neck.

"I've got you," she assured him, smoothing back his damp hair. Her fingers paused for a fraction at the lumps of his scars and the divots in his skull.

His eyes moved frantically beneath their lids, his jaw clenching so tightly she heard his teeth gnashing together. If this night was to be his last night, she wouldn't let him suffer alone. Olun picked up his hand and gave it a squeeze.

"I'm *with you*, Didan," she said. "Let me share your pain."

What happened next, Olun was not ready for. Didan's terror rippled through her body. She'd felt pain and panic before. She'd felt the terror, the hopelessness, and the *helplessness* of her dreams—but this wasn't it. Didan's pain was more than physical, and now she, too, was at its mercy.

CHAPTER 26

Didan

"*L*ET ME UP!" *DIDAN cried, struggling against the hand that pushed his face into the dirt, a knee digging into his back.*

"Only if you take me to the cave portals," Genta sneered. "Take me to the other side of the mountain—"

"How about the other end of Diadasos!" Manuk laughed.

The boys were just into adolescence. Their bodies hardening to men's and their voices occasionally fluctuating between the childish pitch of youth and the low rumble of adulthood. Didan, on the other hand, had maintained the gangliness of childhood. Thin from years of living minimally, while Genta and Manuk ate heartily. His muscles were sparse despite his build, compared to Genta, who wielded hammers, and Manuk, who threw spears. There was no escaping them, though Didan tried.

"Get off me!" He struggled against Genta's hold. "That is not how it works!"

"No? So, you are saying you have been lying?"

"No!" Didan cried. "I never lied!"

Manuk plucked a berry into his mouth, smacking his lips. "I think he stashed that girl's body away all those years ago," he theorized. "I think he did it so that he could 'find' her and make himself look good. But he is just a big fake, like all his stories."

Didan dug his fingers into the dirt, blinking away tears as he remembered her. He'd only meant to tell the desert girl about the cave stars to cheer her up. She loved his stories, and he loved telling them to her. He never thought she'd go off to look for them on her own.

Genta threw a handful of dirt at the other boy. "Shut up, Manuk, he is not that foolish." He turned his attention back to Didan. "I will be chief, but it is you they praise. You are not even Elder, and yet Father hangs on your every word, saying I should, too. Me! As if I take orders from a weakling like you. All you do is run away—you thankless coward!"

"Mad man," Manuk added. "Feeble-minded weakling!"

"You would not dare say those things to Elder Vasc," Didan gasped.

Genta shoved his face further into the dirt. "Yes, but you are not Elder Vasc. You may have had your ceremony, but you are just as useless as you were before."

"If you cannot show us the portals, then show us the cave stars," Manuk suggested, picking a seed from between his teeth. "Or was that something you made up to impress that dirty desert girl?"

"Yes, show me the cave stars you raved about," Genta smirked. "Prove your worth."

Didan couldn't breathe, dirt blocked his nose, and the weight of Genta on his back crushed his lungs. "Fine! I will do it—" he wheezed. "Genta, I cannot breathe!"

Genta climbed off with satisfaction.

The cave yawned like a beast frozen in stone. In its mouth was darkness, and on its breath was death. He knew neither Genta nor Manuk could smell it, for they showed no outward reaction to it. Didan barely reacted to the stench anymore.

"Wait," Genta said, pausing to light the torch he'd brought with them while Manuk danced anxiously from foot to foot.

"What if an echrol is asleep in there?" Manuk asked.

"It is empty," Didan said. At least, where beasts were concerned.

Manuk hesitated at the mouth and backed away. "I will wait here." He grumbled his feeble excuse. "Someone has to keep watch."

Genta rolled his eyes but followed Didan into the cave. Their footfalls echoed through the dark chamber back and back, the only sounds between them.

"Why are you doing this, Didan?" Genta asked suddenly, voice hushed. Was it possible that he was afraid?

"Because you forced me to."

"You could have run," he suggested. "You are good at that, at least. Or fought harder."

Didan stopped and turned toward him, his brother bottom-lit from the torch, his face indiscernible. "I do not want us to fight anymore, Genta," he said. "I want you to understand me—why can you not just try? No one else does."

Genta was quiet for a moment. "Father understands you," he said coldly. "The Doyens will eat out of the palms of your hands if you raise them to their lips. And you want pity from me?"

There was a difference between reverence and understanding. They didn't understand Didan because to understand him meant looking deeper into themselves. It meant finally seeing the cracks they'd made in him. Genta would never understand, Didan realized with a sudden pang. He was and would always be alone.

They walked farther away from the light; the cave stars didn't blink to life. The Cave Man had called to him many times before, lighting his *path through the tunnels. It had been years since he'd come back. Even still, the Cave Man wouldn't have forgotten about him.*

The torch burned out.

"I cannot see anything," Genta called to Didan, falling behind.

Didan couldn't either, but no sooner did the thought cross his mind did the cave stars flickered into existence one by one until he stood beneath the night sky itself. "My dear son . . ." the Cave Man whispered his welcome. The only one to truly understand.

Smiling despite himself, Didan turned just in time to see Genta throw a large rock in his direction. Didan ducked, angry words burning on his tongue, but Genta walked beneath the light, waving his arms in front of him, eyes wide as he strained to see.

"You tricked me!" Genta shouted and picked up another rock. He threw it blindly, with rage laced with fear. "You lying piece of—is this how you get back at me?"

The clacks as the rock bounced off the walls echoed loudly just as the other had, but the moan of the mountain was louder. Rocks began to fall. The cave was collapsing!

"Run!" Didan cried. The cave stars guided him back to the light. He almost made it until he remembered Genta floundering around in the dark. Didan skidded to a stop and turned around. Dust muted the cave stars, and Genta was nowhere in sight. He ran back into the cloud of dust regardless, coughing as he struggled to find his way.

"Genta!" His cries were drowned by the roar of falling rocks, but his brother heard his name. He called back, and Didan grabbed hold of him, towing him back toward the cave mouth. Manuk shouted from outside, and Genta broke free to sprint ahead. Still sore from their earlier fight, Didan willed his stiff limbs to keep up even as rocks the size of his fist pelted his shoulders and head. Dust and debris choked him. Didan

tripped, catching himself painfully on his hands and knees, warm blood coating his palms.

"Genta!" He shouted desperately, coughing and crying out in pain. Every time he rose, he was struck down again. "Genta, help me!"

"Didan! Where are you?" He heard his brother, but all around him, the earth was crumbling. Didan tried to stand again, but the ground shook beneath his feet, pitching him forward and tossing him back. His breath quickened, and the dust that filled his mouth and lungs sent him into a fit of coughs and wheezes. He clutched his throat, unable to breathe.

"Help—" he gasped. He could no longer see his brother, the light of the exit, or the light of the cave stars. They'd all abandoned him!

He heard rather than felt the massive rock come down onto his leg, jerking his crawl to a halt. At first, he thought his robes had caught, but then he saw his leg and screamed. He clawed at the rock, trying with all his strength to move it just enough to roll free, but another stone struck his head, and he went limp. He couldn't speak, couldn't breathe. And now, he could no longer move as his body broke and tore a dozen ways.

"... Let go," the Cave Man whispered. "I let you stay, but look at you now. It is time to come with me into the Great After, my son."

But the nightmare changed, shifting ever so slightly so that a small hand gripped his own.

"I'm here," Olun cooed, her soft voice somehow louder than the roar of the mountain above him. She pulled him against her body, twisting to cover him from the brunt of the debris and shield him from the monsters that inhabited the dark. Didan felt wetness against his face and looked up at her. Though he couldn't see anything but the dark, he knew that she was crying. Was she afraid? Hurt?

"Get out of here," he told her. "You do not belong here!"

"I belong with you," she surprised him by saying. "I may not be able t'save you, or change what happened here, but let me share this so that you don't have t'bear it alone."

Rock after rock assaulted her instead of him. Crushing her legs and her arms. Blood dripped into her eyes as her skull split open. The dust dried her nose until it bled, and he felt it against his face, mixing with her tears. Didan whimpered beneath her, but she only held him tighter. He felt her warmth against his body and her breath against his face. This was not part of his nightmare. The scene had played through his mind again and again for years, always ending with crushing darkness and agonizing hours of silence before they pulled his broken body from the rubble.

When the mountain finally quieted, the silence and the darkness were absolute. Its weight crushing and suffocating.

"Just breathe," Olun soothed, and he felt the rise and fall of her chest. Didan matched its rhythm and found that he could breathe again. With his cheek pressed against her heart, he felt its beating that seemed to beat for only him. His heart slowed to her pace, and he found that he could—and wanted to—live again, too.

"I'm here," her voice echoed through his mind, and one by one, twinkling green lights flickered above them. Didan looked up at the wonder in her face as she watched them twinkle.

He was no longer afraid. No longer alone.

He squeezed her hand, and smiled.

CHAPTER 27

D AWN YAWNED OVER THE mountain peaks. Olun shivered, her hands and body numb from the cold. She unclenched her stiff limbs little by little from the body beside her. Didan was cold and unmoving. She sat up and scrutinized his features. The tension contorting his face eased, and the tightness of his jaw relaxed. He looked peaceful even as dried tears streaked his cheeks, cutting through the blood that had long since stopped leaking from his nose.

Olun stroked his cheek gently and pressed her ear to his chest. *Still breathing.*

"Didan?" She jostled his shoulder. When he didn't move, she tried again, shaking him this time. They couldn't stay up on the ledge, not without warmth. She looked around for the fire stones she'd thrown, but didn't think she could use her hand to strike them.

"Didan, wake up now, ya?" Olun tried to keep her voice calm, but gave him a stern shake.

He scrunched his face, groaning, and shrugged her off. His eyes fluttered open and blinked up at the sky.

"Thank you," Olun said under her breath to whatever god or spirit still lingered and rested her head against his chest. He was alive and awake. Good signs. She had no idea what his triggers were, no idea of their frequency. *It happened before,* Olun reminded herself, thinking of the evening she came up to the ledge and found him bleeding from his nose. *It's happened before, and I hadn't seen him for days because he was like this.*

Didan touched her hair.

"Cold," he mumbled.

"Oh—" Olun wiped her eyes and sat up. "Sorry."

She started tucking the blankets around him, but Didan caught her sleeve.

"No," he rasped drowsily. "You."

He lifted his arm, holding open the blankets for her. Olun hesitated. If it wasn't for the fact that she'd shivered all night beside him, her limbs drawn into her sleeves and tucked beneath her torn dress, she would have declined. But Olun curled awkwardly into his side, her arms wrapped around him to keep both of them inside the blanket. At least, until the sun rose high enough to chase away the cold.

"We have t'get you back t'the village," she told him, tucked against his side. "You need help, and I . . . can't help you alone."

It didn't matter what she could or couldn't do. Didan had already closed his eyes and drifted back to sleep. *Just a little bit longer, then,* she sighed as his face returned to peace. Olun realized that she'd never seen him sleep before. She touched the dark bags beneath his eyes softly, surprised by and slightly jealous of his long, dark lashes. Without the tension he carried like a mask, his face was soft and almost boyish. Less worn out. *Handsome,* even. Olun blushed.

She'd rather see this Didan—without fear, without pain, without heartache and anguish. *What's changed?*

"You . . ." the Shadow Man whispered, drifting away with the night.

***

Didan stirred some time later, jolting Olun to alertness. He sat up and massaged the sleep from his eyes, pausing to stare at the blood on his hand.

"For pity's sake," he muttered, pulling at his tunic to examine the amount of black, crusted blood that stained the front of it, grumbling all the while.

"From your nose," Olun explained, rubbing the sleep from her eyes.

Didan gave a start and swiveled around, realizing her presence beside him for the first time. He stared at her in disbelief, frowning slightly as if trying to discern if he was still asleep. *Doesn't he remember the other night?* Olun put her hand to his forehead in concern. *Doesn't he remember waking up earlier?*

"Some came from your head, too, when you . . ." She trailed off, the memory of his horrible spasms and convulsions flashing before her eyes. Didan had been right, it is such a blessing to be able to forget—She didn't think she would ever forget the other night.

"Do not cry," Didan said quickly, thumbing away her tears. "It—it happens, Olun."

Olun wanted to laugh. *He* was comforting *her?* She stood abruptly, rolling her stiff shoulders and shaking some warmth back into her legs. She wouldn't give either of them the time to feel sorry for themselves.

"Are you well enough t'make it back down?" she asked.

Though he was up and lucid, he looked as if coated in wax. Still in a state of disbelief, Didan struggled to his feet, swaying like a blade of grass caught by the mountain breeze. Without thinking, Olun put her sore hand to his chest to steady him and hissed at the flash of pain.

"What is it?" Didan asked.

"Nothing," she gritted, wrapping her arm around his waist to support his steps. The cold had numbed the pain in her hand, but now it was alive and throbbing.

"Let me see it." Didan took her hand from his chest, holding it carefully in his. It was swollen and bruised.

"What happened?" When Olun didn't respond, the realization set in. "Did—did *I* do this? Have I hurt you?"

"Don't think about it," she pulled her hand away and tugged him into motion. "Let's just get you back in one piece, ya?"

It was a struggle getting him down the path, but he directed her down from the ledge, talking quietly in her ear. Olun had walked this path so many times her feet knew where to go, but she let Didan talk. If he was talking, he was awake, and if he was awake, she could get him to help.

Their progress was slow. She estimated it to be nearly noon when they finally stepped on the footpath that would lead them down to her home. Their return, however, did not go unnoticed. Four villagers who had been part of Manuk's search party spotted them. One raced back toward the village while the other two took Didan between them.

"I'm fine," she waved the fourth away and hurried behind the pair that carried Didan. "Take him t'my home!"

The nearer they drew to the village, the more Didan seemed to wilt. She didn't have to touch him to know he was afraid. It wasn't until they laid him down on her bed that Didan began to panic.

"Get me out of here—" he gasped, taking hold of Olun's sleeve. "I should not be here! Olun, help—" The two men held him down as he thrashed.

"Stop—You'll hurt him!" Olun pushed them aside and took Didan's hand again. "Look at me, ya? I'm here."

The look in his eye—he was a scared boy again. Back in isolation. Back in the dark of the cave. Back in the bed he'd lain in while he recovered from the worst injuries of his life. He'd imprinted all of these experiences on the walls of this home.

"Hold on—" Olun slipped her hand from his and jumped to her feet. She shouldered past the men who took up the small space to the rod and pushed open the hatch above. Didan gazed up as sunlight streamed down onto his face.

"Everything is going to be alright," she said, taking his hand again. "You're going to be alright."

Didan nodded, the worst of his panic fading. His hand closed around hers, and in his touch, she felt his trust in her.

"Where are they?" Genta's voice demanded from outside before he burst through the door flap. He was a mess; sleep-deprived and unkempt, his clothes disheveled. Most of all, his cool demeanor had been replaced with wild panic. He threw himself on the floor beside Olun and bowed his head, his hair falling forward to hide his face. To her surprise, his shoulders shook and his hushed sobs met her ears.

"Please forgive me," he whispered again and again. Whether it was for Olun's ears, Didan's, or the Dark Lady Herself, she didn't know. He kept his head bowed, almost touching the floor.

Olun bit her lip and climbed to her feet, but Didan still held on to her hand.

"I'll be right back," she soothed, giving his hand another squeeze of encouragement and disentangling their fingers. Quietly, she stepped around Genta, who had taken up Didan's other hand. He'd been worried. More than worried—he'd been afraid.

"You cannot reason with Fear," the Shadow Man whispered. *"Fear is a great and terrible thing . . . It can turn a desperate man into a savior, just as it can turn him into a villain."*

"Which one are you . . ." Olun whispered, leaning against the wall of the doorframe lest she collapse from exhaustion. "Savior or Villain?"

Before the Shadow Man could answer—*if* he had an answer for her at all—Syndra came bounding through the gate with Naleda at her heels.

Good, Olun thought as the door flap fell into place again. They knew how to help him better than she could.

They were the healers, after all.

CHAPTER 28

D IDAN AND GENTA'S FIGHT had been all over the village, the gossips not content to stop there. No, even Tula and Genta's subsequent altercation became a thing of topic. "They said Tula and Genta fought something fierce—fiercer than his fight with Didan!" Jorre had told her eagerly. "She made him go out and look for you and told him not to come back until he found you. You should have heard her! *How dare you say those things! How dare you use me tah justify your own miserable life!* or something like that."

Olun knew Tula well enough by now to know she'd never say something so hurtful to someone she loved, even in upset. She also knew Jorre's intentions. "You should go see her if you want to know what she *really* said," Jorre hedged. "I mean, where else is there for you to go?"

The girl was right. With her little hut occupied by Genta, Didan, and Syndra, who cared for him, and Naleda, Zafre, and Bana, who made their appearances, Olun would only be in the way. She'd promised Didan she wouldn't leave him—that she'd only be right back. But there was no place for her. He didn't need her anymore.

Jorre followed her around the yard like a shadow; her attempts to distract her thoughts were obvious. "How about this?" she tried again, taking Olun's arm and all but dragging her toward the path. "Genta is going to stay here for a while, so *you* go get his things from Tula before she burns them in their fire."

Olun grimaced. "She's not going to burn his things over an argument." *Especially about me.*

"You do not know that!" she grinned. "Once, my sister burned Manuk's favorite spear because he looked at that big-toothed woman, Farhana, a little too long. Go! Quickly, I smell smoke!"

Olun was too exhausted to roll her eyes, let alone protest. But when she found herself standing in Tula's yard, Genta's words came flooding back. Tula had to have known what Genta had been doing. There were no secrets between the two. And yet, the look of shock on her face as he said it had been so real. The hurt, too deep to be false. Still, Olun hesitated like a stranger.

"Olun?" Tula said from her doorway. Her eyes were red and puffy as if she'd cried for hours instead of raged as Jorre had said. Tula closed the distance and threw her arms around her.

"I am *so* sorry," she whispered, and in her embrace, Olun felt the truth.

***

Genta sat with Didan night and day. Olun stopped by as often as she could, bringing meals that she and Tula prepared and lingering outside for updates. But she couldn't bring herself to ask after how Didan fared. He was in good hands, she told herself each time she left. Better hands, now with Syndra looking after his health and Genta, his well-being. Olun was glad. She knew the horrors of his mind. She remembered holding on to that terrified boy in the dark, taking the brunt of the rocks, shielding him from the worst of the barrage. He needed people around him who could protect him. He needed his family.

And I am nobody.

"My dear Olun," Zafre said warmly, catching her just as she turned down the street to Tula's home. Behind him, an apprehensive Hujak, a bored Zayeer, and a serene Helima.

"Words cannot thank you enough for bringing my son home," Zafre said, placing his big hands on her shoulders. "Such a curious feat. How is your hand, by the way?"

"It's alright," she mumbled. Two of her fingers had been broken when Didan seized. She tucked her stiff, bandaged hand behind her and glanced at the Doyens at his back. Naleda was not among them.

"You have been doing many intriguing things as of late," Zafre continued gently. "Your dreams pointed us to find Manuk. Did they point you to find Didan as well?"

Olun shook her head mutely. She tried to focus only on Zafre's face—a face that looked so much like her beloved aunt—and not those behind him who looked at her with more accusation than question.

"Do your dreams tell you . . . anything else?" Zafre asked patiently.

"I don't remember." It was the honest truth, but Hujak scoffed.

"I've never been able to remember my dreams," she explained, eyes lowered.

"Perhaps it is too noisy here," Helima suggested with a hint of encouragement. "In Solitude, my young Elder, all distractions will be silenced, and your dreams and memories will come back to you."

Dreams and memories will come back to you. At one point, Olun would have given anything to regain her memories. She would have given anything to know *why* it was she woke up in a cold sweat, hoarse from her screams and exhausted from fighting shadows.

"She is not going anywhere," came Genta's voice from behind her before she could answer. He strode to Olun's side. "She stays *here*."

"That is not for you to decide," Zayeer said, exasperated by the intrusion. "If the girl is to get a better handle on her gifts, she does not need these distractions."

"Tell me what she needs, then," Genta demanded. "You all have kept me ignorant for so long—ignorant of what you did to my own brother. So, tell me—no—tell *her* exactly what it is you are demanding."

"Distance," Helima said coolly. "To quiet the voices of the village."

"To sever the ties of this world so that she may strengthen the ones to the next," Zayeer added. "She is too close to your Bonded, Genta. She does not need *family*. Not anymore."

"Deprivation," Hujak summed up. "The only way to be closer to the Goddess is to lose all worldly possessions and forego unnecessary attachments. The Goddess wants you to *forget* these things."

Genta looked expectantly at his father, waiting for him to add anything the others had missed. Zafre only held his gaze, regarding him with cautious surprise.

"It is time we begin treating her like an Elder, Genta," he said.

"Is an Elder not part of this village?" Genta challenged. He placed a hand on Olun's shoulder. "I have watched you all build walls around Didan for years. Walls so high, he could scarcely see over. It separated him from the village—him from *me!* I said nothing as he declined, never understanding what it was he was going through because I did not see. I chose *not* to see because I respected you, Father. You, who dangled the title of Chief before my eyes. But, Father, I will not stand by again and let you do the same thing to this girl as you did to your own son."

Olun stared up at Genta, just as shocked as the four faces around her.

"What we did was necessary," Zafre said finally. Quietly.

"Have you not listened to Didan? Have you never once wondered at anything he has gone through because of you?" Genta shook his head. His hand tightened on Olun's shoulder as if he prepared to physically remove her from their grasp. "No more."

"She was brought here *to be our Elder!*" Hujak argued. "What is her purpose, then, if she is not?"

Genta gazed down at Olun with such warmth and love that she felt her eyes well. "She was brought here to heal, and *that* is what she will do."

Olun watched a myriad of expressions storm Zafre's face, and considered his frustrations. On the one hand, he knew what the village needed to maintain order. Regardless of where she was, an Elder has always been a bridge linking the living to the spirits and the Afterlife. On the other, Olun saw just how much it tore Zafre apart to stare into Genta's eyes and see all of his faults as truths. To finally see glimpses of the chief his son would be.

With no further comments, Genta spun her around by her shoulder and walked her to his home. Zafre and his Doyens didn't follow, but Olun shrugged off Genta's hand and turned to him just before they entered the yard.

"They were going to take you," Genta explained, staring past her to where the Doyens had gone. "If I had not come, they would have sealed you away just as they had Didan."

"What do you care, ya?" Olun lifted her chin indignantly. She hadn't forgotten what he'd said to her. Whether he'd said it in fear or worry, it'd still hurt.

"What I said was true: I was tasked to be your guardian, and it was—*is*—my duty to keep you safe." Genta's jaw clenched and met her eye. "I blamed Didan's weakness for his madness. His peculiarities, his eccentricities, his anger for me and the village. I wanted to protect you from these things in him, but I should have been listening to what they all meant.

"Didan told me about his so-called training. Days locked away in a cave without food and water. Without light and warmth. I never knew that each time he left us, it was so they could lock him away in *there*. And I—"

His voice broke, and he paused. Olun knew what he would say, though. She'd been there in Didan's dreams, watching as Genta goaded and bullied him back into that place.

"I never wanted him to get hurt. I . . . I do not want to lose him, Olun. The Bright Mother knows I can never apologize enough, least of all to him. But what you heard me say to my father was also true: I will not stand by again. I am truly sorry, Olun, for how I have hurt you. Whether you accept me as your brother or not, I will continue to look after—"

Olun threw her arms around him, and, for the first time, he hugged her fully. "Thank you, brother," she said, her words muffled by his shirt.

"Why aren't you with Didan?" she pulled back.

Genta opened his mouth, swallowed, and met her eyes. "He is gone, Olun."

All at once, her breath stopped.

CHAPTER 29

HOW COULD HE LEAVE without saying goodbye?

At home, Olun scrubbed Didan's blood from her bed and gathered soiled rags to wash. She collected empty bowls and swept the soot back into the oven, drifting through each task as listlessly as a spirit. Her fingers did what they had to do, and her limbs moved her where she needed to go, but Olun felt nothing. Heard nothing.

She'd been naive to think four days—out of *twenty-four years*—would be enough to mend what was broken between him and Genta. How idiotic to believe that a single night sharing his dreams would be enough to cast their hurt away.

Olun shook out the last of her washing, flipped it over the line, and pulled it straight. In her absent state of mind, she pulled too hard, and the blanket began to slip from the line. Olun readjusted its hem to steady it, but a force tugged from the other side, setting it back into place. She backed away, startled, but caught her breath when Didan ducked under the line.

She wanted to fling her arms around his neck and hold him close, but stopped herself short of touching him. This wasn't who they were to each other. He'd been vulnerable and in despair, and she'd been desperate to save him from it. She couldn't trust what she was feeling.

Didan looked tired in the way a sleeping man does when he wakes, but he was no longer the haggard man from before. The bags beneath his eyes had diminished significantly. His face seemed softer—*fresher*—and the tense lines that creased his eyes and mouth had smoothed. He wore Genta's kaftan, the knee-length shirt fitting a bit looser on his slimmer frame, and the tapered trousers bunching slightly at the ankle, but he was neat and clean. Olun wondered when Genta returned home for these things. His hair was still a wild mess of curls, cords, and trinkets, but at least she had no trouble seeing his eyes any longer. They stared down at her so intently, she felt the words he wanted to say. Words she didn't want to hear—not yet. Olun looked away.

"I thought you'd left," she said, nodding to the loaded pack slung over his shoulder and the spear-headed walking stick he leaned on.

"I did . . ." he trailed. "But I forgot something."

Olun glanced up at the line. None of Didan's clothes hung from them, and there was nothing of his inside.

"Walk with me?"

Olun nodded.

They walked around the outskirts of the village in a silence that was neither comfortable nor uncomfortable, stealing glances at each other. Olun fidgeted with her sleeve, growing increasingly nervous as the silence stretched on and searched for a way to fill it.

"You . . . you look better," Olun said awkwardly.

"I do not know if I will ever be better," Didan sighed. "But I *feel* better."

Olun nodded. "That's a start . . ."

"The sky window was a nice touch," he said before the silence had a chance to grow again.

"It was Genta's idea," she said, glancing at him sharply for any sort of reaction to his brother's name. There was none, and she continued.

"It was a wonderful gift he gave me. I missed counting the stars until I fell asleep, and waking to the sun in the morning."

"And yet you still came to do both with me," he chuckled, and Olun's face grew hotter.

"I am only teasing," he said softly with amusement. Despite her embarrassment, it relieved her to hear him laugh and tease. It was nice.

"Well, what if I missed the company, ya?" she grinned, glancing up at him.

"I missed *your* company," he said abruptly. "As I lay bedridden, I hoped I would see you. I wondered why you did not come back."

"I would've been in the way," Olun mumbled. "And—Syndra is more experienced with these things than I am. I couldn't've helped you. And you needed t'talk t'Genta, too, so . . ."

It wasn't necessarily a lie, but it felt like one nonetheless.

Didan said nothing for a moment, but Olun felt the weight of his gaze on her face. "Yes, I suppose you are right," he said quietly and let the matter go.

"Genta and I have said more to each other these few days than we ever had in our entire lives. So, I thank you for that. He even defended me when the Doyens came about Manuk."

Her smile dissipated, and she stopped. *Had they expected to drag a sick man away for questioning?* It angered her—everything about them did! It disappointed her that Zafre had let it happen, too.

"Peace," Didan chuckled, noticing her seething. "It has been resolved."

"They still think you killed Manuk!"

"Hujak still does, yes," Didan said. "But he is one man with more anger than proof. Really, Olun, it is fine."

They resumed their walk in silence for a time. Didan paused to unsnag Olun's robe from a bush.

"This, however, is not," he said glumly, pointing to the dingy wrapping around her hand.

"Oh . . ." she looked down at it. It hurt, but not as terribly as before. "I am sorry, Olun. Truly."

"You couldn't help it, ya?" she waved her hand dismissively. "Don't worry about such things."

"But I *do* worry about such things," he said quietly. "I worry about hurting you again. This thing that is wrong with me will not go away, Olun."

She knew that. Naleda had explained the pitfalls of healing. Pieces could be put back together, but some things—like her memories—would never return. A hand could be splinted and healed, but tremors may still remain. Didan's convulsions and spasms were no different.

"Nothing's *wrong* with you," she said firmly. "This is just another part of you, and we'll manage."

"*We?*" he cocked his head to the side, and Olun widened her eyes at the realization of what she'd let slip.

"Naleda and Genta and me and—you know what I mean!" She turned her attention to her surroundings, flustered and heart thundering in her chest. From the corner of her eye, she saw amusement slant his lips into a smirk.

Their meandering walk had led them toward the valley. Wordlessly, Didan helped her sit on a slab of rock, and they both watched the ootingla graze below. Olun recognized Bana among the other boys, keeping watch over the lazy herd. Didan relaxed back on his elbow, watching Olun pick absently at the wispy blue grass that sprouted from the cracks between the rocks.

"You were in my head," he said. "In the nightmare I have had every night since the accident—*you were there this time.*"

Olun stiffened. What happened was a fluke, and if he asked her to do it again, she wouldn't even know where to start. She'd called on the Shadow Man for help, and perhaps it had been his doing. But fluke or not, she'd heard what the Shadow Man had said back then. He'd called Didan *his son*. Somehow, it wasn't the right time to bring that up.

"That is something I have never been able to do," he muttered. "Never thought of it as something *any* of us could do."

"I can't be a healer anymore, can I?" she said shakily, and Didan took her hand. His thumb made slow circles on the back of it, and in his touch, she no longer felt fear or flickers of pain. She felt how deeply he treasured her.

"No matter what or who you become," he said softly. "You have my mother, Genta, and Tula. Bana, Jorre, and Yadir. You have *people*, Olun. They will support whatever path you take."

What about you? she wanted to ask, but thought the better of it. "What aren't you saying?"

Didan fell silent for a moment, staring at their twined fingers as if they bore all the answers in the world.

"My whole life, I have been told who and what I am. You had asked me once who I was, Olun, and it has become clear to me that I must find out."

"You're leaving, aren't you?" she said flatly, the breath leaving her body.

Didan nodded. "But I *will* come back," he said in earnest. "Olun, I came to tell you that, whether I find the answers I seek or not, I will come back to you. If . . . that is what you want."

She didn't know what she wanted, but she knew at that moment that she didn't want him to leave. Olun squeezed his hand as if it would keep him there beside her forever. Whatever was happening to her—whatever was to come—she wanted him by her side.

Didan nodded solemnly and brought her hand boldly to his lips. "Then I will return."

"Where're you going?" she asked, voice cracking.

"I do not know," he sighed. "There are some things I must reflect on. Answers, I am so used to finding out there. But I want to find Elder Vasc, too. He has spent decades longer than I have in Solitude. The village owes him an apology."

"And he should get to spend the rest of his days in the comforts of the village," Olun added in agreement, wiping her wet eyes.

Didan nodded with a smile. "Yes."

When her tears dried and her sorrow had calmed, Didan came to his feet. "I do not know what we are to each other or what our fates hold, Olun," he said, echoing her earlier thoughts. "Whether this is real or I am still stuck in my head, I do not know. But *please*—wait for me."

"What if you're gone too long and I discover I'm meant to return to my people?" she asked, half-jokingly. After all, the Rohta was her reason for learning under Naleda.

Didan combed his fingers through his locs, isolating one adorned with an off-white cuff the length of her littlest finger. He slipped it off and gave it to her. Olun gazed down at the charm, the phases of the moon etched in its bone surface.

"Wait for me," he repeated. "When you see these phases pass by twice, I will return— even if it is only to say goodbye. Please, allow me the chance to see you one last time."

"Okay," she whispered.

Olun clutched the charm tightly as she watched him go, his back straighter, his steps more purposeful. He would never be whole again, she knew, but this Didan was gathering the pieces to create a new life for himself.

What is the cost of life? Elder Kikyel once asked.

"Living," Olun answered, and said a silent prayer that Didan would keep doing just that. And she would keep on living, as well, like she was meant to do.

End Part I

ACKNOWLEDGEMENTS

IN 2017, I MOVED to a new state where I only knew one person. My mother suggested I join a group or a club to meet people with my interests. Being the Millennial that I am, I turned to the internet and found a great group of writers. It is because of them that I finished this novel—along with four other manuscripts! Their encouragement, support, and feedback not only on my progress but on the changes in my life have been monumental. They helped me realize that writing doesn't have to be lonely. To my writing community (you know who you are), thank you.

To "Merc," "Stun," "RZ," and "SomeGuy:" thank you for reading multiple iterations of this story before it even made it to beta readers . Thank you for putting up with my poor SPAG, anxieties, self-doubts, frustrations; for sharing my excitements, and commiserating in failures. For always remaining encouraging and willing to lend an eye or a voice.

Lastly, I want to acknowledge my husband. Thank you, hubby, for putting up with me during my anti-social times, the stare-off-into-space-as-I-mentally-solved-plot-hole times, the muttering to myself as I worked out dialogues, and the seemingly random

questions I'd poke you about at night times. Thank you for not insti-
tutionalizing me.

Sneak Peek

Part II: Storm Touched and Spirit Bound (Unedited)

Chapter 1

THE BABY WHIMPERED IN his mother's arms, body slick with the fluids and tissue of birth. It wailed with strong lungs and trembled, clenching his fists with all of his little might. Olun took a deep breath and plastered a placid smile on her face as the mother sobbed her joy and cooed her love, all pain forgotten the moment Naleda placed him in her arms. She turned her emotions inward, carefully navigating the space between the massive burning aura of raw emotion that used to engulf her.

Olun had learned quickly the first time she accompanied Naleda to a birth that strong emotions radiated from its hosts, taking up space like steam. The warring miasma of moods had been an assault on her mind and body, crippling and reducing her to a fitful puddle before even entering the home. Such a reaction had been a shock to her as it had to Naleda. Burdensome and embarrassing at the moment. It had been a wonder Naleda kept her at all. But it had been then that Olun realized she did not need to touch skin to feel what they felt.

Today, she'd spent hours at this woman's bedside as she labored. She'd watched unflinchingly as the baby crowned, feeling the delight at his first gasping breaths without being overwhelmed by it. Olun sought the aura of her own treasured memories—sinking her toes into the desert sand, being held in her aunt's arms, the soft medicinal scent of skin marred by many scars—and the feelings they stirred. She let her breath out slowly, centered by these comforts. Grounded.

"Congratulations!" Olun grinned at both mother and baby, fully in control of herself. She kept the cloak of her control tight, careful not to slip, for her duties were far from over.

***

Olun massaged her eyes tiredly as she made her way to the bath caves that evening. Three babies had been delivered over the past four months and Tula, too, seemed ready to burst. Such abundance still filled her with awe. The Ithoumi were a prosperous people in many ways. There hadn't been a child born in her clan in nearly five years by the time Olun had left the Rohta. Illness had made the body frail and famine made it hard for mothers to carry to term. Worst of all were the babies born that didn't survive their first weeks, their mother's breasts dry of milk.

And yet, here she was living in a land of flowing water, fat ootingla, and bountiful crops. Of women who bore healthy children without fear of plague, famine, and death. How ironic that a village beholden to the Dark Lady of Death would be one full of abundance and life.

Olun didn't know whether to laugh at its absurdity or cry. Should she feel guilt for living such a rich life or feel blessed?

"You seemed stressed—is my daughter okay?" Olun jumped as the middle-aged woman materialized in front of her, blocking her way to the vaulted cavern that contained the baths.

"How is my Mela?"

So much for peace. Olun sighed heavily and tried her best to ignore the woman, walking past her without a glance. She was too exhausted to deal with her today. Blocking out the emotions of others took concentration. It was almost as taxing as being inundated by them!

"Any news?" The woman appeared in front of Olun, once again blocking the tunnel. "What of my daughter's child? Do I have a grandson? Granddaughter?"

"I told you, ya?" Olun hissed, glancing around for anyone who might hear. "She hasn't given birth yet."

She stepped around the woman again but stopped short when the steam of the baths dampened her skin. Olun groaned, her own guilt bearing down on her. She didn't *want* to be rude; Olun hadn't even known the woman was a spirit when she'd first encountered her months ago. The woman had gone on about how she disliked her daughter's bonded's family—and how she'd vowed to stay long enough to see her daughter admit the errors of her ways and leave the oaf of a man—but *oh* she'd heard that she was with child and *now* she wanted to stay long enough to meet this grandchild, hoping that it wasn't an idiot like its pa—

Olun had gotten the shock of her life when the fitful woman flitted away through solid rock, muttering to herself all the while. For a time after, she'd been wary of the bath caves, unsure of whether or not the next person she came across was living or dead. She hadn't forgotten what Didan told her. Answering the spirits left her open to more.

But it was already too late for that. The Bath Caves Lady—as she'd begun calling the woman—had attached herself to Olun, knowing just when she'd appear. Twice, Olun had avoided the bath caves, choosing to bathe in the cold stream where Didan used to go, but her thoughts always returned to the Bath Caves Lady waiting for news from the realm of the living.

Mela was the only name the Bath Caves Lady ever said. *Jamela*, Olun had discovered. A pleasant young woman perhaps a year or two her junior. She was due to give birth in the next few weeks. The Bath Caves Lady tried talking to Jamela, Olun had observed, even though she knew her daughter couldn't hear her. Once, the woman followed Jamela's Bonded and plucked the back of his ear. The man waved his hand as if flicking away a buzzing gnat.

"Won't you come in with me?" Olun asked the woman, gesturing further into the cave where the baths awaited. "I promise that I'll listen t'whatever you have t'say, but *please*, I'm tired. Let me bathe first, ya?"

The woman shook her head vehemently. "I cannot go in there, I already told you!" she scoffed.

"I forgot." Olun silently thanked the Goddess for that little gift. She'd have to tell Didan that warmth dissuaded the spirits when he came back. *If* he came back at all.

"You are sad again," the woman noticed.

"Yeah . . ." Olun sighed, and just when she believed the spirit cared, the woman grew anxious again.

"Did something happen to my daughter? What of my grandchild?"

Olun groaned and hurried into the cavern, the spirit shouting at her back.

Part II Coming Summer 2026

ABOUT THE AUTHOR

Jade T. Woodridge was born in Naples, Italy to military parents and raised (for the most part) in the Washington D.C. metro area. She holds a Bachelor's in English Literature and a Master's in Library and Information Sciences. Jade is a Michigan transplant, a public library branch manager, and a person who stutters. Her largely speculative works can be found in *The Great Lakes Review, The Amistad, Obsidian: Literature & Arts in the African Diaspora, Midnight & Indigo, FIYAH Magazine,* and more. *Shadows of Memory* is her first novel.

Keep up with her and her various other works-in-progress on www.jadetwoodridge.com